RUTHLESS RIVALS COLLECTION

KATE BATEMAN

Desert Island Duke, The Phantom Of Drury Lane, and *A Scandal In July* are a works of fiction. Names, places, and incidents either are products of the author's imagination or are used fictitiously. Any resemblance to actual events, locales, or persons, living or dead, is entirely coincidental.

Copyright © 2024 by Kate Bateman

All rights reserved.

No part of this book may be reproduced in any form or by any electronic or mechanical means, including information storage and retrieval systems, without written permission from the author, except for the use of brief quotations in a book review. Not to be used for AI training.

Ruthless Rivals Collection PRINT ISBN: 979-8-9873291-9-1

KATE BATEMAN

Desert Island Duke

The
RUTHLESS RIVALS

CHAPTER 1

*L*ady Caroline Montgomery glared at the body farther down the beach and let out a snort of aggravation. Five minutes ago, she'd thought being shipwrecked alone on a tropical island was the worst thing that could have happened to her.

She'd been wrong. So wrong.

Being shipwrecked *alone* would have been delightful—in comparison. She was clever, resourceful, and accustomed to challenging situations such as this. Alone, she would have been fine.

Fate, however, hadn't granted her that small mercy. Not content with sending a typhoon to wreck the *Artemis* and separate her from her beloved family, the cruel universe had saddled her with *him*.

Maximillian Cavendish.

His Grace, the fourteenth Duke of Hayworth.

The most infuriating man on seven continents and the very last creature Caro would have chosen as a fellow survivor—including the *Artemis's* pig, which she'd affectionately named The Duke of Pork.

Hayworth lay on his side, his face turned away from her, but there was no mistaking his dark, tousled hair or those improbably broad shoulders. For such an indolent scoundrel, he had a remarkably healthy physique.

Caro stomped toward him along the sand, her damp skirts hampering her strides, and tried to squash the tiny kernel of panic at the stillness of his giant frame.

"You'd better not be dead," she panted crossly.

He didn't move when her shadow fell across his face, so she prodded him, none too gently, with the toe of her boot. "Hayworth? Are you dead?"

He wasn't. She could see his shoulder rising and falling as he breathed, and a knot of something she refused to label as relief loosened inside her. She told herself it was because she didn't want to be saddled with a corpse.

Still, he seemed to be unconscious. Considering how obnoxious the man was when awake, she would have preferred to leave him that way, but Caro supposed she had a moral obligation to rouse him. She poked him again in the ribs.

He let out a low groan, but his eyes remained closed.

Caro dropped to her knees beside him, grasped his shoulder, and gave him a hard shake. The muscles beneath the wet material of his jacket were incredibly solid.

She tried not to notice.

"Wake up, you insufferable oaf! It's too hot to dig you a grave."

She gave him another push, then almost jumped out of her skin when he sucked in a gasping breath and began coughing uncontrollably.

Caro gave him a few helpful whacks between his shoulder blades.

He flailed his arm and shoved her away. "Hoi! Stop that! I'm not dead, damn you!"

His voice was rough and raspy and she cursed the little frisson the sound always produced in her stomach. She scuttled backward like a crab as he rolled over onto his back and took a great lungful of air that made his chest expand even more.

He slung his forearm over his forehead, shielding his eyes from the blinding sun, and squinted up at her with a frown.

His eyes were an extraordinary turquoise, the same blue as the lagoon before them. Caro narrowed her own eyes in irritation. It was a stupid color for a man. Truly. It should have made him look pretty and vapid, like a doll, but instead they'd been paired with black-as-night eyebrows, a straight slash of a nose, and cheekbones that could have hewn granite. The effect was aggravatingly attractive.

His chin was covered in a peppering of dark stubble, as fine-grained as the white sand that stuck to his cheek, and Caro caught herself wondering what it would feel like against her palm.

Dear God, she must have sunstroke.

Hayworth, thankfully, was unaware of her ludicrous thoughts. He pushed himself into a sitting position with a groan and rested his head on his bent knees.

Caro scowled. She, no doubt, looked like a drowned rat. *He* somehow managed to look perfectly delicious, in a rumpled, careless, piratical sort of way. How had such an underserving wretch been endowed with such extraordinary good looks? It wasn't fair.

Maximillian Cavendish hadn't just been born with a silver spoon in his mouth – he'd been gifted the entire silver dinner service, too. Ever since his father's death, when Max had been a boy of merely nine, he'd been heir-apparent to his childless uncle, the thirteenth Duke.

Caro had made his acquaintance years ago; he was one of her brother William's closest friends, and she could unwaveringly state that Hayworth had displayed a confidence that bordered on arrogance even *before* his uncle's demise had promoted him from duke-in-waiting to *His Grace* last year.

He was one of those people for whom everything seemed to come easily. In addition to sinful good looks, he possessed a fierce intelligence, a quick wit, and considerable charm—not that he'd ever wasted those last two attributes on her. He was irritatingly good at everything he tried; whether it was fencing, riding, or gaming at his club.

And, it seemed, surviving a shipwreck at sea.

He turned his head and caught her eye, and Caro's heart gave an uncomfortable little thump. She'd always both craved and hated his regard.

"You're right. I'm definitely not dead," he said. "If I was dead, you'd be naked."

CHAPTER 2

*C*aro's mouth fell open in shock. "I beg your pardon?"

"If I was dead," Hayworth repeated, his voice a deliciously low rasp from the salt water he'd ingested, "and in heaven, then the beautiful woman who greeted me would most definitely be naked."

Caro blinked. Beautiful? Had Maximillian Cavendish just called her *beautiful*?

She glanced around at the sky, the white sand, the palm trees swaying on the shore. What bizarre alternate universe was this? Was she *dreaming*? It was the only logical explanation. She pinched herself on the thigh, to make sure.

Nothing happened.

Hayworth didn't seem to notice her confusion.

"Then again," he used one hand to ruffle the sand from his tousled hair, "I might be dead and in hell. That's very possible. In which case, being greeted by a fully-clothed siren who *looks* like she should be naked, but never takes her clothes off, well, that would be the very definition of punishment, wouldn't it?"

Caro assumed that was a rhetorical question.

"You're delirious," she said stoutly. "Did the lifeboat hit you on the head when it overturned?"

He rubbed his scalp again, as if searching for lumps. "Don't think so."

"Look at me."

He glanced at her again, and she stared deeply into his eyes, searching for any sign of recognition. Or, indeed, sanity.

He stared back at her solemnly. And then his mouth curved into a slow, wicked, openly appraising smile that made her stomach swirl dangerously. His gaze dropped to her lips, as if he was thinking of kissing her.

What on earth was happening?

"Stop being ridiculous," she scolded. "I'm not an angel or a devil. You know who I am. I'm Caroline. Caro Montgomery. William's sister."

"Caro." He repeated the name with a kind of wonder, rolling it around his mouth as though saying it for the first time. "Hello Caro. I'm glad you're not dead."

"As am I," she muttered uncertainly.

Maybe that was it. Maybe *she* was the one who was dead, and in some dreadful underworld where her only companion was the one man guaranteed to drive her mad for all eternity. It made a horrible kind of sense. He'd cursed her when she was alive. It stood to reason that he'd haunt her when she was dead, with his irresistible smirk and his perfect, unattainable body.

He reached out and smoothed a strand of salt-encrusted hair back from her forehead. His palm stroked her cheek, and Caro froze in surprise at the appreciative look on his face.

What was *wrong* with him? He'd never looked at her in such a way before. He usually regarded her with a mocking expression that suggested she was the amusing, unwitting, butt of his jokes. Did he *really* not recognize her?

"So, we've established that you're Caro," he murmured.

"Which would make me . . ?" He let the sentence trail off in a questioning uplift of sound.

"Cavendish," Caro said irritably. The idiot was clearly fooling with her, pretending he'd forgotten his own name.

"Huh," he said, sounding surprised. "Do people call me Cav?"

She was getting more exasperated by the second. "No, they don't. Cavendish isn't your first name. It's your family name, you dolt. Your Christian name is Max."

"Short for Maximillian, I assume?"

She batted his hand away. "Yes. Stop pretending you don't remember."

He let out a short laugh. "You think I'm *feigning amnesia*?"

"Of course you are. It's precisely the kind of thing you'd do. Teasing me is one of your favorite pastimes."

His lips twitched again. "It is? Teasing you?"

"Yes," she gritted out. "You've been mocking me and laughing at me from the first moment we met." That was absolutely true.

"And when was that?" he prompted.

"Years ago. You used to come and visit Will during the school holidays. And since then, every time we were in London, whenever my family was between expeditions."

"Expeditions?"

"My father's one of England's best-known butterfly experts. We travel all around the world looking for them."

"Hmm." His reply was non-committal, and she studied him again, more closely.

"Do you really not remember?"

"I remember your face," he said vaguely, "But as to the rest—" he gave a shrug that lifted his broad shoulders.

Caro was still suspicious. How could he remember her, but not his own name? It was extremely unlikely. Then again, the odds of them both surviving a shipwreck and being washed up, alive, on this same stretch of sand were infinitesimally small too. Perhaps he *was* telling the truth.

"Do you remember being a soldier? You served with Will at Waterloo."

His brow furrowed again. "Yes, I do remember that. My horse was shot out from under me."

Caro bit her lip. She'd heard the same thing from her brother's account of the battle. It was yet another example of Hayworth's charmed life that he'd emerged from that infamous bloodbath with hardly a scratch.

"Do you remember anything else about yourself?" Surely the man would recall he was a *duke,* for heaven's sake.

He paused, as if racking his brains. "I know I like peppermint."

Caro almost threw her hands up. This simply couldn't be true.

And then the most wicked thought bubbled up in her brain. Perhaps he really *didn't* remember. Perhaps fate was giving her this tiny sliver of opportunity to bring the arrogant devil down a peg or two. To level the playing field between them.

On this island, he wouldn't be the smug, superior friend of her brother, the high-and-mighty Duke of Hayworth. And she wouldn't be his best friend's little sister. They could start again, as equals. As simply Caro and Max. A man and a woman. Two people stuck on an island, working together.

It was an extremely alluring thought.

He was still staring at her in that strange, slightly besotted way, and Caro schooled her face into a bland expression.

"It's good that you remember your time in the army." She patted him consolingly on the arm. "Do you remember what you did after that?"

She waited for him to shake his head, then sent him a wide smile. The kind of bright, reassuring smile she used to cheer up children when they'd scraped their knees or been bitten by an ant. "After you left the army you discovered your uncle—you're his heir, by the way—had left you nothing but an enormous pile of debt."

Caro had to bite her lip to stop herself from laughing at this monstrous falsehood. His uncle had indeed left him an enormous pile—of *money*—and a lovely country estate named Gatcombe Park which boasted no fewer than twenty-three bedrooms and a ballroom big enough to play cricket in.

Oh, she would roast in hell for this, but it was worth it. Even if she was greeted at the fiery gates by a fully-clothed Maximillian Cavendish who teased her for eternity with the possibility of seeing him naked, it would be worth it.

"My uncle?" Hayworth repeated slowly. "A mountain of debt. Are you sure?"

"Oh yes, very sure. William felt so sorry for you, having fallen on such hard times, that he offered you a job."

Now Hayworth was delightfully confused, and Caro couldn't resist giving him the *piece de resistance*. She cast around for a suitably lowering position.

"You're a groom at our house in Lincolnshire. William says you're wonderful with the horses."

The incredulous look on Hayworth's face—as if the very idea of being a groom offended him to the core—made Caro's heart pound with the certainty that he'd recognize the lie and call her out.

Instead, he squinted up at the sun. "If I'm a groom, what am I doing here?"

"You're doubling up as Will's valet," Caro temporized quickly. "His usual man, Timms, got sick the week before we were due to sail for Madagascar, so you came along instead."

She waited for him to explode in outrage at her perjury. In truth, he'd only been a passenger on the *Artemis* because he'd been returning from a visit to see his cousin in India.

Hayworth's lips did an odd little twitch, as if he was about to laugh, but then his expression sobered and he nodded. "Ah. A groomsman and sometime-valet. That makes sense. I *do* like horses. And I definitely remember how to tie a decent cravat."

His hand strayed to this throat, where his own bedraggled

neckcloth still hung incongruously about his neck. That it had survived the chaos of the pounding waves when they'd both been tossed from the lifeboat and thrust onto this sandy shore was another miracle.

He untied the sodden knot and tugged the thin strip of linen from his shoulders, revealing an intriguing wedge of tanned chest in the deep open V of his shirt.

Caro averted her eyes, but only after an indecently long look. When she glanced back up at him, guiltily, he'd turned his head away and was gazing out over the blue expanse of water in front of them.

"So. I'm Max and you're Caro," he said easily, and she was struck with the renewed suspicion that he was teasing her.

He squinted at the green shape of another island, visible on the near horizon. "How did we get here?"

CHAPTER 3

Caro couldn't quite believe that Hayworth was accepting her story so readily, but she swiveled around to face the water, too.

Playful waves tickled the white sand, and the surface of the water within the enclosure of the reef was as smooth as glass. Huge waves still crashed against the outer ring of coral, spending their force with a constant low rumble, but it was hard to reconcile this same scene with the furious, churning cauldron of wind and waves that had flung them both ashore the previous night. Apart from a few tangled piles of driftwood and other flotsam higher up on the beach, there was hardly a trace of the storm.

"The *Artemis* lost her topsail, then her rudder," Caro said evenly. "She was blown onto the rocks over there." She pointed westward. Another island could be seen in the distance, and the ship lay just offshore, lilting badly to one side. It had clearly sustained serious damage.

"When Captain Thomas gave the order to abandon ship, there was a great deal of confusion on deck. You and I somehow ended up in the same lifeboat. You tried to row us ashore, to that other island, but the waves kept pushing us this way. When we neared the reef, a huge wave overturned us; I remember rolling over and over in the water, certain I was about to drown, but I awoke this morning here, on the sand."

Caro shook her head in amazement. It all felt like a terrible dream.

Hayworth frowned. "So where are the rest of the passengers? Dear God, they didn't all drown? What of your family?"

Caro smiled at the bombardment of questions. He might have lost his memory, but his imperious, demanding ways were still intact.

"My family was in another lifeboat." She gestured toward the sliver of beach just visible across the strait. "They made it to shore, along with the rest of the passengers. Look, you can see them, moving about on the sand. I've counted them, and everyone seems to be there."

Hayworth gave a grunt. "Everyone except us."

"At least we're alive."

"What happened to our lifeboat?"

"I assume it must have smashed on the reef. I walked a little way up the beach, but I didn't see it."

Hayworth grunted again, then narrowed his eyes at the other island. It seemed tantalizingly close, but Caro knew that the distance was deceptive.

"It's too far to swim," he said, as if reading her thoughts. "Even if we held onto driftwood or made a raft. That's at least two miles, maybe three, and we already know there are hideously strong currents out there."

"And sharks." Caro added helpfully. "And probably jellyfish."

"Quite so." He slapped his hands on his thighs and stood, full of renewed purpose. "Seems we're stuck here until we're rescued, then."

"It shouldn't be long," Caro said, more to comfort herself than him. "They must have some undamaged lifeboats over there. They'll row over and save us."

"They *might*," Hayworth sounded skeptical. "But it would be extremely risky. A small rowboat could easily get swept out to sea and lost. It's more likely they'll see we're alive and decide not to chance it. If we can see them, they must be able to see us." He sent a jaunty wave toward the opposite beach.

Caro shielded her eyes and could just make out an answering wave from one of the little figures on the shore.

"If that's my father, I can guarantee he's got a spyglass trained on us right now."

Hayworth stretched his hand out to pull her up from the sand. "In that case, I'll be on my very best behavior."

Her stomach flipped as his large fingers enfolded hers, and she struggled gamely to her feet. He brushed a small avalanche of sand from his thighs and turned to survey the lush forest that ringed the perfect crescent of beach.

A series of tree-covered slopes rose steeply toward the center of the island, and Caro sent up a prayer of thanks that they weren't on a windswept, treeless speck of land no bigger than a handkerchief.

"Look at this place. It's paradise." He gestured at the foliage. "I see coconuts, and we can fish in the sea. All we need is a source of fresh water and some shelter, and we'll be able to survive here for weeks."

"*Weeks?*" Caro gaped. "We won't need to survive for weeks. People will come looking for us as soon as they realize the *Artemis* is overdue in Cape Town."

Hayworth raised his brows. "I bet we were blown off course. You said we were on our way from Madagascar?"

Caro nodded. "I heard Captain Thomas say we were being pushed north, towards the Seychelles."

"Well, there are hundreds of islands dotted about in these waters. Unless some local fisherman happens upon us, it really *could* take weeks for us to be found. We should hope for the best, but prepare for the worst."

"Dear God," Caro muttered, appalled. This wasn't Paradise; it was Purgatory.

Hayworth, however, seemed remarkably upbeat about the prospect of being stranded. Perhaps he really *had* taken a blow to the head. He strode purposely off across the beach, his long legs eating up the distance. "Come on, we need to get out of the sun."

Since there was nothing else to do, Caro followed him, trying not to notice the way his fawn breeches clung to his long legs.

As soon as they reached the shade of the coconut palms, he turned back to her. "Right. First things first. We need water, fire, and shelter."

"Agreed. This isn't the first time I've had to make camp, you know. I spent several months in the rainforests of Brazil, before we sailed to Madagascar."

Of course, in Brazil she'd had the support of her family and a small army of local helpers, but there was no way she'd admit that to Hayworth. She might not have much practical experience, but she was confident in her own resourcefulness.

"How fortunate, to have been stranded with someone so perfect," he said smoothly, and Caro narrowed her eyes, unsure whether he was being sarcastic or not.

"Between my time in the army," he continued, "and your experience of living in all sorts of exciting places, we should make an excellent team."

Caro gave an unconvinced sniff.

He spread his cravat over a nearby bush, then patted his sodden jacket. With a triumphant crow, he reached into a pocket and withdrew a brass object, about three inches long.

"Ha, look at this! A folding knife. Past Max was clearly a man of foresight."

"You don't remember putting it in your pocket?"

"No. But I *do* remember winning it from a rifleman in a game of cards in Portugal. It was just after Salamanca."

"You remember your time as a soldier, four years ago, but not what happened last week?" Caro couldn't keep the skepticism out of her voice.

Hayworth grinned. "I'm sure it'll all come back to me eventually."

Caro prayed that day came long *after* they'd both left this island. She was already regretting her impulsive fabrication. As soon as Hayworth remembered he was a duke, and not a groomsman, there would be hell to pay. He'd probably strangle her in fury—if this blasted island didn't finish her off first.

He coaxed the small silver blade from the handle with a practiced flick of his thumbnail and held it up for her inspection.

"Now, I know what you're thinking," he said, with a wicked smirk. "But size isn't everything. It's what you do with it that counts."

Caro's cheeks heated at his bawdy inference. She wasn't so innocent as to misunderstand his meaning. Men loved embarrassing women by alluding to the size of their manly accoutrements. Considering Hayworth's monumental confidence, she had little doubt that his own personal 'blade' was more than adequate. She made a concerted effort not to look down at the front of his breeches.

"It's not going to be much good for cutting down trees," she said briskly, "but it's better than nothing, I suppose."

"Exactly. This little blade might be the difference between life and death out here."

He placed it on a piece of driftwood, then stripped off his jacket and spread it on the bush next to his cravat. His still-damp shirt clung to him like a spurned lover, and when he tugged the bottom of it from the waistband of his breeches, Caro let out a strangled gasp.

"Wait! What are you doing?" Her voice had risen an octave in shock.

He paused with the hem of his shirt halfway up his torso.

"Taking my shirt off, of course. We need to dry out." He

gestured at her own wet clothing. "Come on. Off with 'em. This is no time to be missish."

Before Caro could argue, he'd whipped the shirt over his head to reveal a muscular chest that made her catch her breath.

Dear God, the man was indecently well-built. She'd always suspected it, thanks to the cut of his jackets and the snugness of his breeches, but having it confirmed so emphatically made her a little lightheaded.

He turned, completely at ease with being half-naked in front of her, and began draping the shirt over the bushes. Caro couldn't help staring at the incredible play of muscles rippling beneath his lightly tanned skin. He'd clearly spent time without his shirt in India. He was golden all over. Far more like a groomsman than a duke, in fact.

When his fingers dropped to the buttons of his falls, however, she put her hands on her hips in outrage. "You absolutely *cannot* remove your breeches!"

CHAPTER 4

Hayworth sent her an amused glance, and Caro had the distinct impression that he'd had no intention of removing his breeches at all—that he'd only done it to get a rise out of her.

"Oh, very well. I suppose we should try to preserve your modesty. Although considering where we are, it's rather pointless. The rules of polite society can't possibly be upheld in a place like this."

Caro frowned. He had a good point. And she was definitely still damp.

Her dress—a sheer, sprigged muslin that was the perfect weight to counter the oppressive heat of the tropics—was practically transparent when wet, as it was now. Mercifully, she was also wearing her favorite long cotton petticoat, a set of short stays, and a knee-length cotton chemise as the final layer against her skin.

When the order to abandon ship had come last night, she'd tugged her leather ankle boots over her stockings and thrown a thin woolen shawl around her shoulders before her father had bustled her out into the passageway and up onto the heaving deck.

Her shawl had been lost to the churning waves, and in hindsight it was lucky her skirts hadn't prevented her from swimming. The weightless fabric had billowed up in the water, like a jellyfish, allowing her to kick her legs. If she'd been wearing a thick woolen skirt, and multiple petticoats, she would probably have been dragged down to a watery grave.

Still, perhaps learning the contents of Davy Jones's locker would have been preferable to disrobing in front of Maximillian Cavendish right now.

"I'm not taking *anything* off," Caro said stubbornly. "Except for my boots." She bent to undo the laces.

Hayworth merely shrugged and, after kicking a driftwood log over and checking it for insects, sat down to remove his own boots. He gripped the heel of one and tugged, and when it slid free, a stream of water and sand poured out onto the ground.

He sighed, as if pained. "They'll never be the same now, you know."

Caro was about to retort with a sarcastic comment about how he could afford ten more pairs, then remembered he was supposed to be a penniless groomsman and closed her mouth.

Since her stockings were wet, she took them off too, and wriggled her toes in the pleasantly warm sand.

Hayworth did the same, and she shot a sneaky glance over at his bare feet, hoping they'd prove to be one part of his body that was ugly, but they were long and elegant, just like the rest of him.

"You really should take more off," he said.

His tone made it sound like a perfectly reasonable suggestion, instead of perfectly indecent.

"You can't be comfortable, and there's no point in suffering just for the sake of propriety. I hate to break it to you, Miss Montgomery, but whatever reputation you might have had before this disaster has long since evaporated."

He sounded annoyingly pleased at the prospect that she might be ruined.

"My reputation, or lack of it, is the least of my problems right now, *Mister* Cavendish."

Caro took a gleeful delight in omitting his honorific title. "I'm sure there are scores of young ladies back in London who'd choose death over dishonor, but I'm not one of them. I'm glad to be alive. If the *ton* considers me ruined because I've been marooned on an island with an unmarried gentleman—through absolutely no fault of my own—then there's very little I can do about it. Fortunately, I care far less about finding a husband than I do about finding something to eat and drink."

He grinned. "A woman of independence. I like that. But still, we can't have you catching a fever from lounging about in damp clothing. If there was one thing the army taught me, it was to always stay warm and dry."

Caro let out an exasperated groan. In truth, she *was* uncomfortable. The steel wires in her stays were pressing into her ribs, and every inch of her was covered in scratchy sand.

"Oh, *fine*."

Turning her back to him, she slipped out of her dress and stepped out of her petticoat. After a moment of indecision, comfort won out over modesty, and she unlaced the front of her stays, too. She slipped the garment from her shoulders with a sigh of relief, and draped it over a piece of driftwood in the sun.

Risking a glance over her shoulder, she found Hayworth shirtless in just his breeches, looking like a sun-kissed Robinson Crusoe. She, now in nothing but her knee-length cotton chemise, probably looked like an escapee from an asylum. Or a very bedraggled ghost.

The only way to get through this situation was obviously to ignore her embarrassment and concentrate on the task in hand, namely: survival.

"It's still early. We should walk up the beach and try to find fresh water. There's no point setting up a camp miles away from something drinkable."

Hayworth nodded. "Agreed. If we can't find a stream, then we'll have to bash open some coconuts. Or find a puddle of rainwater. We can leave our clothes here to dry."

The two of them set off, keeping to the shade of the trees that fringed the beach as much as possible. The sandy bay ended in a rocky headland, which they reached without finding any stream or even trickle of water running onto the beach.

"We have to see what's around these rocks. Hopefully it's another bay."

Caro glanced at her bare feet. "They look too sharp to climb over. We should wade around, if it's not too deep."

Hayworth ventured into the shallow water, keeping to the sandy spaces between the rocks, and Caro followed in his wake. The water was astonishingly clear, and shoals of colorful fishes raced around their legs.

"Watch out for sea urchins," she warned.

"I wish we had a fishing pole. Or even just a hook and line. I could catch us some dinner."

"You could make a spear out of a stick," she suggested. "That might work. Or we could try to catch some of those crabs."

Scores of the armored little creatures crowded the rocks, scuttling into hiding holes whenever they got near.

With a final clamber over some partly-submerged rocks, they rounded the headland and discovered another perfect crescent, this one a little smaller than the one they'd been on before. Caro's heart gave a jolt as she noticed a disrupted section of sand about a hundred yards away.

"Look! Is that a stream?"

Hayworth set off at a brisk jog, and Caro let him go, disgusted with his athleticism. It was far too hot to run.

"It could just be seawater!" she shouted after him.

Before she was even halfway there, he dropped to his knees

and lifted a handful of liquid to his mouth. His whoop of triumph made her quicken her pace, and as she neared, she saw a steady trickle of clear water flowing out from the forest and down to the water's edge.

"Is it drinkable?"

He splashed his face with a laugh of delight. "Yes. It's wonderful! Have some."

She crouched at his side and scooped a handful to her lips, so desperate for a drink she didn't even care about the leaves and sticks floating about in it. She closed her eyes on a groan of pleasure. "Oh, dear God, that's good."

She took another long drink, then splashed her face, glad to remove the sticky salt and sand from her skin. When she glanced at Hayworth, she blushed to find his gaze fixed on her wet lips.

He coughed, as if there was something in his throat, and looked quickly away, then busied himself with washing the back of his neck.

When he finally stood, it was to inspect the foliage around them. He indicated a little clearing set back from the beach, sheltered by the trees, beyond the line of debris left by the high tide.

"We should make camp here. It's stupid to try to carry water back around to the other beach."

"But we'll be out of sight of the other island. My family will think something terrible has happened to us if we disappear."

"We'll go back and wave twice a day, so they can see us."

Caro sighed, accepting defeat. "Fair enough. If you go back for our clothes, I'll gather some sticks and branches to make a shelter."

He nodded, and Caro watched him retreat. Realizing she was staring at the tempting curves of his buttocks outlined by his tight, damp breeches, she forced herself to look away and get to work.

CHAPTER 5

As soon as he was sufficiently far away, Max allowed the laugh that had been brewing in his chest for the past hour erupt. He shook his head at the shameless tales Caro Montgomery had concocted.

Destitute groomsman, indeed!

Oh, she was a little minx.

When he'd first opened his eyes this morning and seen her angelic features surrounded by a blinding halo of sunlight, he'd experienced a brief, understandable, moment of confusion. Since he only awoke next to Caro Montgomery in his wildest, most wicked dreams, he'd assumed he was still asleep.

That delusion had disappeared almost immediately, but when Caro had started spouting her outrageous torrent of misinformation—presumably just for the perverse pleasure of bedeviling him—he'd been so entertained that he hadn't bothered to correct her.

It had ever been thus between them.

She'd been right to say that he loved to tease her. As a schoolboy, he'd looked forward to his visits to her family home with breathless anticipation, hiding his delight at sparring with her behind mock disapproval and counter-teasing that had developed into a dangerously thrilling flirtation.

Fantasies of kissing her, and more, had invaded his dreams for years.

As they'd grown older, and Caro had ventured out into society, he'd watched with increasing disapproval as other young men had begun to appreciate her sparkling eyes and irreverent wit. But despite lusting after her to an inordinate degree, she was still his best friend's sister—which meant she was not the girl for a quick tumble in the sheets, but rather the kind of girl one married.

Back then, Max had considered himself far too young to settle down, but he'd breathed a silent sigh of relief each time he'd heard she'd turned down another marriage proposal.

In his foolish immaturity, he'd been a classic dog-in-the-manger; he hadn't been able to admit that he wanted her for himself, but he hadn't wanted anyone else to have her, either.

He shook his head at his own youthful stupidity.

Caro put him in mind of the butterflies her father was so fond of studying; effortlessly beautiful and yet elusive, flitting from one group of people to another, delighting all she encountered, but never settling in one place for too long. A transitory beauty as beguiling as a South American swallowtail.

He'd missed her whenever she'd accompanied her parents and twin sisters on their various specimen-hunting expeditions around the world.

When he'd defied society's expectations and joined the fight against Napoleon as a cavalryman alongside her brother William, he'd come to realize just how much she meant to him. His numerous brushes with death, culminating in the nightmare of Waterloo, had solidified his feelings. He loved Caroline Montgomery with every thump of his still-beating heart.

Unfortunately, his determination to court her in earnest had been stymied by the fact that she'd left for a six-month-long trip to Brazil not three weeks after he'd returned to England. They'd been like ships that passed in the night.

Since London was a miserable place without her in it, Max had headed to his country seat, Gatcombe Park, and busied himself with setting the affairs of the estate in order. His uncle, the thirteenth duke, had—contrary to Caro's assertions—left the tenants happy and the ducal coffers full, and Max had quickly grown restless.

To pass the time until Caro came home, he'd taken a long-overdue trip to see his cousin in India. When Will had written to him, mentioning that Caro and the rest of her family would be traveling to Madagascar, in the Indian Ocean, the following month, Max had decided the fates were finally smiling down upon him.

He'd hastily arranged his own passage to the island to intercept them, and secured a cabin on their return ship, the *Artemis*, with the delightful prospect of spending the journey back to England wooing Caro so thoroughly that she'd finally see him as her perfect match.

That, clearly, hadn't gone to plan, but Max found that he couldn't be annoyed at the situation they'd suddenly found themselves in.

Was there such a thing as wishing for something *too hard*? He'd wanted to be alone with Caro, after all. Perhaps destiny had concocted this unlikely state of affairs to grant him his heart's desire in the most emphatic, inescapable way possible.

Because now he had her, all to himself.

For days, if not for weeks.

It was either the very best, or the very *worst* thing that could possibly have happened to him.

Obviously, he would have preferred somewhere a little less life-threatening. To be snowed in together at a cozy coaching inn, for example. Or stranded at a house party in the Highlands. Somewhere with decent food and adequate facilities.

Here there was the possibility of real bodily harm. Either one of them could get sick, or injured. They could slowly starve to death.

Max shook his head again. No. No harm would come to Caro. He'd die before he'd ever let that happen.

His protective instincts had always been strong, perhaps from having lost his father at such a young age, and he'd cared for the men under his command in the army as if they'd been his own flesh and blood. He'd done as much as humanly possible to keep them all alive while on campaign, and he would do exactly the same for Caro, now.

Not that he didn't think she was perfectly capable of surviving out here on her own. Caro was one of the most competent people he knew, male or female; it was one of the many things he loved about her. Most women of his acquaintance would have been swooning about on the sand right now, bemoaning their fate. Caro merely looked disappointed at the size of his pocket knife.

Max let out another snort of amusement. She hadn't been disappointed by the sight of his chest, though. She hadn't been able to look away when he'd stripped off his shirt.

The knowledge buoyed his spirits immensely.

He'd done a better job of pretending not to notice *her* body, although it had been a Herculean task. When she'd removed her damp dress, petticoat, and stays, it had taken a great deal of fortitude not stare at the tantalizing outline of her body so barely concealed by her chemise. He'd wanted to gather in his arms and never let her go, but such a move would have been met with either astonishment or fury from Caro.

He would have to bide his time.

Realizing he'd reached their clothes, Max gathered them up and started back along the sand.

CHAPTER 6

Caro had gathered a decent pile of driftwood by the time Hayworth returned. He arranged their still-damp clothes over some nearby rocks, then approached her with a grin.

"I have another surprise. When I picked up my jacket, I discovered my pocket watch."

The metal case glinted as he held it up. "It appears to be solid gold." He sent her a sideways, questioning look. "Which is odd."

"Why is it odd?"

"Well, this must be worth a few hundred pounds, at least. If I'm so short of money, how come I haven't sold it, to pay off some of my debts?"

Caro cursed inwardly. Was he trying to catch her out in her lie? Or did he truly not remember his own lofty position?

"It has sentimental value," she said quickly, praying it was true. "It belonged to your father. You couldn't bear to sell it."

Her pulse pounded as he flipped open the case and peered at an inscription engraved on the underside of the lid. Please, God, it hadn't been a gift from a friend, or, worse still, a mistress. If it said *'To Max, from your darling Sally,'* or something equally damning, she would be in a whole world of trouble.

"H.E.C." he read.

Caro breathed a silent sigh of relief at her lucky guess. "That stands for Henry Edward Cavendish. Your father."

"Ah. Excellent." He snapped the cover shut. "Not that having a watch will be very useful here. It's not as though we'll be receiving any visitors." He suddenly slapped his open palm against the back of his neck. "Ugh. Something bit me!"

"We need to make a fire. Smoke will keep the insects away."

"True, but how? If you think I'm going to spend hours rubbing sticks together, you can think again. One of my lieutenants tried it once, in Spain, and all he got for his trouble was blistered palms and an aching back."

"You won't need to rub sticks together."

His lips gave an amused little curl. "You've got a tinderbox hidden under that delightful chemise, have you? A brace of pistols, perhaps?"

Caro tried not to flush at the reminder of her state of undress. "Sadly not, but we can make a fire with that." She pointed at the timepiece in his hand.

"How? The hands are steel, I grant you, but they're tiny, and we don't have a flint to strike against them."

"No, look." She held her hand out, and he passed her the watch. She flicked it open. "The glass is curved. We can use it like a prism, to focus the sun's rays onto some tinder."

Caro bit back a little smile. This was one practical skill she *had* learned in Brazil, even though she and the twins had only done it for fun, and not for necessity. They'd burned patterns into leaves and set fire to Louisa's straw bonnet with their father's magnifying glass.

She glanced upward. "Unfortunately, we don't have any sun." Despite the oppressive heat, the sky was overcast. "But as soon as those clouds disappear, we can try it."

Hayworth nodded. "Let's make a shelter, then. It's bound to rain at some point. We'll need to keep dry, and so will our tinder."

He glanced up at the trees. "I don't think we should build directly under a coconut palm. I've heard of people being killed by falling coconuts."

Caro wondered if he'd heard those tales from the cousin he'd been visiting in India, but held her tongue. Perhaps he really *didn't* remember that part of his life. It seemed odd, that he should remember some things, but not others, but she was certainly no expert on head injuries.

He picked up a palm frond and began to sweep the area clear of debris. "This is a good spot. The rocks will shelter us from the worst of the weather."

Caro bit her lip at the unexpected sight of him performing the task of a scullery maid. "Have you ever made a shelter? Did you use tents in the army?"

"Well, as an officer, I was generally billeted in a local farmhouse whenever possible, but I did spend a few nights under the stars." The muscles in his arms flexed as he gathered a few fallen branches from among the trees. "We can make these into a frame, and then cover them with palm fronds and leaves."

"How will we tie them together? I didn't see any rope washed up on the shore, sadly."

Caro was loath to suggest they start ripping up her petticoats to make ties. She had few enough layers as it was. "I'll go look for some vines. And some food."

Hayward sent her an easy smile that made her heart patter. "Thank you."

"You should start by making a platform, raised off the ground," Caro added. "That's what we did in Brazil. There are all manner of things crawling about. Snakes and spiders and centipedes and whatnot."

He gave a theatrical shudder. "Good point. Scorpions I can deal with, but I am *not* a fan of spiders. Nasty, leggy things."

Caro pulled her still-damp boots back on and left him snapping branches and gathering lengths of wood. She ventured up the beach, on the lookout for anything that might be useful.

A few years ago, she'd read Daniel Defoe's novel *Robinson Crusoe*. The author had given his fictional castaway a host of tools and other items for *his* adventure. Crusoe had scavenged all manner of things from his ship, from blades and carpenter's saws, to sailcloth sheets and yards of rope and twine.

She and Hayworth, in contrast, had a folding knife, a pocket watch, and the clothes they stood up in.

Caro let out another huff of irritation. The fates, clearly, wanted them to suffer. Would it be too much to send them a bit of canvas and a nice long length of rigging?

She scanned the beach and then the lagoon, praying for a miracle, but there was nothing to see but sand and sparkling waves.

Several coconuts had washed up on the shore, so she collected them into a little pile for her return trip, along with some empty scallop-type shells. Then she ventured inland, careful to note her path by snapping twigs so she didn't get lost.

The foliage was much like the jungles she'd encountered in Brazil, a riot of green, but there were scores of plants she didn't recognize. Brightly-colored birds called to one another in the trees and butterflies flitted lazily between flowers.

A flash of red caught her eye, and she discovered a tree laden with fruit. The flesh resembled a huge, elongated peach, graduating from red, through orange and green.

Hardly daring to believe her good fortune, she picked one and sniffed it, then took a tentative bite and groaned in happiness as the sweet, familiar taste of mango filled her mouth. She'd tried this tropical fruit in Brazil, and it had quickly become one of her favorites.

Filled with excitement, she picked four of the ripest fruits and hurried back to the beach.

She didn't have enough hands to carry all the mangos, shells, and coconuts, but she was reluctant to make another trip in the smothering heat. Pushing aside her natural embarrassment, she placed everything in the bottom half of her chemise, and lifted the hem to form a rudimentary sling.

She kept the material as low as possible, praying that Hayworth would be so busy gathering wood that he wouldn't notice her arrival, but the sound of movement stopped abruptly as she neared the camp. She looked up to find his avid gaze fixed firmly on her bare thighs.

Caro knelt as quickly as she could and deposited her bounty on the sand.

The movement seemed to snap Hayworth out of his trance, and he busied himself with covering the roof of the shelter he'd constructed in her absence. Much to her disappointment, he'd put his shirt back on, hiding all those glorious muscles of his.

"What have you got there?" he asked gruffly.

She held up a blushing fruit. "I found a mango tree."

He sent her a dubious look. "You're *sure* it's edible? The last thing we want is for one of us to get sick."

She rolled her eyes at his skepticism. "Yes, I'm sure. I've already eaten some, and I'm not frothing at the mouth or rolling around on the floor in agony. We ate these all the time in Brazil."

She pushed some lumps of driftwood together to make a rudimentary table and set the mangoes and coconuts on it, then held up more of her discoveries.

"We can use these empty coconut shells as cups for water, and these big seashells as spoons, or even plates."

"Good work."

She squashed down the glow of happiness his praise produced in her chest. "That looks like a good shelter."

He grunted, as if unimpressed with his work. "It'll do for now. It's off the ground, at least. And it should keep off the worst of the rain. It's hard not having an axe or a saw to cut branches."

"It looks wonderful," Caro said, genuinely impressed at what he'd constructed.

A few years ago, she would have bet her life on Max Cavendish not being able to put his own boots on without assistance, but his time in the army had clearly given him skills the average aristocrat did not possess.

He made a theatrical sweep of his arm. "Welcome to Chateau Cavendish, mademoiselle. The finest residence this side of Madagascar."

Caro smiled at his teasing, self-deprecating humor. The 'chateau' was a basic A frame of branches and leaves supported at the far end by three huge boulders. "It's certainly the finest edifice on *this island*," she said judiciously.

"May I give you a tour?"

"Please do."

"The floor, as you see, is the very latest in split bamboo construction, with a generous covering of palm fronds."

Caro bit her lip to stop a laugh escaping. She schooled her expression into one of mock gravity, as if she were being given a tour of one of England's finest mansions. "I believe the great architect Robert Adam uses exactly the same materials."

His lips quirked.

"And the roof?" she queried.

"The finest timber-frame, secured with vines, finished with the highest quality overlapping leaves."

Caro tapped her lips with her finger, as if giving it serious consideration. "Such an innovative technique. I'll be sure to mention it to my cousin Tristan when we're back in England. He's an architect, too."

Hayworth gestured grandly at their surroundings. "The lady will note the agreeable aspect to the south, and the unparalleled sea view."

"Magnificent," Caro crooned.

"There's the very latest in alfresco dining." He waved at her impromptu table. "And let us not forget the innovative arrangement of the facilities for personal hygiene."

"The what?"

"There aren't any chamber pots," he said, straight faced. "You're going to have to go round the back of that tree."

Caro flushed but still chuckled at his bawdy humor. She appreciated the attempt to put her at ease.

He pointed at the stream. "Not to mention the hot and cold running water."

She lifted her brows. "Hot *and* cold?"

He smiled again, and her heart gave another little jolt. He was irresistible when he was teasing.

"Hot in the afternoon when the sun's been on it. Cold in the morning, for milady's ablutions."

"Ah. And how many do you think it will accommodate? I may have a guest to stay."

His eyes twinkled. "A guest, you say? Hmm. This residence is extremely compact. In fact, it might be a bit of a crush, when one's actually inside. But provided you and your guest are on friendly terms, I don't think it will pose a problem."

Caro knew her cheeks were heating at the thought of the two of them having to take shelter inside. It barely looked big enough for them to lie side by side without touching. Still, it was better than nothing.

"I'm sure we can come to an amicable arrangement," she said smoothly. "What's the asking price?"

His sparkling gaze caught hers and for a moment she was sure he was about to ask for something outrageous, like a kiss. His gaze *did* drop to her mouth for a second, before he gave a gallant shrug.

"There's been a great deal of interest, madam. Properties on this stretch of the coast are few and far between. This wonderful estate will set you back . . . two coconuts and a mango."

"Done!"

Caro brushed her hand on her shift and then stuck it out toward him to shake. He took it, and her stomach swooped as his fingers closed around hers. He gave her hand a firm squeeze to cement the 'deal', and she squashed her feeling of disappointment when he released her and let his hand drop.

She took a cooling step back.

"If you'll give me your knife, I'll cut up the mango."

CHAPTER 7

Caro sneaked furtive glances at Hayworth as he picked up one of the coconuts she'd gathered.

"So, how do we get into these then?"

"The green ones, like that one—" she pointed to one on the ground, "have a refreshing water inside them that we can drink. We should be able to open them with your knife."

He shook the one he was holding. It made a liquid, sloshing sound. "And these darker ones? Do they have the nut inside?"

"Yes. But you have to pull off the outer husk to get to it. Without a decent blade, the best way is probably to hit it with a rock until you can peel it off."

"Right."

He set off for the water's edge and she watched as he wedged the coconut between two boulders. Then he selected another large rock, lifted it to shoulder height, and dropped it onto the top of the nut with a loud crack.

He repeated the action several times, and eventually pulled the hairy covering free. He held up the resulting nut in triumph, as if he'd captured the enemy's standard during a battle.

"Success!"

Caro smiled at his enthusiasm. For all his sophistication when he was in the *Ton*, she had the feeling that she was finally getting a glimpse of the real Max Cavendish. The man who lurked beneath the civilized, cynical veneer. A man who took a simple, primitive pleasure in doing something so physical.

A man she found extraordinarily attractive, damn it.

He strode back up the beach, clutching his prize. The coconut looked surprisingly small in his big hands.

"Now what?"

Caro took it from him and balanced it carefully between her knees. "If we open it up, we can drink the milk that's inside." She located the three darker spots on the top, and used the tip of the penknife to bore a small hole. She held it up toward him. "Try it."

"Oh no, ladies first, I insist."

She gave a wry smile. "You just want to make sure it's drinkable."

He grinned. "Maybe."

Caro put the coconut to her lips and took a sip, savoring the sweet, refreshing taste. Then she held it out for Hayworth, and her stomach clenched a little as he placed his mouth directly over the same spot hers had been without even wiping the surface.

His throat bobbed as tipped his head back and swallowed, and she clenched her fingers into a fist against the desire to reach out and touch his skin.

"Ahh," he sighed. "Now. Shall I bash this open?"

She waved him back toward the rocks. "Bash away." She *almost* finished with 'Your Grace,' but stopped herself just in time.

By the time he returned, she'd sliced up two of the mangos, and they sat on opposite logs with her makeshift table between them. Caro used the knife to hack out a few chunks of the white coconut meat from the split shell.

"I've never had mango before," Hayworth said, taking a slice. "At least, I don't *think* I have. Who knows, maybe I've eaten mango every day for weeks and don't remember? I presumably ate mango in Madagascar?"

Caro rolled her eyes, still not entirely convinced he wasn't playing an elaborate hoax on her. "Indeed, you did. Perhaps the taste will remind you. It's a little like a peach, only sweeter, with more juice."

She watched in fascination as he took a tentative bite, unable to tear her eyes away from his mouth.

His lips had always drawn her. They were firm and finely molded, and she'd spent far too many nights wondering what they would feel like pressed against her own. The juice from the mango coated the lower one in a wet sheen, and she had the sudden insane urge to lean forward and lick it off, to taste the sticky sweetness on him.

The heat was clearly making her delirious.

"Delicious," he murmured, and she glanced up to find his eyes fixed on her.

For a moment she imagined he was describing *her*, and unbidden heat flooded her cheeks. Flustered, she popped a sliver of mango between her own lips and concentrated on the heady perfume and fragrant flesh.

"Don't eat too much, or you'll get stomach ache," she murmured, between chews.

He raised his brows. "That sounds like the voice of experience."

She nodded. "Lenore once bet her favorite ribbon that I couldn't eat three in one sitting. I proved her wrong—but I wish I hadn't. I spent the rest of the day in bed, feeling terrible."

He chuckled at her wry expression.

Suddenly uncomfortable with his gaze, she glanced out at the horizon. The sun, already past its zenith and on the descent, was visible, but the patchy clouds precluded any rays that could be used to start a fire.

"It's a shame the sun isn't coming out," she grumbled. "It would be nice to get a fire going."

Hayworth stood and rinsed his hands in the stream. "Well, I for one think we've had a very successful first day, all things considered. We've found water and food. And we've got somewhere to sleep. I'd say we make a good team."

Caro shrugged, even though she was secretly thrilled at his praise. She'd never thought to hear him say something so complimentary. In fact, she suddenly realized she'd become accustomed to men viewing her as some sort of overeducated freak—a woman with far too many 'unfeminine' skills and not enough 'desirable' traits like simpering ignorance and a willingness to laugh at a man's jokes, however feeble.

"We've been incredibly fortunate," she said levelly. "I don't know what we would have done if there hadn't been fresh water." She glanced back along the beach, toward the rocky headland. "I hope the others have been so lucky."

"I'd be surprised if they hadn't. That other island looks bigger than this one, and they might even be able to row back to the ship and save the supplies that are on it. We can walk back around and see, if you like."

"Very well."

They set off, with Caro clambering over the rocks this time, since she still wore her boots. She squinted over at the island on the horizon, and gave a gasp as she spied a flicker of light.

"They've made a fire! Look!"

CHAPTER 8

A plume of smoke rose against the sky, and Hayworth let out a long whistle. "So they have. Lucky devils. I wonder how they managed that."

Caro couldn't conceal her envious groan. "I wish we were on *that* island."

He bumped her shoulder with his own in a friendly nudge, exactly as she'd seen him do with her brother. "Oh, come now. It's not so bad here. We're alive, aren't we? *'Dum Spiro Spero'*, and all that."

"While I breathe, I hope?"

He looked suitably impressed by her ability to translate the Latin, and she quashed a little spark of pride. Her Latin was excellent, thanks to her father's need for help in classifying his various butterfly species.

"Exactly. One of those crusty old Romans said it. Cicero, maybe? Or Herodotus. Either way, it was something I told myself every day when I was in Portugal. Each time I lived to see another sunset—no matter how hungry, or hurting, or tired—it was a reminder that at least I wasn't dead. Dead is final. Alive, there's a chance you'll see home again, see the people you care about. The people you love."

Caro glanced at him, surprised and oddly touched that he'd shared something so personal with her. She'd always thought of him as invincible; the untouchable, unruffled Duke of Hayworth. It was rather comforting to know that he was human, and prone to the same fears and insecurities as she herself. It made her admire him even more.

Ugh. Why couldn't he have stayed all irritating and aloof, as he'd always been in the past?

She forced herself to give a light, teasing laugh. "*Love?* I didn't think gentlemen believed in love. Will always swore he'd never fall prey to such a ridiculous emotion. He says love is only for women and fools."

Hayworth slanted her an enigmatic look. "I used to think the same, but war changes a man. I hope to find a woman to love me, flawed as I am." He stopped abruptly on the sand. "Wait! I'm not *married*, am I? I haven't a wife back in England? A fiancée? A mistress?"

Caro laughed. If he was only pretending to have lost his memory, he was doing an admirable job of it. "You do not have a wife. Nor a fiancée, as far as I know. You didn't have one when I left for Brazil eight months ago, at least."

He heaved a sigh of apparent relief.

"As to a mistress," she couldn't resist teasing, even though the topic would have been distinctly off-limits under normal circumstances, "you could well have one of those. Or several. I wouldn't know."

He'd definitely had paramours in the past. The rumor mill in the *Ton* was always whispering about him. Her heart gave a jealous little squeeze in her chest.

"I don't suppose many women want to marry an ex-soldier, turned groomsman and valet," he said evenly.

She almost snorted. She knew a hundred women who'd marry him, even if he didn't have a penny to his name. The man looked like a Greek god. And he had a title. That alone made him matrimonial gold. Add an obscene amount of money to the mix, and it was a miracle he hadn't been snapped up already.

Hayworth seemed to be expecting a response, so she feigned a look of sympathy. "You'll get back on your feet. Who knows? In a year or two you might even be promoted to stablemaster."

"Assuming we ever get off this island."

They both gazed enviously over at the glowing orange flames. Hayworth waved, and received an answering signal from a figure on the shore.

He bent and started gathering an armful of driftwood. "We should prepare our own signal fire. That way, when a ship comes, we'll be ready."

Caro nodded, pleased with his confidence that she would, indeed, be able to make a spark for them soon. His belief in her abilities was heartening. So many men she knew would have tried to do the task themselves, or dismissed her idea out of hand, and insisted on trying a hundred other ways to start a fire.

They spent the next half hour stacking a pyramid of driftwood beneath the trees, then made their way back to camp.

The sun was slipping closer to the horizon, and the sky was beginning to turn a gorgeous mix of purples and pinks. It was going to be a spectacular sunset. Caro began collecting more driftwood in readiness for the morning, but Hayworth ventured to the water's edge.

"I'm going for a swim."

He tugged off his shirt and threw it up onto the dry rocks.

"You might want to look away, Miss Montgomery," he warned with a low laugh, "because I am about to remove my breeches."

Caro sucked in a breath and willed herself to turn and face the shelter, even though every fiber of her being wanted to turn around and peek. Her ears strained to hear the rasp of fabric being shed, then she heard the splash as he waded out into the shallows.

A larger splash, and she heard him call, "You can turn around now."

She did so, and pretended she was perfectly used to seeing a partially submerged, naked man swimming in the sea not fifty paces from her.

Despite the clearness of the water, the lengthening shadows and unhelpful movement of the waves prevented her from seeing more than the briefest flashes of skin. But just the knowledge that he was there, *perfectly naked*, was enough to make her feel decidedly on edge.

The rosy glow of the setting sun gilded his broad shoulders and set the droplets of water in his hair sparkling. He ducked beneath the surface and reappeared, running his hands through his wet hair like some mythical merman, or Poseidon, emerging from the deep to claim a mortal lover from the land.

Caro could quite see how a girl might be tempted. The curve of his biceps and ridged perfection of his chest made her mouth run dry. The suspicion that he might be flaunting himself deliberately, to try to attract her, formed in her brain, but she dismissed it almost immediately. A man like Hayworth would never be interested in a woman like her.

"Are you coming in?" he demanded playfully. "You must be hot."

Caro was decidedly warm – and not just from collecting the wood. She would have loved to take a refreshing dip, but there was no way she was going to take off any more clothing in Hayworth's distracting presence.

"Maybe tomorrow. May hair will take too long to dry without the sun, and I can't sleep if it's wet."

She doubted she'd be doing much sleeping at all, with that divine body right next to her in that ridiculously small shelter, but that was beside the point.

Hayworth sent her a chiding look that suggested she was a spoilsport, but she forced herself to cross to the stream instead and wash her face and hands. She kept her back turned when he finally left the water, and waited until he'd had ample time to dress before she looked at him again.

They ate the remaining mangoes as the light began to fade and the purple shadows lengthened.

"Tomorrow, we should try to walk around the island and see how big it is." Hayworth said, and Caro had a flash of what he must have been like as a Captain in the army, planning the next day's excursions into enemy territory.

"Then we can venture inland," he continued, unaware of her perusal. "We can follow this stream and see where it leads. There might be a lake or larger river further up the hill that we can wash our clothes in. Salt water leaves them all crunchy."

Caro nodded. "Yes. It would be nice to bathe in fresh water. We can look for more food, too. I remember where my mango tree is, but there will probably be others."

"You don't have to come," he offered. "It might be quite strenuous."

"Ha! I'll wager I've crossed more difficult terrain than you have, Max Cavendish. I once had to cross a river while balancing between two suspended ropes. I'm not some simpering debutante who's never been farther afield than Brighton."

His mouth quirked in appreciation. "You're an extraordinary woman, Caroline Montgomery. Which is why I can honestly say there's no one I'd rather be shipwrecked with than you."

Caro scoffed at his blatant attempt to butter her up. She didn't believe him for a minute—no doubt he would have preferred to be marooned with one of his mistresses, who would have offered him the most basic of human comforts. But her heart still glowed at his praise. It was nice to be considered competent, at least.

"So," Hayworth said. "Time for bed?"

CHAPTER 9

"Which side do you prefer?" Hayworth asked cheerfully.

Caro's heart began to pound. She had no idea *which* side she preferred, never having shared a bed with anyone—a fact Hayworth must surely know, or at least assume, since she was clearly a lady—but she refused to let him needle her.

"The right," she said.

His smile widened. "That's good. Because I prefer the left."

She glared at him and crossed her arms defensively over her chest. "You do realize that this shelter is the *only* thing we'll be sharing tonight, Maximillian Cavendish. I'm not some London trollop you can—" she paused, unsure quite where she'd been going with that sentence.

"—use for bodily warmth?" he supplied with a laugh. "Seduce into a quivering pile of limbs?"

"Something like that," she muttered.

He lifted both hands up in a gesture of innocence. "I swear, I'll be the perfect gentleman."

"Well, good."

Caro stalked to the rocks and retrieved her dress and petticoats. Both had dried, so she went behind a bush and put her dress back on, then rolled her petticoats up into a bundle to use as a pillow. Her stays were also dry, but she couldn't face the thought of putting them back on to sleep, even if they would provide an extra layer of protection. She left them hanging on the bush.

When she emerged, Hayworth was already lying in the shelter, looking out, so she removed her boots and crawled in beside him, stockinged feet first.

The two of them lay side by side on their stomachs, supported on their elbows, and looked out at the darkening sea. Their shoulders almost touched.

"It shouldn't get too cold, even without a fire," he said. "But if, at any time, you feel the need for extra body heat, you only have to ask."

Caro gave an amused little snort. "I'm sure I'll be fine."

She tucked her petticoat pillow under her head and turned her back to him, but despite her physical exhaustion, her mind refused to calm. She'd shared a tent with her sisters, on occasion, but she'd never slept this close to a man.

In the enclosed space she could smell him—a pleasant mix of salt-clean skin and some indefinable masculine scent that made her toes curl in her stockings. The even sound of his breathing and the various rustlings of the leaves as he tried to make himself comfortable filled her ears and made her very aware of the crowded space.

Some part of him brushed her bottom, and she wriggled away, glad that he wouldn't be able to see her pink cheeks.

"Sorry," he muttered.

Caro yawned. The floor of the hut was not at all comfortable; she was going to have bruises on her hip and shoulder by the morning. Willing herself to relax, she closed her eyes and had just begun to doze when a loud 'thump' nearby made her jolt back awake with a start.

"What was that?" she yelped, her heart racing.

"Falling coconut," Hayworth muttered, apparently less alarmed than herself. "Told you we shouldn't build under the palms."

It was almost fully dark now, but the moon was out, and Caro could make out a bank of clouds above them. With a sudden patter, a barrage of raindrops began to fall, slowly at first, and then in a steady rhythmic hiss all around.

"Oh, wonderful," Hayworth groaned dryly. "Just what the doctor ordered."

Caro moved deeper into the shelter, away from the drips that now fell from the open entrance. She waited for more to start falling in through the leafy 'roof', but Hayworth must have done a decent job of covering it because no water managed to seep in.

Relieved that at least they would stay relatively dry, she closed her eyes again, oddly soothed by the sound of the rain hitting the leaves and the reassuring male presence next to her. Some primal, base part of her felt infinitely safe with Hayworth at her side. That, in itself, was a troublesome thought, but she was too tired to dissect it.

"Good night, Cavendish," she murmured.

There was a smile in his voice as he answered. "Good night, Montgomery. Sweet dreams."

CHAPTER 10

When Caro awoke, she frowned at the slanted patch of leaves in front of her nose for a few moments, utterly disoriented. Her whole body ached, and she had a vague recollection of being cold in the night, but now she felt deliciously warm—at least along the back side of her body.

The rosy glow of sunrise warmed the inside of the shelter and recollection returned with a flash of alarm. The heavy weight slung over her waist was *Hayworth's arm*. The pleasantly warm feeling behind her was *his body*, pressed against hers, full length.

Caro sucked in a scandalized breath. *Was Hayworth already awake?*

She strained her ears, her heart pounding, and identified strong, even breathing that suggested he was still deeply asleep.

Thank the Lord! She had no memory of how they'd ended up in this situation, but they'd clearly become entwined at some point during the night.

Her cheeks heated in mortification, even as she tried to stay absolutely still to catalogue the extraordinary sensations.

He was hard, and warm, and all-encompassing. He was pressed against her back so closely she could feel the rise and fall of his chest as he breathed, and the tickle of his exhalations against her neck. His knee was pressed against the back of her leg, and—oh, God!—her bottom was nestled quite wonderfully in the lee of his lap.

She'd never in her life expected to wake in his arms. Hayworth undoubtedly had no idea of what he was doing; he was probably so used to sharing a bed with a woman that his body had automatically reached out to hers in the night.

Determined to extricate herself from this mortifying situation, she slid out of his embrace as quietly as possible. She paused, pulse racing, when he mumbled something incoherent and rolled over onto his back, but thankfully he did not wake.

When she was fully out of the shelter, she risked a glance back at him, giving into the urge to watch him as he slept. It was such a privilege, a secret moment she'd keep with her forever. The dawn's rays highlighted the slope of his nose and the stubble on his cheek. Caro took one last longing glance and forced herself to go for a head-clearing walk up the beach.

She felt more awake when she'd taken off her stockings and paddled in the sea. She gathered a few more coconuts, and when she returned to camp it was to find Hayworth sitting on an upturned log with his penknife in one hand and her stays in the other.

She dropped the coconuts and rushed toward him.

"Hoi! What on earth are you doing?"

He continued merrily ripping through the stitching of her stays with the blade. "I'm taking them apart so we can use the steel wires to make a fish hook."

Caro's whole body flushed at seeing her private underwear in his big hands. "What? No!"

"You're going to have to make sacrifices for survival. You can either have fish for dinner or a well-supported bosom. Which is it to be?"

His unrepentant gaze flickered to her breasts, and Caro

cursed the way her nipples seemed to tingle in response. She crossed her arms in front of her. "Fine. Fish."

"Good choice," he grinned, even though she hadn't really been given a choice at all. With a rip and a tug, he pulled one of the thin metal strips from its setting, and proceeded to bend it into a curve. With his knife he cut it down to size and sharpened the end into a point.

"What are you going to use for string?" Caro groused.

He pointed behind him, at her petticoats, and she cursed herself for leaving them behind. She should have known better than to trust him with anything.

"I've already pulled a good long piece of thread from the bottom," he said, clearly relishing her displeasure. "Don't worry, it's still perfectly wearable."

With an irritated huff, Caro sank down onto her own piece of driftwood. The sun had risen, but clouds dotted the sky. Still, there was hope that they might disperse as the day wore on. She might be able to make a fire after all.

She nibbled on a bit of coconut and watched with silent appreciation as Hayworth set about making a rudimentary fishing pole from a stick, the length of cotton thread, and his newly-made hook.

Not wanting to be accused of idleness, she wandered to the rocks and inspected the rock pools, then pried a limpet from its home. She tried to catch some crabs, but the little devils were too fast.

"Here," she held the limpet out to Hayworth. "You'll be needing something for bait."

His smile of thanks made her stomach somersault. She told herself it was hunger, not attraction.

She'd thought he'd try to catch something immediately, but instead he placed the rod inside the shelter. "No point catching a fish until we have a fire to cook it on. I don't fancy eating it raw." He glanced at the sky. "When those clouds move off, we can try your idea with the watch. Until then, how about we follow the stream inland?"

"Excellent plan."

Caro pulled on her boots, and he did the same, and together they set off into the trees, following the trickle of water.

The land started to rise almost immediately, and they were forced to scramble up muddy banks and rocky outcrops. Tangled tree roots provided countless handholds, but wet leaves and slippery slopes made progress slow.

They found the place where their trickle split off from a larger stream, and continued following that uphill.

At one particularly rocky part Hayworth reached back and offered Caro his hand. Her heart fluttered as she took it, and she marveled at his strength as he effortlessly pulled her upward. Her attention snagged on the play of sinews in his forearm—he'd rolled the sleeves of his shirt up—but just as she was wondering what they must feel like, her foot slipped and she scraped her knee on the jagged rocks.

"Owww!" Her shout was as much annoyance at her own stupidity as it was due to pain.

"Careful!" Hayworth hauled her up the last rocks and onto more even ground.

She hopped on one leg, then grabbed a nearby tree for support as he dropped to his knees in front of her and caught her ankle.

"Hush!" he commanded, anticipating her disapproval. "Let me look."

He pushed up the bottom of her dress without waiting for permission, and she bent to inspect the damage. Her stockings had protected her knee a little, but a fair-sized scrape oozed blood, staining the ripped white cotton a deep red.

Hayworth made a clucking sound with his tongue. She wasn't sure if it was meant to be chiding or sympathetic. She winced as he scooped a handful of cold water from the stream and washed the wound, but pushed him away as soon as he'd finished his ministrations. He took his time releasing her ankle.

"Sure you don't want me to kiss it better?" he teased.

"I'm fine. It's just a scratch."

He stood and peered down at her with a frown. "I know. But you still need to tend to it. Wash it in salt water when we get back to the beach. The last thing we need is for you to get an infection out here with no access to any medicine."

Caro blushed, embarrassed by her own carelessness, and relished the sting in her knee. She deserved it for being an ogling idiot. She, more than anyone, knew that the jungle, while beautiful, could be deadly.

Hayworth, however, seemed to have forgotten his irritation. He turned his head and held his hand up as if for quiet. "Do you hear that?"

Caro frowned. She *could* hear a faint rushing sound, but she'd assumed it was the frantic beating of her heart. Now she concentrated, it was plainly audible above the general noise of the forest.

"It sounds like a waterfall," she said, excitement lifting her tone.

Hayworth caught her hand. "It does indeed. Come on!"

CHAPTER 11

With Caro in tow, Hayworth pushed through the jungle, staying close to the banks of the stream. The sound of rushing water grew ever louder until they burst out of the undergrowth and into a clearing bathed in sunlight.

"Oh, goodness!" Caro's mouth opened on a gasp of delight.

A torrent of water rushed from the top of a rocky cliff and tumbled at least thirty feet into the pool before them. A fine mist spray clouded the base of the falls, creating a permanent rainbow where the sun caught it.

"Do you think it's safe to swim?" She had to raise her voice to be heard over the sound of the water.

"I don't see why not, as long as we mind the slippery rocks." Hayworth sent her one of his irresistible grins. Before she could blink, he'd tugged off his boots and stockings, stripped off his shirt, and began making his way carefully into the pool.

Caro bit back a smile. She'd never met anyone who could undress so quickly.

He set off swimming with long strokes toward the base of the falls, his strong arms pushing against the current, then turned to face her, treading water.

"What are you waiting for?" he shouted. "I promise I won't look at your unmentionables."

To emphasize his point, he turned so his glistening shoulders faced her.

After a brief moment of indecision, Caro threw propriety to the wind. She was desperate for a swim, and the water looked incredibly inviting. She stepped behind a tree, removed everything except for her shift, and peered out at the pool. Hayworth's back was still turned, so she made her way gingerly over the rocks and into the water.

Compared to the sea, it was bracingly cold, and she shrieked as she made the final plunge. She came up for air, then ducked below the surface again, fanning her hair to rinse out every last grain of sand and salt.

"Oh, that feels so good!"

Hayworth, swimming in lazy circles across the pool, grinned at her enthusiasm. She tried to swim close to the base of the falls, as he had, but the push of the water was so strong she gave up after only a few strokes, arms aching with the effort.

She turned to find him right in front of her. Sunlight glinted off his slicked-back hair and glimmered like diamonds on his muscled shoulders. Water droplets trickled down his nose and gathered at the corners of his mouth.

Caro couldn't look away. She had the most insane urge to lick those drops from his lips, to taste the cool water on his warm skin.

He drifted closer. "Caro." His voice was a deep growl, almost a warning.

Her gaze flicked up to his. "Yes?"

"When you look at me like that—"

"Yes?" she prompted, half teasing, half terrified of what he was going to say. Her heart was pounding against her ribs, and not just because of the unaccustomed exercise.

He took a deep breath. "Never mind." A rueful smile curved

his lips as he reached out and smoothed a strand of wet hair from her cheek. "Is 'disheveled castaway' a fashion style back in London? Because if it's not, it should be. It suits you."

She let out a snort and tried to stay afloat. He was tall enough to stand, but her toes barely touched the bottom of the pool.

"Pfft. You're only saying that because there's no other woman on this whole island for you to flirt with. You, Max Cavendish, are a scoundrel."

"That may be true, but that doesn't alter the facts. You're beautiful. I've always thought so."

Caro's pulse skipped a beat, but she feigned airy amusement. "And *you've* clearly had a blow to the head that's affecting your judgment."

A wave buffeted them, and she grabbed his arm to steady herself—then immediately regretted it as the muscle flexed beneath her fingers, slick and impressively solid. Her stomach flipped, but before she could push herself away from temptation, he caught both her shoulders in his hands.

The upper part of his chest rose above the lapping water, mere inches from her own. Caro glanced down and realized she might as well have removed her chemise, for all the coverage it was providing. The cold had peaked her nipples into tight buds and their dark tips were clearly visible through the near-transparent fabric.

Heat scalded her cheeks as she realized Hayworth had noticed, as well. His sea-blue gaze roamed over her and his fingers tightened on her upper arms. For a blissful moment she thought he was going to drag her against his chest and kiss her, but he pushed himself away with an almighty splash.

She quashed a groan of disappointment.

"You should get dressed." His voice was deeper than she'd ever heard it. "I'll wait until you're done before I get out."

Thoroughly flustered, Caro nodded. She swam to the shallows and made her way out, but when she glanced back to see if

Hayworth was watching her, he was swimming with purposeful strokes to the far side of the pool.

* * *

Bloody hell.

Max ducked under that water and blew out a stream of frustrated bubbles, willing the chill of the pool to cool his ardor.

Had he really thought this place was heaven? It was hell. Pure hell. And he'd been sentenced to a never-ending state of aching, yearning lust.

He was deliberately *not* looking at Caro, but the image of her was seared into his brain. Her shift had been rendered completely sheer by the water. It looked like a sheen of icing. Her perfect breasts had reminded him of glazed buns; each with a gorgeous cherry nipple on the top begging for his mouth.

God, he wanted to taste them. To taste *her*.

He'd been a split second away from doing it, too. The interest, the invitation, in her eyes had been unmistakable, and it had sent a punch of primal satisfaction to his gut. But she was an innocent, and he would *not* seduce her until he was absolutely sure she wanted him as much as he wanted her.

His cock, however, needed no further convincing. He was as hard as an iron bar in his breeches and he couldn't leave the water until the damn thing had subsided—which was unlikely with Caro half-naked just a few paces away on the bank.

Max ducked beneath the water again and scrubbed his hair vigorously. By the time he resurfaced, slightly more in control of himself, Caro was dressed and loitering in the shade of the trees with her back turned to give him privacy.

With a resigned sigh, he waded from the water, dried himself as best he could with his shirt, and pulled it on, along with his boots and stockings. If he'd been alone, he would have swum naked—and wouldn't now be saddled with wet breeches trickling water into his boots. He sent a silent apology to his bootmaker, Hoby, back in London, who would have an apoplexy to see his finest—and most expensive—creations in such a pitiful state.

Giving Caro a wide berth, he started down the trail. "Let's get back to the beach."

They walked in silence, with Max acutely aware of her behind him, when he suddenly heard her stop.

"Max."

He turned. It was the first time she'd ever used his given name. "What's the matter?"

"Stay still and do not be alarmed."

He frowned. "What do you mean 'don't be alarmed.' That's precisely the kind of thing someone says when the other person should be *very alarmed indeed.*"

Her lips curved up in an easy smile. "There's a spider on your back, that's all."

He froze, suppressing the urge to look over his shoulder or to start brushing his hands all over himself to get rid of the thing. "What kind of a spider? A big one? Get it off!"

She caught his forearm and turned him slowly back around. "It's only a little one. Here, let me."

He quelled an instinctive shudder as he felt movement on his back. He hoped to God it was her hands.

"There!"

Her confident tone lowered his pulse rate a little, but it ratcheted back up when he discovered her cupping the biggest spider he'd ever seen in his life in her hands.

He took an involuntary step back. "Bloody hell, woman! Kill it!"

She sent him a laughing glance and bent her head to address the spider.

"Oh, don't you listen to him," she crooned, as one might to a lap dog or small child. "He's just grouchy. You are *such* a *handsome* fellow, aren't you?"

Max broke out into a cold sweat. "Put it down! Are you mad?"

Caro laughed—actually laughed. The girl was out of her mind.

She raised the monstrosity up to eye level. "This is a tarantula. Rather sweet, if a little hairy. I had one as a pet in Brazil. His name was Timothy. I was very sad to leave him behind."

Max fought the need to slap it out of her hand and run screaming into the forest. "You are *not* keeping that thing as a pet. I forbid it."

With a grin, she extended her hand close to a branch and the nightmare creature slowly ambled off her skin and onto the twig.

He let out a relieved huff. "You shouldn't take such chances. What if it had bitten you?"

"Tarantulas aren't usually aggressive and rarely bite. But even if he had bitten me, I would have been fine. Have you ever been stung by a bee? It feels like that."

Max felt his jaw drop open. "You've been bitten by one *before?*"

"Just once. Timmy didn't want to share his mouse." She watched in obvious fascination as the newly-released specimen clambered up the tree. "Timmy was a lovely blue color, but this one, you see, is black and brown."

"I thought your family studied butterflies," he said hoarsely. "Pretty, harmless butterflies."

"We do. At least, father does, and we all help him. But one can't walk ten feet in a jungle without encountering things that are *not* butterflies."

Max shook his head, stoutly refusing to think about all the other *not butterflies* that might be close to him at that very moment. *Dear God.*

"Thank you for removing it," he said stiffly.

Caro sent him a beatific smile. "You're very welcome."

CHAPTER 12

Caro bit back her laugh at Max's reaction to the spider as they made their way back to the beach. For some reason the knowledge that the man who had led his troops into battle, who'd faced the horror of Napoleon's army without flinching, was afraid of spiders, was incredibly endearing.

Perhaps feeling that his masculine aura of invincibility had been tarnished, he stomped to the shelter when they reached the beach, collected his fishing pole and knife, and set off toward the promontory with a grunt about "catching us some dinner."

Caro let out a little chuckle. If anything, her admiration for him had only increased. The tarantula had been far larger than anything he would have previously encountered in England, and she'd been pleased that he'd obeyed her command to stay still, rather than flailing around and trying to dislodge it himself.

She only hoped that her unladylike display of affection for the eight-legged creature hadn't lowered her in *his* estimation. It was perfectly acceptable for a lady to like kittens or puppies, but an interest in arachnids was rather less common.

She finger-combed her damp hair in an attempt to remove some of the tangles, and when the sun broke through the clouds, her spirits lifted. She hastened to Max's jacket and pulled the watch from his pocket, then gathered the tinder necessary to start a fire.

Cross-legged, she directed the bright circle of reflected light onto a pile of shredded coconut bark, and watched in excitement as a dark spot appeared. The singed area began to smolder, and she heaped more dried grass on top of it, blowing carefully. The sudden bright flare of a flame was like a tiny miracle.

"Yes!"

Careful not to swamp the flame, she added larger twigs, and when she was sure it was past the danger point, she sat back on her bottom with a sigh of satisfaction.

A glance up the beach showed Max had his back to her; he was casting his makeshift fishing hook into the shallows. With a sudden jerk he pulled back his arm and tugged a silvery, glittering fish from the waves. He almost lost his balance trying to land the thing on the rocks, but managed it at last, and his whoop of triumph echoed across the bay.

He straightened, fish in hand, and held it up to show her—and it was then that he noticed the smoke and her fire.

Caro grinned and waved, and he waved back, leaping athletically down from the rocks and jogging back along the sand.

"You made a fire!" His sun-flushed face was wreathed in a smile. "You marvelous thing!"

"And you caught us some dinner," she countered, nodding at the fish in his hand.

"I did. I've no idea what it is, but it saves us from eating nothing but mango."

He headed back the water and made quick work of cleaning the fish, while Caro piled more wood on the fire until it was a steady blaze. When he returned, he sank to the sand next to her and held his hands out toward the flames with a sigh of satisfaction.

"Now this is excellent. We'll dine like kings tonight."

Caro stilled as a sudden thought occurred to her. "Wait, what day is it?"

He shrugged. "Don't ask me."

"We left Madagascar on December the twenty first, and the storm was the night of the twenty second. Which means we woke up on the beach here yesterday, the twenty third—"

"—which makes *today* Christmas Eve!" he finished. "Tomorrow's Christmas day."

"We're missing Christmas!"

"We're not *missing* it," he smiled. "We're just having it somewhere else, that's all. Somewhere interesting. What would you usually do? If you were in England, that is. Sing carols? Decorate the house?" His eyes twinkled. "Hang a branch of mistletoe over the doorframe, hoping for a kiss?"

He glanced up, as if expecting a similar branch to be suspended above their heads, but there was only the swaying green lattice of palm fronds. He puffed his lower lip in a disappointed pout.

"We usually spend Christmas with the family, if we're in England." Caro said. "Especially the cousins. We've been absent so often that it's lovely when we all manage to get together."

"I know your cousins. Tristan and I were at university together."

"I was sorry to miss his wedding. But father *insisted* on going to Brazil. Whoever imagined a Montgomery would fall in love with a *Davies*? First Maddie married Gryff, and then Tristan married Carys." She frowned. "Wait, you were invited to their wedding, I'm sure of it. Don't you remember?"

If he could remember Tristan's wedding, a few months ago, then surely he'd remember attending as a duke, and not as a stable hand?

"I'm still a bit hazy about England."

"I can't believe you don't remember my great aunts," she prodded. "Constance and Prudence? They're infamous in the *Ton* for their indiscretion."

He shook his head. "Sorry."

Caro breathed a silent sigh of relief. Her deception was safe—for now.

The fish, whatever it was, turned out to be delicious, and they washed it down with fresh water and mango.

By unspoken agreement they built the fire into a roaring blaze. Max withdrew a long stick from the embers, and together they carried it over the rocks, and onto the adjacent beach. Several of the *Artemis's* passengers could be seen across the strait, and Max waved the smoking torch in their general direction.

Two of them waved back, and Caro liked to think it was her father, or perhaps her mother. At least they'd know that she and Hayworth hadn't murdered each other. Yet.

The sun set as they walked back to camp, and Caro let out a jaw-cracking yawn. Max bumped his shoulder against hers.

"Early night for you, sleepyhead." He motioned to the shelter. "In you go. I'm going to stay up for a while and make sure the fire doesn't go out."

Caro didn't bother to argue. As the sun dipped beyond the horizon in an extravagant display of salmon pink and lavender, she shuffled beneath the leaves. The light from the fire was extraordinarily comforting. It flickered shadows on the sand, and she dozed, half-listening to Max moving around the clearing, and adding fuel to the fire.

"'Night Caro."

His low tones drifted through her fuzzy brain, and she managed to mumble, "'Night, Max."

Her last thought, as she drifted off to sleep, was; *When had she started thinking of him as Max, and not Hayworth?*

CHAPTER 13

Max was already up and fishing when Caro awoke. She had no recollection of him sleeping next to her at all. Had he stayed up all night with the fire? Had he decided to forgo the shelter entirely and sleep elsewhere? Was the idea of sleeping next to her so unpalatable? *She didn't snore, did she? Or smell?*

Surreptitiously, she lifted the collar of her shift and took a sniff.

She pushed away such depressing thoughts as she splashed her face and plaited her hair. This might be the most unexpected Christmas day she'd ever spent, but she would contribute her share to the day's bounty.

She gathered some mangos, then returned to the beach. Wading into the turquoise shallows, she rearranged several small rocks into a V shape that funneled into a shallow rock pool. Then she splashed about, trying to herd shoals of fish into her trap, as a farmer's dog might drive a flock of sheep.

It took numerous attempts—the fish presumably being more intelligent than sheep—but eventually six small silver-blue fish raced into the pool. She quickly closed the exit with a rock, then used her petticoats as a rudimentary net to catch them.

By the time she returned, panting, wet, but victorious, Max was cooking something over the fire. He squinted at her against the sun, and her heart gave a little thump at his rumpled, piratical appearance. Even without decent sleep and a daily shave the man was obnoxiously attractive.

"What have you there?"

"More fish. And mangos."

"I caught a lobster between the rocks." He gestured at the crustacean suspended on a stick over the fire. "Not exactly what I imagined we'd be eating for Christmas dinner, but never mind. Let's pretend we're in England, at your house, with no expense spared. What are we eating?"

Caro smiled at his attempt to stay positive. "Well, I suppose we would have roast beef, or roast duck. Roast potatoes, carrots, peas, and parsnips. And gravy, of course."

"Mmm." Max smacked his lips in appreciation and held up a coconut shell full of water. "And presumably some wine from the cellar." He took a sip, then passed it to her. "An excellent vintage."

Caro took a seat next to him by the fire and sampled the 'wine'.

"What would be for dessert?" he urged.

"Ah, well, that would be Christmas pudding."

"Set alight with brandy?"

"Of course. And topped with cream, or brandy butter, or custard."

"I'd have all three," he said solemnly.

"And if you still had room after that, then I suppose we'd have a few mince pies and a sherry."

"I feel full just thinking about it." He glanced sideways at her, and the laughter lingered in his eyes as he lifted his hand and trailed his finger down the bridge of her nose and across her cheek.

"You've caught the sun," he murmured. "You're all pink."

She flushed even more at his unexpected touch, certain she must be the same color as the lobster. Her stomach somersaulted, but she tried to brush off her nervousness with a joke.

"Oh, the shame! My vouchers to Almacks will be withdrawn."

He leaned in conspiratorially. "I'll make sure you get in."

Caro stilled. Did he realize what he'd just said? A mere stablemaster wouldn't have any sway with patronesses like Lady Jersey. Such confidence could only come from the Duke of Hayworth.

Did he remember who he was?

She gazed at him suspiciously, but the intent look on his face distracted her. He hadn't lowered his hand. Instead, he slipped it around her head to cradle the back of her skull.

Caro sucked in a breath. His eyes flicked to her lips, and everything inside her tensed in wicked anticipation.

"All this talk of pudding has me craving something sweet," he murmured. "Do you know what would be sweet?"

She managed a slight shake of her head.

"Kissing you."

She couldn't frame a response. Her wits had gone begging.

"Let's just pretend there's mistletoe," he said huskily.

And then he kissed her.

For a full second Caro was so surprised that she didn't move. And then she melted against him like a candle held too close to the fire. She'd dreamed of kissing him for years, but the reality was better than she'd ever imagined.

His lips were firm, and a little rough. Caro kissed him back, inexpertly, and when his tongue slipped between her lips to tangle with her own, she gave a gasp of delight. She closed her eyes, drowning in the taste, the feel of him. Experimentally, she swirled her own tongue against his, and he groaned deep in his chest. His fingers tightened for a moment against her nape, and then he drew back.

She stared at him, panting and breathless.

"Merry Christmas," he rasped.

"Merry Christmas."

He released her head and returned his attention to the fire, as if the earth hadn't just shifted on its axis.

Caro drew her knees up to her chest and stared blindly into the flames. Her whole body was tingling and she pressed her lips together to stop herself from begging him to do it again. And again. And again.

"Oh, I almost forgot." Max reached behind him into the shelter. "I got you a present."

Caro lifted her brows. He caught her wrist and pressed something into her palm. "It's only a stone with a hole in it. I thought you could put it on a necklace or something."

A pink flush rose on his cheekbones and Caro came to the delightful realization that he was blushing.

"Thank you," she said solemnly. She closed her fingers around it, as pleased as if he'd presented her with a diamond the size of a robin's egg. "I'm sorry, I haven't got anything for you."

"That's all right."

Silence reigned as they shared the lobster, but Caro's thoughts kept returning to the kiss.

"A penny for your thoughts."

She jumped at his question and cast around for an entirely different subject. "Do you know, I promised my parents that when we got back to England, I'd start seriously considering my suitors."

His brows rose.

"But now," she continued, "even if by some miracle we *do* get rescued, I doubt I'll have any suitors to consider. Who's going to believe I'm still an innocent when I've been alone with you for so long? I'll be completely unmarriageable."

"You don't sound particularly distressed by the prospect," he observed carefully.

"Well, in all honesty, I'm not. It's not as if I've ever met a man I wanted to marry."

Caro avoided his eyes as she spouted that disgraceful lie. The one man she'd secretly dreamed of marrying was sitting right beside her on the sand.

Not that he needed to know that mortifying piece of information.

Max rubbed the stubble on his chin and looked thoughtful. "Hmm. It's true, I'm afraid. Your reputation might already be beyond repair. People love to gossip, and they'll always think the worst. Whether you're innocent or not is largely irrelevant. They'll never believe a man and a woman could spend as long as we have together in such circumstances and not be . . . intimate."

His blue eyes caught hers and held. "There's really only one thing you can do." His expression was perfectly serious.

"What's that?"

"Seduce me and make the best of it." The laughter spilled back into his eyes. "You might as well be hanged for a sheep as for a lamb."

Caro gave a choked gasp. "Are you propositioning me?"

"Of course not. That would be highly inappropriate. I'm a lowly stable hand and you're a lady. I'm suggesting *you* proposition *me*."

He sent her an amused look that also managed to make her heart beat faster in her chest, even though she knew he wasn't being serious. "I promise to be an easy conquest. You can have your wicked way with me and I won't put up any resistance at all."

Caro whacked him on the arm for his teasing and decided it was time to come clean about his true station in life.

"You're not actually a—"

"—scoundrel?" he interrupted, before she could finish. "I beg to differ. I'm having the most ungentlemanly thoughts about all the ways you can besmirch my reputation."

She shook her head, both flattered and a little scandalized.

"You're ridiculous. You'd be saying the same thing to *any* woman you were stuck here with, whether duchess or dairymaid."

He clapped his hand over his heart in a mock show of hurt. "You wound me, milady."

With a laugh to cover her fluttering pulse, she got to her feet and brushed the sand from her skirts. "I'm going to the waterfall for a swim."

Max accepted her retreat with a knowing look that suggested he knew she was running away. He picked up his pocket watch from where it rested on a piece of driftwood, flicked open the lid, and glanced at the dial.

"If you're not back in an hour I'll assume you've been eaten by tarantulas and send out a search party."

"You'd brave such monsters to come looking for me?"

His lips quirked, but his expression was somehow earnest. "If I thought you'd show your appreciation in a suitably enthusiastic manner—" His gaze on her lips left no doubt that he was talking about kissing, "Then yes. I think I'd brave anything at all."

Flustered yet again, Caro took her leave.

As she stomped through the forest toward the waterfall, she tried to remember all the reasons she shouldn't be flirting with Maximillian Cavendish, but his teasing words kept swirling around her brain.

He was right. She *would* be judged when she got back to England. Rumors would fly, and the more she and her family tried to protest her innocence, the more people would suspect the worst.

If this escapade had really rendered her unmarriageable, then why *shouldn't* she satisfy her curiosity about lovemaking? Fate had stranded her with the only man she'd ever desired, and he seemed perfectly willing to seduce her, or to allow himself to be seduced.

If she was doomed to a life of spinsterhood for the rest of her days, why shouldn't she seize this chance to experience real passion, just once?

CHAPTER 14

"Bloody woman."

Max strode up the hill toward the waterfall, muttering under his breath. She'd been away for far longer than her allotted hour, and his heart pounded as he alternated between frustration and worry.

What if she'd had an accident? What if she'd slipped on the rocks and broken her ankle, or cracked her head?

He increased his pace, his thighs burning as he pushed through the trees and burst into the clearing, braced to either rescue her, or to scold her for needlessly worrying him.

His words died on his lips.

Caro was still in the pool.

Naked.

Max was quite sure his heart stopped beating before roaring back to life.

He checked the pile of white cotton at his feet—yes, her shift was definitely there, along with her petticoats and dress—then he glanced back up at the undeniable flash of pale skin beneath the rippling water.

His brain went a little fuzzy.

Years of ingrained gentlemanly conduct urged him to turn around, immediately, and give her some privacy.

Years of desiring the bloody woman had him staying precisely where he was.

Cara turned in the water and saw him, and he braced himself for shrieks of maidenly outrage, but instead she started toward him with slow, deliberate strokes.

He was utterly incapable of looking away. He'd seen countless naked women, but never *her*, and his gaze flickered over her pale limbs, so teasingly suggested by the moving water that alternately cloaked and revealed.

She met his eyes as she reached the shallows, and he experienced the stab in the gut her direct look always gave him. He opened his mouth to apologize, but before he could say a word her lips quirked up in a devilish smile.

"You should come in," she said softly.

He coughed to clear his throat. "That's . . . probably not a good idea."

She tilted her head, as if considering. "I won't tell anyone if you don't."

The naughty, teasing note in her voice had him panting in disbelief. His blood was a dull roar in his ears, his cock already hard in his breeches.

"You've been longer than an hour," he growled, trying to look stern.

"I know."

Not even an apology, damn her, for worrying him.

She lifted her hand, beckoning him like a siren, and like the poor sailors of the Odyssey, he couldn't resist. Almost in a trance, he stripped off his boots and his shirt and started forward in his breeches, then stopped when she shook her head and tilted her chin at his lower half.

"Off with them, Cavendish. This is no time to be missish. Can't have you catching a fever gadding about in wet clothes, can we?"

His blood rose at her mocking repetition of his own words.

Little minx. What game was she playing? Did she think he'd be immune to her nakedness? Was this some ridiculous, misguided way of proving to herself that he didn't truly desire her? If so, she was in for a rude awakening. He'd never wanted anyone more in his life.

He sent her a dark look, a warning not to play with fire, and rested one hand causally at the top button of his falls.

"You want me to remove these?"

"I do."

He made one last, desperate attempt to make her see reason. She wasn't a complete innocent. She had to know what she was inviting. What she was risking.

"Have you ever seen a naked man, Caro?"

A delicate flush mottled her cheeks, but she held his gaze.

"An *aroused* naked man?" he pushed.

Her eyes widened, but she didn't back down. "No. But I want to."

His heart skipped another beat.

He shouldn't. He absolutely—

She stood up.

The water was only waist deep. She emerged, wet and glistening; shoulders, breasts, the sinful curve of her waist.

Oh, God. She was perfection. Pale, creamy skin, pink-tipped breasts, water droplets sliding over her like little pearls.

Maybe he'd truly died and gone to heaven. Maybe he'd been bitten by some hideous snake or terrible spider and was even now hallucinating this exquisite, deliberate provocation.

She didn't lift her hands to cover her breasts. Instead, she stood there, letting him look his fill.

"Caro," he croaked, desperate.

Her mouth curved. "I'm seducing you, Cavendish. In case you haven't noticed."

"Oh, believe me, I've noticed. What I'm wondering is why?"

"Why not?" she countered. "It was your idea. And besides, nobody has to know."

There was challenge in her tone, daring him to disagree, and a flash of annoyance warmed him. He didn't want to be her secret experiment, some nameless fling she could forget as soon as they were rescued.

He wanted forever.

But his thoughts scattered as she leaned back in the water and pushed off, and his fingers unbuttoned his breeches without consulting his brain. He shucked the fabric down his thighs, kicked them off, and dove into the water.

The invigorating chill did nothing to cool his ardor. The moment he resurfaced Caro threw herself at him and he almost went under again at the feel of her naked body pressed against his.

Her arms slid around his neck, the hard tips of her breasts squashed against his chest, and he groaned aloud in pleasure.

He was lost.

It was the most natural thing in the world to wrap his own arms around her, to urge her legs around his waist, using the buoyancy of the water to maximum effect.

God, the slip-slide feel of skin on skin was almost his undoing.

His erection was trapped between them, pressed against his stomach, and, impassioned, he caught the back of her head and pulled her in for a soul-stealing kiss.

This was nothing like the slow, leisurely exploration of before. This was openmouthed and hungry, hot and wet. She moaned into his mouth as he devoured her, holding nothing back, showing her the full force of his need.

It should have scared her. Should have had her pulling back in alarm. But Caroline Montgomery had never done the expected. She fisted the wet hair at the back of his head and tugged him closer, kissing him back as if her life depended on it.

God, she was a fast learner. Each time he angled his head to get a better taste, she angled hers the opposite way, fusing them together, giving more. Taking it all.

Unable to help himself, he traced his hand down the curve of her back and cupped her backside, squeezing the rounded flesh until she was squirming against him.

"God, Caro. Let me pleasure you. Please." He panted it against her neck.

She pressed frantic kisses along his jawline, then leaned back in his arms. "Yes."

His heart thundered in relief.

"Not here," he managed. He surged for the shallows, and she clung to him like a starfish. He carried her from the pool, barely making it to their discarded pile of clothes before he lowered her to the ground and pressed her beneath him for another mind-numbing kiss.

Scarcely able to believe it was happening, he kissed his way down her throat, then licked the water droplets from her skin as he moved lower. His hand cupped her left breast while his mouth found the right, and he relished the choked little gasp that escaped her as he swirled his tongue around her peaked nipple.

"Max!"

He opened his mouth and took more of her, his senses reeling at the taste. Sweet and clean, like the water. Bright, like sunlight.

She caught the back of his head, tugging him closer with a wordless plea. He chuckled. "You like that, Caro?"

"Oh, yes!"

His entire body was on fire, desperate for her, but he couldn't forget that she was a virgin. He had to slow down, to make it good for her. He stroked her sleek curves, shaping her ribs, her waist, her thighs. Breathing pleas and praises against her skin.

"You're beautiful, Caro."

He slid his hand over her stomach then down, into the springy triangle of hair. She tensed for a moment, and he waited for her to push him away, but instead she arched her back and tugged him closer still. He kissed her, long drugging kisses, as his fingers slid between her legs to toy with her folds. She was wet, both from the water and her own excitement, and his heart hammered in his chest at the proof of her desire.

She wanted him. *Finally.*

He slipped his finger into her, just a little, and she gasped, then writhed against him. In and out, slowly, showing her the way. He swirled his thumb over the hard little bead at the top of her sex, teasing her mercilessly, and she cried out against his throat, arching into him. Her hands roamed his skin, clutching at his shoulders, his back, his arms, but he was too intent on bringing her to her first crisis to fully savor her touch.

Her breathing hitched and he quickened the pace, pushing deeper, loving the little sounds of pleasure that escaped her. Was she pretending he was a stable hand? Or the Duke of Hayworth, having his wicked way with her? It didn't matter. He was Max, and she was Caro, and he'd wanted to do this to her for a thousand years.

She was hot, and slick, her inner muscles clutching at him, and for a split second he considered withdrawing his hand and sliding his cock inside her instead.

No. This time wasn't for him. And he couldn't risk her getting pregnant, either.

He claimed her mouth, thrusting his tongue in a wicked counterpoint to the movement of his hand, and she surged against him.

"Let it happen, sweeting," he whispered against her lips. "Chase it."

"Oh!"

He felt her climax with a rush of primal satisfaction. Her body squeezed his fingers as she arched up, riding the waves of pleasure with a cry that echoed around the clearing and sent birds flapping from the trees.

When it was over, she simply collapsed. Her arms flopped to the ground and her limbs went lax, and for a moment he feared she'd passed out. And then she let out a sigh of pure happiness and nestled her head beneath his chin.

"My God, no wonder nobody tells young ladies about this," she breathed in awed tones. "There wouldn't be a virgin left in England if they knew how lovely ruination feels."

Max propped himself on his elbows and smiled down at her. Her face was flushed, her skin dewy, and his heart gave a funny little flip inside his chest.

His cock still throbbed in painful urgency, but he smoothed her hair away from her face with a gentle hand. "Nice?"

She sent him an incredulous, laughing look. "More than nice. Astonishing. Thank you."

He bit back a smile at her earnestness. "Thank *you*," he echoed solemnly. "One does one's best to help a damsel in distress. You were clearly drowning and in need of rescue."

Her clear gaze met his as she turned on her side to face him. "But what about you?" Her hand stroked his shoulder, then trailed with casual devastation down over his chest. She flattened her palm directly over his pounding heart. There was no chance that she wouldn't be able to feel it.

"What about me?" he drawled.

She bit her lip and took a deep breath as if steeling herself, then slid her hand down over the muscled ridges of his abdomen and into the line of hair that arrowed from his navel to his groin.

"I think *you* need rescuing, too. Show me what to do."

CHAPTER 15

Max caught Caro's wrist to slow her southward exploration.

"You don't need to do that. I'm fine."

Her eyes twinkled as she slid a sly, frankly curious look down between their bodies. "You don't look fine," she said with a laugh that made his toes curl. "You look . . . uncomfortable. *Swollen*, even."

"It'll go down," he growled. "Just—"

He hissed to a stop, his mind suddenly blank as she slid her fingers around his cock and squeezed gently.

"Oh, my," she breathed in wonder. "Does that hurt?"

Max ground his teeth against the blinding urge to thrust into her hand. "No, but—"

She opened her fingers and stroked him, and her touch sent bolts of lightning shooting up his spine.

"Show me how to please you. It's only fair."

With a groan, Max gave in. Gazing deep into her eyes, he reached down, caught her hand, and showed her how to hold him. He wrapped his own fingers around hers and watched her eyes widen as she caught the rhythm.

It didn't take long. The feel of her, the scent of her filling his nose, the soft touch of her hand—the combination undid him. After only a few strokes his stomach muscles tensed, and with a smothered cry he pulsed in her hand, spending himself against his stomach.

She didn't seem to be disgusted. She watched him with a kind of fascinated interest, and he realized with a flash of humor that it was the same look she'd given that damned tarantula; awe mingled with respect.

With a chuckle he rolled over and sat up, then went to wash himself in the pool. When he returned, she'd pulled her dress over her nakedness and he bit back a disappointed huff.

"You could have stayed naked. There's no-one else to see."

Her cheeks were a becoming pink, and he wondered if she was embarrassed or, worse, regretting what they'd just done, but then she sent him a cheeky smile of her own.

"True, but it's not very practical if we encounter a *real* serpent." She sent a meaningful glance at his crotch. "Or another spider."

Max pulled his breeches on with a grin. "You're right. Sunburn might be a problem too. Clothes it is."

* * *

CARO HAD to force herself to look away from the golden, muscled perfection of Max's body. A body that had just introduced her an incredible new world of pleasure.

Even though she was dressed again, she felt naked, stripped bare by the astonishingly intimate things they'd just done.

She told herself there was no need to be embarrassed. She was a scientist, after all. She would treat the past half hour as an interesting physical experiment. She could be cool, mature, sophisticated. Like his previous lovers.

As Max donned his shirt and boots, Caro tugged on the rest

of her clothes and followed him down the hill, silently drinking in the breadth of his shoulders and the beautiful curves of his backside.

She'd been touching him mere moments ago. Already it seemed unreal, like a fever-dream, and yet her every step made her aware of the new sensitivity of her skin; the cotton shift brushing her breasts, the unexpected ache between her thighs.

She'd made a mistake in allowing Max to touch her. Instead of satisfying her curiosity about lovemaking, as she'd hoped, it had done the exact opposite.

She wanted more.

There *was* more, too. She'd been around farm animals long enough to know that the male put his member *inside* the female. She pressed her fist to the center of her chest and tried to ignore the ache that throbbed beneath her skin. What would *that* feel like?

She tore her eyes from the tempting curls at the back of Max's head, and turned her attention to the lush green forest instead.

"Max, wait."

He stilled immediately. "Oh, God, no. Don't tell me it's another spider. Because if it is, I—"

"No, it's a nice surprise. Look." She pointed upward. "Bananas."

A relieved smile broke out on his face. "That is *much* better than a spider."

With the help of a fallen tree, he detached a bunch of the yellow-green fruit and as he jumped down Caro realized she was grinning at him like a simpleton. A shocking possibility dawned on her.

Dear God, was she *in love with him*?

She'd always found him attractive, always enjoyed their sparring and craved their interactions, but this warm, glowing satisfaction whenever she was in his presence was new.

He was so much more than just his title. He was an aristocrat who wasn't afraid to get his hands dirty, a gorgeous, physical specimen who, astonishingly, appreciated her and her myriad eccentricities.

He was, in fact, everything she wanted in a man; strong, amusing, protective, resourceful, intelligent.

Oh, she was in so much trouble.

"We should take some of the leaves, too," she said, mainly to distract herself. "We can use them on the roof of the shelter. They'll be much better than the palm fronds."

Max dutifully collected an armful of the large, flat leaves, and they set off.

Caro was silent as they walked back down the beach, and it was only Max's shout that finally snapped her out of her brooding.

"Hoi, come look at this!"

He was at the high tide mark, standing over a large brown spherical object. It was quite a bit larger than a coconut, and Caro smiled at his bemused expression.

"It's a coco de mer nut," she said. "I saw one in Madagascar, at the King's palace. They're extremely rare."

Max tilted his head. "It looks just like—"

"—a woman's bare bottom?" she finished with a smile. "Yes, it does."

It was true. The twin curves of the smooth nut were separated by a central cleft that made it look exactly like a curvy woman's derriere.

"You should see the other side," she said.

"It's not the same?"

She shook her head.

Max dropped the banana leaves and rolled the nut over, and despite knowing what to expect, Caro still felt a blush rise on her cheeks. The reverse looked just like her own rounded belly and thighs, complete with the triangle-shaped juncture where Max had touched her to such devastating effect.

Avoiding his eye, she adopted her most scholarly tones. "Because of its ... er ..."

"Erotic shape?"

"*Unusual appearance*, the coco de mer is thought to have mythological, even magical properties."

Max grunted. "I can see why. It's quite something."

"Legend has it that the trees make passionate love on stormy nights. They say the male trees uproot themselves and approach the female trees, and because they're so shy and secretive, anyone who sees them mating will either die, or go blind."

"Well, that's comforting." Max said. "Let's hope this one floated here from somewhere else. Even so, I'll keep my eyes closed, next time there's a storm. Wouldn't want to be an accidental voyeur."

Caro chuckled. Max's relaxed attitude made it impossible for her to be awkward about what they'd done together. She supposed she ought to be feeling ashamed for having allowed him such liberties, but she couldn't seem to dredge up an ounce of regret.

He insisted on carrying the nut back to camp, so Caro gathered the banana leaves and used them to improve the roof of their shelter. As the sun became hotter, she rested in the shade, half hoping Max would find an excuse to join her, but he took off around the headland, so she entertained herself by weaving palm fronds together to make a rudimentary sunhat.

If only she could read Max's thoughts. Was he thinking of her? If he truly believed himself a down-on-his-luck stable hand, might he be feeling guilty for giving in to her seduction?

Or was she just one more woman in a long line of conquests?

She'd remember the feel of his bare chest pressing her down, the wicked play of his fingers, for as long as she lived, but perhaps men were different. He could well have already dismissed the entire incident from his mind. She wasn't his first lover, after all.

Her heart gave a miserable little squeeze.

The heat was as draining and oppressive as her thoughts. She lay in the shelter and must have dozed, because when she awoke the sun was much lower in the sky and there was no sign of Max anywhere.

A flash of alarm caught her. He'd been gone for *hours*. What if he'd had an accident?

He wasn't on the adjacent beach, so she stacked more wood on the signal fire and waved half-heartedly over at the other island. She was just debating whether to carry on when she heard a whistle and looked up to see him appear over the promontory of rocks at the far end of the beach.

Her heart soared in relief. She might have wished to be alone when they'd first been washed ashore, but now she couldn't imagine not having his companionship.

For one foolish moment she wondered what it would be like if they were *never* rescued.

She could be happy, here, with him.

A rogue wave splashed her feet and she let out a soft snort at her own idiocy. This situation wasn't permanent. They would be rescued, eventually, and reality would intrude like a bucket of cold water to the face. Max would regain his memory, and they would each go their separate ways.

If she was truly unmarriageable when they reached London, she would remain a spinster, traveling the world and assisting her parents in their scientific endeavors. Max wouldn't consider her as his potential duchess. She was too unconventional, too unusual. And staying in England to watch him marry someone else would hurt.

"I thought you'd come to grief," she scolded when he was close enough to hear. "What will I do if you break your leg or get bitten by a shark?"

His teeth flashed in his tanned face. "I expect you'll put me out of my misery and finish me off with the pocket knife."

She shuddered at his morbid sense of humor. "Don't say that!"

"Oh, so you'd nurse me back to health?"

"I'd certainly *try*."

He snorted. "Only because it's too hot to dig me a grave. I heard what you said that first morning. You called me an insufferable oaf."

Caro turned her face away to hide her blush.

"I'm hoping your opinion of me has improved?" he pressed.

She started back toward camp, but he kept pace beside her easily, with his longer stride.

"Marginally," she conceded.

She caught his grin from the corner of her eye and felt an answering smile tug her own lips.

"Well, that's a relief. I won't be afraid of sharpening the blade."

"Perhaps you can use it to shave?"

He drew his fingers over his cheek and chin. "You don't like my stubble?"

Caro clenched her hands against the desire to stroke his cheek. "You look like a pirate."

His smile widened. "That's not an answer."

She lifted her nose in the air and ignored his taunting. The man's opinion of himself was high enough already. There was no need to admit she found him devastatingly attractive.

To cool off, she waded out into the shallows, lifting her skirts above her knees. Max started to clamber over the rocks, but she hadn't gone far when something brushed her calf and a stinging sensation prickled her skin.

She glanced down, and saw the clear dome and gently waving tentacles of a jellyfish, bobbing in the waves.

CHAPTER 16

"Oww! Jellyfish!"

Caro splashed ashore and bent to inspect her leg. The burning sensation had increased to pain, and even as she watched, a series of thin red stripes like rope burns appeared on her skin.

Max raced to her side and threw his arm around her shoulder, supporting her as she sank onto the sand. "Hold still."

"It really stings!" Caro bit her lip as a wave of light-headedness threatened.

"You're white as a sheet. Damn it."

"I'm feeling a little—"

"Hold on." He caught her under the knees and lifted her. Caro put her arms around his neck and held on, praying she wouldn't faint.

Her leg hurt like the devil, and she pressed her face into his chest and inhaled deeply. The wonderful musky scent of him filled her nose, and the racing of her heart slowed a little.

Back at camp he deposited her gently on the palm leaves she'd spread in front of the shelter, then rushed to fill one of the coconut bowls with fresh water.

"Here, drink this."

She sent him a wobbly smile of thanks.

A line of pale welts, like a beaded necklace, had now appeared within the red lesions on her leg. Max winced when he saw them, and he looked so worried that Caro felt the bizarre need to reassure him.

"It's not so bad," she said. "It just feels like I've been stung by a hundred stinging nettles."

He raked his hand through his hair. "God, if this was a musket wound, I'd know what to do, but I've never treated a jellyfish sting before. Any ideas?"

Caro took another sip of water and stretched out her leg. "Father was stung once, in Spain. I think they poured vinegar on it." She frowned. "Or maybe be it was wine? I was only ten, I can't remember."

"Well, we don't have either of those," Max growled. "Damn it."

"I seem to remember they also tried hot water."

"Now that I *can* do. Lie down."

Caro lay back weakly and watched as Max filled another of the coconut shells and nestled it among the glowing embers.

"Hold on, brave girl. It will take a while to heat." He bent to brush her hair back from her forehead. Caro closed her eyes and tried to concentrate on anything except the searing pain in her leg.

She heard Max moving around, and then felt the gentle brush of his hand on her arm. "Caro, sweetheart. The water's ready."

Max's unexpected endearment made her open her eyes. She found him leaning over her, the shocking blue of his stare unexpectedly close.

He sent her another of his heart-stopping smiles and his knuckles brushed her cheek. "Come on, soldier, sit up."

He'd folded his cravat into a makeshift pad, and she bit back an unladylike curse when he dipped it into the warm water and pressed it to the sting. Eventually, however, the pain subsided, and she sent him a relieved smile.

"It's working. It's not so bad now."

He let out an audible huff. "Thank God. It's too hot to dig you a grave."

Caro chuckled.

"I expect it'll hurt for a while, though" he continued. "Still, you can consider this just one more exotic injury to add to your tally. Was it worse than being bitten by a tarantula?"

"Definitely."

He shook his head. "You are a remarkable woman, Caro Montgomery. I've seen soldiers with a tiny splinter make more fuss than you. I swear, some of them cried for their mothers if they even grazed a knuckle."

Caro's cheeks heated at his compliment.

He rose to his feet. "Now, you stay right there while I go and get us some dinner."

True to his word, he managed to chase two silver-blue fish into her rock pool, and by the time the sun began to set the delicious scent of grilled fish made Caro's stomach rumble in anticipation.

The throbbing in her leg had almost completely subsided, so she hobbled over to the 'table' and sliced up the mangos and bananas. They ate the fish with their fingers from banana leaves, and Caro decided she'd never tasted anything so good in her life.

"Well, what a day."

Max leaned back against one of the palm trees with one knee bent, as relaxed as Caro had ever seen him. She tried to recall him back in England, perfectly attired and stiffly polite in some society ballroom, and failed.

"This is certainly the strangest Christmas day I've ever spent," she agreed.

A gust of wind fanned the fire and ruffled her hair and she

sighed, grateful for the breeze, but Max frowned over at the horizon.

"I don't like the look of those clouds. We're in for another storm."

She followed the direction of his gaze. It was almost dark, but she could just make out a bank of purple clouds rolling toward them. As if to confirm his theory a jagged bolt of lightning flickered along the underside of the dark mass, briefly illuminating it.

"One. Two." Caro began counting aloud to estimate how far away the storm was. Father had always taught her that one second equaled one mile, if one counted from the flash of lightning to the corresponding sound of thunder.

"Eleven. Twelve—" An ominous rumble boomed across the sea, as if a brewer was rolling heavy barrels of ale across a flagstone floor above them.

Max rose to his feet, filled with new purpose. "I'll secure the roof of the shelter. If the wind gets up, we don't want it blowing away. Or falling in on us."

"Would it be better to go inland? What if the waves come up this far?"

"I think we should be safe here. We're above the highest tide line, after all. And the reef should protect us from the worst of the waves. I'd rather stay here where it's more open than risk getting hit in the head by a falling branch or stray coconut."

The light was fading fast, and Max hurried to collect more strips of vine to secure the roof. Caro gathered extra firewood and stacked it under a pile of palm leaves to stay dry, then built up the fire into an impressive blaze.

She wondered if those on the other island would be able to see the glow of it over the headland, and prayed that they would be safe from the oncoming storm, too.

The flashes of lightning were almost constant now, and definitely closer. The thunder reverberated through her chest, but by the time the first raindrops spattered onto the fire they were as well-prepared as they could be.

Caro ducked under the leaves and shouted at Max over the rising wind.

"Come inside. You'll get drenched!"

He heeded her command, and she shuffled sideways to give him room. The open front of the shelter was high enough for them to sit up, and she pulled her knees to her chest as the rain began to come down in earnest.

Beside her, Max crossed his legs, tailor fashion, and the two of them watched as the fire leaped and sizzled in protest and the glowing red embers swirled in the wind. The surface of the lagoon danced with the downpour.

"Do you think the fire will withstand the storm?" She had to lean closer to Max to be heard over the steady drumming of the rain.

"I hope so," he answered, his lips close to her ear. "But I wouldn't bank on it."

A flash of lightning split the sky directly overhead followed by an ear-splitting crackle of thunder, and Caro let out an instinctive shriek that turned into a peal of laughter at her own foolishness.

"I've always loved storms," she shouted. "They make me feel funny—sort of tingly and excited and nervous at the same time. I can *feel* it, right here." She pressed her palm to her chest.

Max's answering amusement was clearly illuminated by the flickering red firelight. "Me, too. The power of nature is amazing, isn't it?"

His laughing gaze dropped to her hand, still pressed between her breasts, and Caro's pulse leapt in sudden awareness of their proximity. His shoulder was mere inches from her own, his knee pressing her leg, and the curtain of rain seemed to enclose them in their own private world.

"Just think," his lips lifted in a wicked smile, "Somewhere, out there, far from prying eyes, the coco de mer trees are uprooting themselves and making mad, passionate love."

His eyes flicked back to hers and held, and Caro's heart gave another jolt. Quick as lightning, her body was hot with desire, tingling with anticipation.

She licked her suddenly-dry lips. "I can't say I blame them. I mean, what else is there to do in weather like this?"

His gaze sharpened with a look that had her stomach clenching with excitement.

"Nothing," he murmured. "There's really nothing else to do."

"Except sleep," she said, perversely determined to tease him. "We could always try to sleep."

His dark brows rose. "Do you *want* to sleep Caro?"

CHAPTER 17

Caro could barely breathe. She knew what he was asking, what she desired. If she was a good girl, a dutiful girl, a girl who followed the rules, she would tell him yes, she wanted to sleep.

But the wildness of the storm had stirred up an answering wildness inside her. Something deep and yearning and primitive. She wanted his strong arms around her, his big body on hers. She wanted the same passion and intensity as the lightning, the thunder, the rain.

She might not have this man forever. But she had him here, now. Life was precarious at best. She could have drowned the night of the storm. And what if she'd stepped on a deadly lionfish today, instead of a relatively innocuous jellyfish? She would have been dead by now. She'd be a fool not to seize her chance.

Decision made, she lifted her hand and traced her fingers across his lips, then trailed them along his prickly jaw. His eyes flared and he opened his mouth to say something, but she didn't let him speak.

"No, Max. I don't want to sleep."

Caro held her breath. The incessant pounding of the rain matched the roar of her own pulse in her ears.

For a heartbeat Max sat frozen, and she wondered if he'd turn her down, but then his hand shot out to cup her nape and he tugged her forward for a kiss as intense as the storm outside.

His lips played over hers again and again, increasing her desire to a fever pitch, and a wicked, throbbing ache pulsed between her thighs. She pressed herself against him, stroking his hair, his shoulders.

"Please, make love to me."

He pulled back, just a fraction. "Caro. Are you sure?"

She nodded, then realized he probably couldn't see her; the fire was almost completely out, vanquished by the relentless deluge.

"Yes," she said. "I'm sure."

"I can make certain you don't get with child," he said gruffly. His voice was a low rasp, as if speaking was an effort. "I can pull out, before I finish."

She cupped his jaw. "I trust you. Yes. Please."

Max groaned, and then his lips claimed hers, melding them together into one being. Caro leaned into him, but when he tried to take her in his arms his shoulder hit the wooden frame and the whole shelter shook alarmingly.

"Damn it, I wish we were in a bed," he growled.

Caro smiled into the darkness. "Should we lie down?"

"That's an excellent idea."

He pulled away from her and she stretched out, stifling a laugh at the sound of his frantic movements as he tried to shed his shirt and wriggle out of his breeches in the enclosed space. Several muffled expletives echoed from his side as she pulled her own dress up over her head, but her amusement fled as he rolled back toward her and found her mouth again.

He half-covered her with his body and the incredible heat of him seeped through the cotton of her shift. His palm slid up the outside of her thigh, rough and urgent against her skin, and she writhed against him, desperate for more.

He obliged. Her senses swam as his hair-roughened leg slid between hers and she groaned into his mouth. And when his hand moved to her breast, squeezing and fondling, she cried out her pleasure.

Lightning crackled overhead, briefly illuminating his chest and arms as he held himself over her, then they were plunged into darkness once more. His breath was hot as he kissed his way down the side of her throat, interspersing his kisses with mumbled terms of encouragement.

"God, Caro, yes. That's right. Touch me."

She ran her fingers through his hair, then did some exploring of her own; tracing the curves of his shoulders, the muscles that bracketed his spine. Beyond shame, she dug her nails into his curved buttocks and received a groan of encouragement against her breast as he teethed the stiff nipple through the fabric.

Waves crashed on the shore, but Caro could barely hear them over the pounding of her own heartbeat. Max was everywhere, all around her, his taste, his scent.

He moved fully over her, supporting himself with bent elbows on either side of her head. His flat stomach pressed hers and the hard shaft of his manhood notched in the lee of her spread legs.

Caro tensed as he slid his hand between them and touched her, as he'd done at the waterfall. Her breath was coming in excited pants, but she arched up wordlessly into him, silently begging for more of that glorious pleasure he'd shown her before.

He didn't disappoint. His wicked fingers swirled and teased, driving her higher before leaving her cruelly unsatisfied. But her groan of complaint died on her lips as he reached down and positioned the head of his cock to her slippery entrance.

They both stilled.

"You're sure?" he breathed against her lips. "Last chance to say no."

She lifted up and pressed her mouth to his. "Do it, Cavendish, or I'll stab you with that stupid knife of yours."

His chuckle morphed into a low growl of pleasure as he pressed his hips forward and slowly, slowly entered her.

Caro opened her eyes wide in the darkness, absorbing this astonishing new sensation with a sense of awe. He pulled out a little, then he slid back inside, even further this time, and a shimmer of dark delight raced along her limbs.

"That's it," he whispered against her temple. "Let me in. Let me love you, Caro."

He pressed further, stretching her, but her body yielded to his invasion. He rocked back and forth in a maddening rhythm that made her catch her breath and arch up, straining for more of the delicious friction.

She gripped his hair, urging him on, as tension built in her muscles, clamoring for release. His movements rubbed a spot deep inside that built and built until suddenly, with a cry of elation, her entire body flew apart.

Lightning flashed behind her closed eyelids as pleasure pulsed through her body. Max wasn't far behind. With a groan that seemed dragged from the center of his chest, he thrust once more inside her then withdrew from her body. He pressed himself, full weight, upon her and Caro felt the hot tide of his release against her stomach.

For a brief moment they lay completely still, hearts hammering in tandem. And then Max rolled off her with a sound that was half groan, half exhausted chuckle.

"Dear God, I knew you'd be the end of me, Montgomery."

Caro tried hard to catch her breath. Her entire body was glowing, replete with a wonderful lethargy.

"Well, if it's any consolation, you've killed me too," she managed weakly.

He cleaned them both off with his discarded cravat, then shifted back to her. Silently, he rolled her so that she was facing away from him, then threw his arm over her waist and tugged her backward, nestling her bottom into the curve of his groin, surrounding her with his body.

Caro had no objections. Their exertions had brought a sheen of sweat to her skin, but now she was cooling off. A gust of wind battered the shelter and she shivered involuntarily.

"Cold?" Max's voice was muffled as he pressed his mouth to her neck.

"A little."

His arm tightened, drawing her closer into the shelter of his body, and she let out a little sigh of contentment.

"Don't worry. I'll keep you warm."

CHAPTER 18

Caro awoke at dawn, still in Max's arms. She must have turned over in the night, because now the top of her head was tucked under his chin and her flattened hand rested on his glorious chest. His left arm was thrown over her waist, and his heart beat, sure and steady, thumped beneath her palm.

"Ah, awake at last."

Max's voice, deep and gravelly with sleep, rumbled above her, and she pulled back to look up into his face.

Despite her resolution to be mature and sophisticated, the feel of his body pressed so intimately to hers made heat rise to her cheeks.

The storm had passed. The rising sun warmed the angles of his cheeks and gilded the straight line of his nose, and Caro's heart gave a little squeeze inside her chest.

Oh, she was going to miss him.

She tried to memorize every detail, to burn it into her memory so that when she was back in cold, rainy old England she would be able to remember the sheer heaven of being held like this, in his arms.

"Still deciding whether to stab me?" Max's blue eyes twinkled at her. "Because I distinctly remember you threatening me with such a thing last night."

"Only if you didn't make love to me."

"Which I did." He narrowed his eyes at her. "Was it not satisfactory?"

"Oh, it was *very* satisfactory. As well you know, you scoundrel."

"Glad to hear it. Wouldn't want the woman I plan to marry dissatisfied with my performance."

Caro stilled, gazing up at him in shock. "Wait. Marry? What?"

Max smoothed a strand of hair from her cheek and stared deep into her eyes. "I'd like to marry you, Caroline Montgomery. If you'll have me, of course."

Her heart began to pound. "You don't mean that. You don't know what you're saying. You don't even know who you are. I mean—"

"You don't want to marry a stable hand?"

"It's not that. It's just that . . . you don't have to marry me just because we've—you know—"

She waved her hand vaguely between them, horribly aware that she was babbling.

Oh, this was both the best and worst day of her life. She'd never imagined she'd receive a proposal of marriage from Max, and while there was nothing she wanted more than to be his wife, how could she say yes, when he had no idea who he was?

To accept would be to entrap him in the worst possible way. As a gentleman, he'd be too honorable to withdraw his offer, once he learned he was a duke. He'd regret it, and come to resent her in the process.

"Cavorted?" he supplied. "Made love?"

"Because I'm ruined," she managed. "There's no need. Honestly. I don't care what the gossips will say back in London. Please don't feel like you have to offer just to save my reputation."

Max's laugh cut off her protests. He pressed a kiss to her forehead and pulled back, shaking his head.

"Oh, Caro. That's not why I want you to marry me. I love you. I want you beside me. Forever."

"You're not a groom," she blurted out desperately. "I lied. You're not penniless either. Your uncle left you an enormous house and a huge pile of money and you're—"

"The Duke of Hayworth?" He grinned down at her, his blue eyes twinkling with devilry.

Caro was certain her heart actually stopped.

"You remember?" she croaked.

"Never forgot."

She scowled up at him in dawning horror, then whacked him on the chest with her balled fist. "You know you're a duke?"

"Of course."

"How long have you known?"

He *laughed*, the beast.

"Since about five minutes after I opened my eyes on the beach that first day."

"Ohhh, you monster—"

"A groomsman?!" he chided. "Really? Was that the best you could do? Why not make me a chimney sweep or a tinker? Or one of those mudlarks, who wade about on the side of the Thames at low tide picking up rubbish?"

"I think I might stab you, after all," she growled.

He caught her wrists and restrained her with the lightest of holds.

"I love you," he repeated softly. "Of all the people in the world I could have wished to be shipwrecked with, I'd always and forever choose you."

Caro could barely think. Happiness was constricting her chest, but she was afraid to believe that this was real, and not a cruel dream.

"But I love *you*," she said, almost accusingly. "I think I always have."

He released her wrists and slid his fingers between hers so their hands were entwined.

"Is that a yes? You'll be my duchess? Just think, if we can get along under trying conditions like this, we'll have no problem living together in my London town house, or at Gatcombe Park."

He slanted her a hungry, heated look that made her pulse race. "I want to make love to you in a bathtub filled with rose petals, in a huge soft feather bed piled high with cushions—"

Caro groaned. "Ohh, you beast. Don't tempt me. What if we're never rescued?"

"Then I'll be perfectly happy making love to you right here, in this awful, uncomfortable hut, for the rest of my days. We'll be the duke and duchess of Heaven-Knows-Where." Max's hands cupped her cheeks as he tilted her face up to his. "Say yes, Caro."

The sun burst over the horizon, flooding them both with light, and Caro pressed her lips to his. "In that case, Maximillian Cavendish, yes. I'll marry you."

CHAPTER 19

On the thirty first day of December, New Year's Eve, Caro glanced up from her hibiscus flower tea and saw a tall plume of smoke rising over the headland.

"Max! The other island's signal fire!"

Max, who had been dozing in the shelter after a night of lovemaking that made Caro blush to recall it—*who knew a man could do such wicked, exquisite things with his tongue, for heaven's sake?*—leapt to his feet.

"Quick!"

He snatched a stick from the fire, and together they raced along the beach and clambered onto the rocks.

Sure enough, a fire blazed on the opposite beach, and Caro gave a whoop of sheer elation as she spied a ship with billowing white sails heading toward the strait.

"We're saved!"

Max caught her in an impulsive hug, then leaped down and put the glowing torch to the tinder beneath their own signal fire. Since they'd been diligently keeping it ready, it caught almost immediately, and Caro heaped handfuls of damp leaves onto it to make it smoke.

As the ship drew closer, they could see crew members moving about on the deck, and Max squinted to make out the flag that fluttered from the rigging.

"It's a Royal Naval ship," he grinned. "I wonder how they found us."

"Who cares!" Caro laughed, giddy with relief. "We're going back to hot baths and soft beds and food that isn't mango. I never want to eat another mango ever again."

Max kissed the top of her head. "Very well. If that's your wish." He smiled down at her. "Would you like to be married at St. George's, Hanover Square?"

Caro wrinkled her nose. "I don't mind. Wherever you want."

"Because I was thinking..."

"What?"

"What if we present everyone with a fait accompli and get married before we get back to London? The ship's captain can marry us. We could do it here, before we set sail."

Caro went up on tiptoe and pressed a kiss to his cheek. "Oh, yes, I love that idea! My clothes should still be on the *Artemis*. We can marry on the deck, in front of my family."

"I'll have to formally ask your father permission to court you."

Caro snorted. "It's a little late for that. And besides, they've always liked you. I can't imagine they'll be disappointed that you're joining the family. You're not a *Davies*, after all."

* * *

CAROLINE MONTGOMERY AND MAXIMILLIAN CAVENDISH, his Grace, the fourteenth Duke of Hayworth, were married at sunset on the deck of *HMS Carron*. The bride's immediate family were in attendance, and the bride carried a bouquet of tropical blooms.

As the sky turned an extravagant array of pinks and reds, Max joined Caro at the ship's rail and they both gazed back at the tiny island that had been their home for the past ten eventful days.

Caro leaned her head against her new husband's shoulder. "This might sound strange, but I'm going to miss this place. Despite all the hardships, we had some truly memorable moments. I'm glad we were stranded. Together. Alone."

Max put his arm around her waist and pulled her into his side. "Me too."

"I can't believe you insisted on bringing the coco de mer home, though."

"And why not? We might be the only couple in England to have one. And how could I leave it behind? It has such fond memories attached to it."

"As do thunderstorms," she added, blushing.

He chuckled. "Plenty of those in England, too."

Caro shook her head. "We might have missed Christmas, but we'll be home in time for the twins to make their debut in society. I wonder what they'll make of the *Ton*."

Max gave her a loving squeeze. "The real question is, what will the *Ton* make of the twins? They're going to cause chaos, I guarantee."

"At least they'll have an older sister who's a duchess."

"A *scandalous* duchess." Max turned her in his arms. "A desert island duchess."

Caro glanced over her shoulder and was relieved to find the remaining crew members had all discreetly found engrossing things to do elsewhere. She lifted her face for a kiss.

"Well, if I'm a desert island duchess, then that makes you my desert island duke," she smiled. "I hope this won't be our last adventure together, Your Grace."

Max kissed her soundly. "It won't be. I have a feeling our adventures are only just beginning, my love."

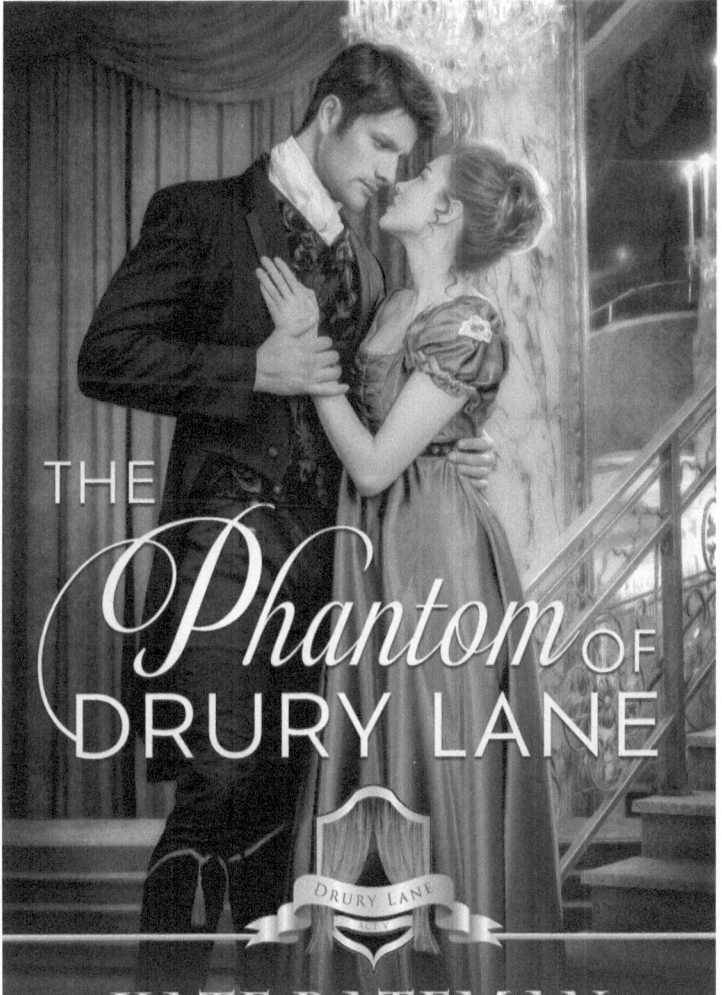

Man is least himself when he talks in his own person. Give him a mask and he will tell you the truth.
   - Oscar Wilde.

CHAPTER 1

The Theater Royal, Drury Lane, London – 1817

LUCY MONTGOMERY HAD MISSED many things about England, but William Arden, Viscount Ware, had *not* been one of them.

Three years had not been long enough.

Three decades probably wouldn't suffice.

Some men were simply too vexing for words.

Her stomach somersaulted with an unwelcome combination of anticipation and dread as the man in question pushed through the crowd, making a beeline for the quiet corner she'd chosen for herself in Lady Carrington's ballroom.

His desire to torture her clearly hadn't abated during her time abroad.

Lucy narrowed her eyes, studying him as she'd once studied a jaguar in the steamy jungles of Brazil; with the same fascinated wariness. She hadn't seen him since her family had docked in London several weeks ago, and despite her dislike of the man, she could grudgingly admit his physical appeal.

He'd always been attractive, but the scar that now slashed across his eyebrow and cheekbone—courtesy of a French saber at Waterloo—had inexplicably *improved* his appearance. There was no justice in this world. He'd been annoyingly handsome before; a dark-haired, indolent playboy, but this new imperfection added an air of dangerous, rugged maturity that had been previously lacking.

Damn him.

Lucy took a fortifying swig of punch and schooled her expression into one of polite neutrality even as her heart beat faster in her chest. She was three years older now. Three years wiser. She'd survived a shipwreck off Madagascar and the snake-infested forests of South America. She could certainly face one infuriating, sarcastic scoundrel in a ballroom.

However handsome he might be.

Still, her stomach tightened as he stopped in front of her.

"Lucia."

He said it the Italian way, as he'd always done. *Lou-chee-ah*. Three syllables, drawing it out like honey gliding from a spoon, and all her good intentions evaporated at the hint of teasing laughter in his gravel-deep voice.

"Don't call me that," she snapped. "It's *Lucy*. Only my mother ever calls me Lucia—and only then if I've done something particularly dreadful."

His dark brows rose in amusement. "I expect you hear it on a weekly basis, then."

She ground her teeth, and the corner of his mouth twitched as if he knew precisely the effect he had on her. Had *always* had on her, ever since he'd first come to stay with her older brother during the school holidays, when she'd been a girl.

She forced a sunny smile. "Not at all. I haven't done anything dreadful for weeks. Months, even."

"Then you're probably long overdue."

An inelegant snort escaped her. "Not me. *Lenore's* the scandalous one."

She tilted her head toward the dance floor, where her twin sister was laughing up into the face of a clearly besotted partner. "Most people still get us mixed up. Although I don't see why, when we're hardly identical."

"Ah, but I'm not 'most people,' am I? I've never confused the two of you." Arden's mocking expression didn't change, but something flashed in his eyes as he studied her. "You, Lucy Montgomery, are . . . unforgettable."

His deliberate pause—and choice of verb—were hardly flattering, and Lucy tried not to wince at the reminder that he'd been witness to some of her most humiliating childhood escapades. She hated the way he always seemed to be laughing at her.

"Yes, well, I'm a grown woman of twenty-three now," she said haughtily. "I'm past all that foolishness."

It was Arden's turn to snort. "Really? Because the Lucy *I* remember couldn't pass up the opportunity for an adventure. Or refuse a dare."

She lifted her chin and met his eyes, despite the quivery, weightless feeling it always produced.

"Not true."

"*So* true," he drawled. "Which is why I bet you'll be the one to unmask the Phantom of Drury Lane."

Her own brows rose; she was intrigued despite herself.

"The what of where? I'm not up to date with all the London gossip yet. You're going to have to enlighten me."

"It's been the talk of Covent Garden for months. I'm surprised it hasn't reached your ears."

"I don't frequent the area as often as you do," Lucy said sweetly, relishing the way his lips compressed at her saucy inference. Covent Garden was known for its proliferation of brothels and taverns. Arden, she was sure, was no stranger to either.

"Lenore mentioned that you were 'particular friends' with an actress?"

Lucy had digested that news with hardly a pang. Arden always had a woman on his arm. He attracted everyone, from dairymaid to duchess, and he rarely denied himself female company.

The twinge in her midsection had *definitely not* been jealousy.

He sent her an easy smile. "You're referring to Kitty? Or maybe Barbara? Either way, we've parted company. But that's beside the point. I know the gossip about Drury Lane Theater because I have a financial stake in the place."

"How so?"

"When the previous building burned down, my father donated funds to rebuild it and became one of the major shareholders. He gifted me his stake three years ago. Just after you left for lands unknown."

"Oh."

Lucy couldn't quite hide her surprise. She'd never imagined Arden as having any interest in business. He'd always seemed too carefree to bother with such serious matters, but perhaps he wasn't quite such a dedicated libertine as he'd once been. Perhaps the war had changed more than his physical appearance.

The thought was intriguing, but she quashed it. Leopards didn't change their spots.

"Tell me about this Phantom, then," she prompted.

Arden glanced over his shoulder and then leaned in, as if imparting a great secret, and her heart stuttered as she caught a delicious whiff of his cologne.

God, he always smelled delicious. One day she was going to find out exactly which scent he wore and buy a bottle for herself. For no particular reason, of course. She most certainly wouldn't put a drop of it on her pillow so she could breathe it in while she slept.

His broad shoulders blocked out the rest of the room as she pressed back into the corner, simultaneously breathless at his proximity and irritated at herself for such a reaction.

Her body clearly wasn't as discerning as her brain.

"The Phantom is a masked figure who's haunted the theater for months," Arden said.

"He sits alone, in the highest box on the left-hand side of the stage. Sometimes he stays for an entire performance. Other times he only appears for a moment, then vanishes before he can be accosted. Everyone's desperate to know who he is. And whether he's real, or an apparition."

Lucy rolled her eyes. "Of course he's real. There's no such thing as ghosts."

Arden raised his brows. "Are you sure?"

"Your 'phantom' is flesh-and-bone, Arden, I guarantee it. But why are you so keen to unmask him? If he's got people talking about the theater, and buying tickets on the off-chance that they might see him, you should be grateful for the free publicity."

He tilted his head in wry acknowledgment. "I can't deny he's been good for business, but it irks me not to know who the fellow is."

"Have you ever seen him?"

"Not personally. But plenty of other people have. The rumor is that he's a veteran, hideously scarred by a grenade. He wears a mask so people don't scream in terror when they see him."

Without meaning to, Lucy glanced at Arden's own injury, and his lips quirked as he noted the direction of her gaze.

"Do you find *me* hideous now, Lucia?" he teased, clearly unworried about his own scar. "Do I make you want to scream?"

Lucy's heart was hammering against her ribs. His words sounded as if they had another, far more seductive, meaning. How had things suddenly become so intimate? It felt as if they were the only two people in the ballroom.

She clenched her fingers into a fist against the sudden bizarre desire to touch his injured face, and rallied gamely. "Scream? Only in aggravation."

His gaze dropped to her lips. "Hmm."

Heat washed over her skin at the intense way he studied her mouth. She bit her lower lip, suddenly self-conscious, and he let out a low sound that made her belly tingle.

She'd kissed *his* mouth. Just once. Four years ago, before she'd left for Brazil. The shameful episode was etched into her brain. As was the subsequent humiliation.

"You mentioned a bet?" she said breathlessly.

"I did. Kit Hollingsworth is offering a hundred pounds to whoever unmasks the Phantom."

"And you think that person will be me?"

His gaze flashed back up to hers. "I do. Because if anyone loves meddling and mysteries, it's you. You've been back in London for weeks without a scandal to your name, which means you must be desperate for something to do."

Lucy tried not to look interested. She *had* been getting a little bored. Life in the *ton* was so restrictive compared to the wonderful freedoms she'd enjoyed for the past three years, traveling the globe with her intrepid parents.

Still, the fact that Arden knew her well enough to guess that she'd been longing for a challenge was annoying, to say the least. She hated to be so predictable.

She tilted her head and pretended to give the matter serious thought, despite already knowing she couldn't refuse such an enticing challenge.

"Let me just make sure I have this right. Kit Hollingsworth will give me a hundred pounds if I prove the Phantom of Drury Lane is a person and not a ghost?"

Arden nodded. "You must provide a name."

"Very well. It's father's birthday coming up next month. I'll use the money to buy him a new microscope. His favorite one was damaged when we were shipwrecked a few months ago."

Arden's lips curved at her confidence, and he moved back, giving her some space. The noise of the crowd intruded again. "I wish you the best of luck. When will you start your investigation?"

"As soon as possible." Lucy sent him a questioning glance. "I assume, as one of the theater's backers, that you have access to the place whenever you like?"

"I have a key to the side entrance, if that's what you mean. But I'm not trusting you with it, Lucy Lockit."

Lucy scowled at the teasing nickname. Lucy Lockit was a character from John Gay's comedy, The Beggar's Opera—the foolish daughter of the fictional warden of Newgate, who stole the keys to free her bigamous, cheating lover from debtor's prison.

"How am I supposed to investigate, then?"

His easy smile made her feel like she'd walked into a trap. "I'll escort you, if you like."

Lucy blinked. Arden had never offered to take her anywhere before. In the past, he'd gone out of his way to *avoid* her company.

She narrowed her eyes. "You? Escort me?"

He looked almost offended by her skepticism. "Yes, me. We can go tomorrow morning. Hard as this may be for you to believe, Montgomery, but I do occasionally get out of bed before noon."

A sudden, unwanted mental image of him, sprawled in an artfully concealing tangle of bed sheets, heated her cheeks. He sent her an amused, wicked glance, as if he knew precisely the direction of her wayward thoughts.

"I'll be there, I promise," he said. "The entrance for the boxes is on Brydges Street. I'll meet you there at ten."

He didn't wait for her agreement. He simply turned on his heel and walked away.

Lucy watched him leave with mingled relief and regret. Interacting with Arden always left her slightly on edge, but the thought of having something to enliven her day tomorrow was enough to lift her spirits.

Discovering the identity of the mysterious Phantom would be gratifying, but not half as satisfying as proving to Arden that she was a clever, capable woman, and not the foolish girl he'd kissed and then rejected with such obvious loathing four years ago.

CHAPTER 2

*A*rden was waiting at the Brydges Street entrance to the theater when Lucy's carriage pulled up the following morning. Her parents had insisted that she be accompanied by Rebecca, her long-suffering maid, for propriety's sake, but since the girl was desperate to finish reading her book, Lucy laughingly told her to stay in the carriage with *Emma* and Jane Austen.

Arden took her hand to help her down the step, but he released her with unflattering haste, and Lucy bit back a sigh.

He tilted his head toward the theater door. "There's probably a rehearsal going on at the moment. The company can't afford to close between productions, so they practice the upcoming play during the day, and perform the current one at night."

He unlocked the door with a key from his jacket and ushered her inside. A handsome pillared hallway led into a square salon with plenty of gilt scrollwork.

Arden pointed to their left. "That staircase leads directly up to the private boxes, so the lucky few don't have to mingle with the general rabble."

"Do you have your own box?"

"No. I could have one, as a shareholder, but I prefer to be down in the stalls. That's where all the action is."

And all the harlots, Lucy added silently.

The sound of voices and general activity grew louder as they moved further into the building, and she smiled as they entered the auditorium itself. The stage at the front was framed by an impressive proscenium arch and flanked on each side by four tiers of private boxes, each with its own sparkling glass chandelier.

A sunken orchestra pit was positioned directly in front of the stage, next to where the cheapest spectators sat. Behind that rose rows of red velvet seating, sloping toward the stage, while three tiers of long, curved balconies soared up to the ceiling. The red, cream, and gold color scheme was both sumptuous and welcoming, and Lucy inhaled the pleasing scents of fresh paint and sawdust with a happy sigh. She'd missed the theater when she was on her travels. Performing plays with her sisters was hardly a decent substitute.

The stage was a hive of activity. A red-haired female carpenter was directing two men to reposition the sliding scenery of a castle, while a young painter perched precariously atop some wooden scaffolding to decorate a fabric backdrop.

"This is actually the fourth theater that's been built on this site," Arden said softly at her side. "The last three all burned down."

Lucy frowned. "My goodness! I hope you're taking care when it comes to naked flames."

"We are. I certainly don't want to see my investment going up in smoke. The chandeliers are currently lit by candles, which is not only time-consuming, but also has the unfortunate side-effect of dripping hot wax onto the people below. The other lights are oil, but we're trying to raise enough to install new gas lighting, both for the house lights and the stage."

"Gas? That doesn't sound much safer than candles. Isn't there a risk of an explosion?"

"There is, but it's small when managed correctly. We intend to take considerable care to avoid that scenario."

On stage, a gorgeous, statuesque blonde woman was arguing with a portly gentleman, while another man appeared to be trying to diffuse the situation.

"That's Sarah Beckwith, our leading lady," Arden explained. "She's playing Lady Drusilla. The man she's arguing with is Thomas Cotton, her leading man, who's the Earl of Pudding."

"What play are they rehearsing?"

"It's a new comedy called 'The Lady Of The Scullery.' It's a ridiculous farce about a duke's daughter who disguises herself as a maid in an earl's household." Arden's tone was dry. "They fall in love, of course, after the requisite number of complications and misunderstandings."

A shriek of irritation emanated from the blonde, and Arden shook his head. "The two of them are going to have to use all their acting skills to pretend to fall in love by the end of the third act. They've been bickering for weeks."

He pointed to the harried-looking gentleman standing alongside them. "Poor Holland has been driven to distraction. He's the Stage Manager."

"Maybe people will come just to see if Mrs. Beckwith can endure kissing Mr. Cotton every night. Perhaps she'll crack and punch him in the face instead."

Arden grinned. "One can only hope. Scandals like that are box office gold. And the theater needs every penny it can get to stay open when there's so much competition."

"All the more reason to encourage your Phantom, then," Lucy said. "If he's filling seats, you should be happy for him to keep haunting the place. Provided he isn't hurting anyone. He isn't, is he?"

"No. He's never done anything threatening or dangerous. I'd

never have suggested you try to unmask him if that was the case. I'd never put you in harm's way."

Lucy snorted. "Ha! You spent *years* when we were younger putting me in harm's way, Arden. What about the time my horse lost a shoe and you refused to give me a lift back home, and I had to walk three miles in the mud? Or the time I cut my finger and you told me to squeeze *lemon juice* on it to stop the sting?"

Or the time you kissed me, and broke my heart?

She didn't say *that* out loud.

Arden's grin was unrepentant. "Disgraceful behavior, I admit. But I was young and foolish. Please allow that being in harm's way myself for several years has changed my perspective considerably."

Lucy stilled, surprised. She hadn't expected him to discuss his wartime experiences, but the scar on his face was a clear indication that he'd known suffering of his own. Had he really changed so much?

He spoke again before she could ask.

"I'd never do such things to a lady now. Not even *you*, Montgomery."

She rolled her eyes. "Only because my brother would box your ears if anything happened to me. And my parents would still give you a dressing down, too, viscount or not."

He chuckled. "True. Not one member of your family has ever demonstrated the proper respect for my title."

"An elevated rank does not necessarily equate to elevated intelligence," Lucy countered pertly. "True nobility is proved by someone's actions, not by some dusty old piece of parchment."

Arden clutched his chest and staggered backward in feigned horror. "Dear God! That sounds dangerously like something a Bonapartist would say. Don't tell me you've returned to London to start a revolution. I've spent enough of my life fighting, thank you very much. I plan to live a life of peaceful indolence from now on."

Lucy laughed. "Fair enough. I promise not to incite any revolutions. Not even the smallest riot, I swear."

He looked doubtful. "Hmmm. You Montgomerys have a penchant for trouble, but we've had plenty of riots here without your interference. The Prince Regent's coach was attacked on the way back from the state opening of Parliament in January, and just this March, in Manchester, a bunch of weavers gathered to protest against their working conditions. You need to be careful. There's a great deal more unrest than there was when you left."

"Duly noted. Although I hardly think it's more dangerous here than being on a ship in a storm in the middle of the ocean. Or traipsing through the jungles of Brazil. Now tell me, which is the Phantom's box?"

Arden pointed to the left of the stage. "There, the highest of the private boxes. He sent a note addressed to the directors requesting that it be kept empty for his exclusive use, and asking that the candles in that particular chandelier remain unlit."

"How long ago was that?"

"Two, maybe three months ago."

"Did he say what would happen if his demands weren't met?"

"No. He just said he was a theater lover who valued his privacy. And since his note was accompanied by five hundred pounds, *in cash*, the directors unanimously agreed to humor him."

"Well, now I feel indignant of the Phantom's behalf," Lucy said. "The poor soul clearly just wants to enjoy his evenings in peace, but now Kit Hollingsworth has gone and put a price on his head. I bet scores of people are lurking about, trying to win that hundred pounds."

Arden shrugged. "People have been interested ever since he made his first appearance. You know how London is for gossip. Once an article about the 'mysterious masked stranger in box number four' appeared in the newspapers, rumors spread like wildfire." He tilted his head. "But if you ask me, I think the Phantom secretly *likes* the attention."

"Why do you say that?"

"Well, he could simply stay at home, couldn't he? If he didn't want to engage. Then, he wouldn't run the risk of being unmasked. But since he *chooses* to keep appearing, it makes me think he likes the thrill of the chase."

"Hmmm, it's an interesting theory," Lucy mused. "And you might be right. Perhaps, if he's as scarred as everyone says, and doesn't go out much in society, then playing a game of cat and mouse here at the theater could be a form of entertainment in itself." She squinted up at the darkened box. "Can we go up there and take a look?"

"Of course, this way."

A side door led into a corridor, which in turn led to a set of stairs. Arden set off up them with athletic enthusiasm, while Lucy picked up her skirts and mentally cursed the Phantom, whoever he might be.

Of course he'd choose to haunt the highest box in the entire theater. He didn't have to contend with yards of petticoats and a stupid corset, did he?

She hadn't worn a corset for months while she was abroad. It chafed to wear the restriction now, purely for propriety's sake. Still, there was no denying it did wonderful things for her bosom.

Her thighs were burning by the time she reached the final flight of stairs, and she tried to distract herself from the pain by noting how delightful Arden's posterior looked as he climbed ahead of her. His buckskin breeches molded faithfully to his muscled flanks and she sent up a silent toast to the tailors of London who could produce such a form-fitting miracle.

Perhaps being back in England wasn't *so bad*, after all.

Arden was waiting for her in the shadowy hallway when she reached the top, looking irritatingly normal, while she tried to slow her panting breaths. Her heart was pounding against her ribs, and for once it had nothing to do with his proximity.

The last time she'd been this out of breath was when she'd

raced down the beach toward the Royal Navy warship, *HMS Carron*, on the way to being rescued after a shipwreck near Madagascar.

She pressed her palm to her chest, and Arden's gaze dropped to the square-cut neckline of her pelisse, where her breasts rose and fell in time to her erratic breathing.

A muscle twitched in his jaw and he turned away abruptly.

"In here." His voice was gruff, as if he had to clear his throat.

Just as the staircases had grown narrower with each successive flight, so the corridor that let into the private box had become smaller. Arden pushed open the slim door, ignoring the sign that read 'PRIVATE BOX, RESERVED,' and Lucy followed him into the Phantom's lair.

It was not large, perhaps only ten feet wide, with a waist-high curved balcony overlooking the stage. The floor was split level, with two red velvet upholstered chairs on the upper level, and a two-person red velvet seat on the lower tier. The walls were upholstered in a patterned red silk damask, and despite being unlit, the facets of the crystal chandelier that hung overhead still glimmered faintly in the light from the stage below.

Lucy looked around with interest. The back of the box was shadowed, and hung with deep red velvet drapes.

Arden leaned on the balcony and looked down at the crowded stage. The bickering of the actors could still be heard, but since they weren't speaking too loudly the words were indistinct.

"So, tell me, what else do you know about this Phantom?" Lucy demanded. "Is he tall or short? Stocky or slim? Does he have a beard or mustache? How big is his mask?"

Arden turned, shaking his head at her barrage of questions. "By all accounts, he's of average height, maybe a little taller than most, and as to his build, he's neither fat nor overly lean."

Lucy gave a huff of frustration. "That's not very helpful. That could be half the men in London."

"He always wears evening dress; black jacket and breeches,

white shirt and cravat. His mask is black, and fitted to cover the top half of his face. His mouth and chin are visible, and those who've seen him say he's clean shaven. He's also dark haired, although it's possible he's wearing a wig."

Lucy frowned. "I assume people have already tried the obvious, like waiting for him outside the door, once they see he's here in the box?"

"Of course. But the Phantom is wonderfully elusive. He seems to have the ability to vanish into thin air."

"Like the actors in Shakespeare's *Tempest*," Lucy murmured absently.

"What?"

"Oh, Prospero, I think it is, says something like that at the end of the play. *'Our revels are now ended. These our actors . . . were all spirits and are melted into air, into thin air'.*"

Arden shook his head. "You're a fan of Shakespeare, I take it?"

"I am. I took his *Complete Works* with me on my travels. Caro, Lenore, and I used to act them out, playing all the parts between us. I make an excellent Lady Macbeth." Lucy turned in a slow circle, then crossed to the walls and began sliding her hands over them.

"What are you doing now?" Arden's sigh was thick with resignation.

"Looking for a hidden entrance. Perhaps the Phantom sneaks in here from a hidden closet, or escapes via a secret passage." She tapped the walls, listening for a change in tone that would indicate a hollow space, then looked behind the curtains.

Arden perched himself on the gilt arm of the settee and watched her with the air of someone humoring an inmate from Bedlam.

"There are passageways all over this place, actually. They allow the production team and actors to move about the theater without being seen by the audience. The stage itself has at least three different trap doors that let into the space below, and there are cellars and store rooms down there, too."

Lucy gave a frustrated huff as her search for a hidden door yielded nothing. She pointed to the decorated ceiling of the main auditorium.

"What's above us?"

"The roof, naturally, but also a huge attic space between the rafters that's used for storing costumes and scenery."

"Can you get down to the street from the roof?"

He nodded. "Since the last three theaters burned down, there are now multiple means of escape for people in the case of fire. There are metal rungs attached to the outside of the building that can be climbed down to the road."

"Perhaps that's how the Phantom arrives, then."

He gave a derisive snort. "Sounds like a lot of hard work."

"I suppose you have a better idea?"

His lips twitched at her irritated tone. "All I'm saying is, why go to such drastic lengths? Half the men who come here dress in evening wear. The Phantom could just arrive with everyone else and mingle with the crowd with his mask off until he's about to enter the box."

"That wouldn't be possible if he's as scarred as everyone says. He'd be too recognizable. People would be bound to notice him."

"Maybe he isn't disfigured at all? Maybe the mask is just to hide his identity. He might simply be some bored aristocrat out for a lark."

Lucy frowned. Those were all definite possibilities.

Arden stood, and despite the fact that he was on the lower tier, the top of her head still only came up to his nose. Her heart started to pound at his nearness. She'd been too preoccupied looking for a secret door to realize quite how *small* this box was. How intimate. She only had to stretch out her arm and she'd brush his hand, or his thigh.

Arden shifted his weight, and she caught a whiff of his delicious cologne, then shook her head to dislodge the sudden, foolish desire to step forward and bury her face in his snowy white cravat.

No man had the right to smell so good. It wasn't fair.

Or, rather, it was wonderful that a man smelled so delicious, but why did it have to be *Arden*? A man so unattainable she might as well be a goat for all the chance she had of securing his interest. The one man who'd rejected her so unequivocally.

He cleared his throat, jerking her from her daydreaming.

"So, what's the plan now?"

Lucy made a concerted effort to pull herself together and sound capable and businesslike. She reached into her reticule and withdrew a folded piece of paper.

He squinted at it in the gloom. "What's that?"

"A letter. For the Phantom."

She held it out for him to take.

"Dear Phantom," he read aloud. *"Please forgive my forwardness, but I desire to speak with you in private. To that end, I shall be sitting in your box this evening, and every evening henceforth, in the hope that you will grant me an audience. Be assured that I wish you no harm. Sincerely, Lucy Montgomery."*

Lucy gave a pleased nod. "Short, and to the point, I think."

Arden shook his head. "It's certainly direct. But you have to assume this Phantom won't want to make *your* acquaintance. The man specifically asked for solitude. He might not take too kindly to someone thrusting themselves into his private domain."

"Nobody's *thrusting* themselves anywhere," Lucy said peevishly.

Arden's lips twitched, but she continued before he could make some childish, ribald comment. "I am merely being upfront about my intentions. If the Phantom wishes for privacy, then he can simply stay away. It's his choice."

He gave a skeptical shrug. "You have no idea who this person is. What if they're dangerous? What if your presence offends them so much, they decide to throw you off the balcony?"

She peered past him, over the edge, and her knees went a little weak. The rail was only waist high, and it was an extremely long way down.

"You said he'd never done anything threatening. But I shall bring my knife for protection. Father made sure all three of us girls could defend ourselves if necessary. And I learned some extra tricks from the King of Madagascar's bodyguard."

Arden made a derisive sound. "That may be true, but I still doubt you'd stand a chance against a fully grown man. He could be ex-military. What if he tries to hurt you? Or molest you?"

He took a step closer, deliberately crowding her with his body, looming over her to reinforce his point. "You're *small*, Montgomery. Delicate." His eyes held hers, and his pupils seemed huge in the shadows. "I could overpower you in a heartbeat. I could *kiss* you—right now—if I wanted to. And I could have you flat on your back on that sofa with your skirts up around your waist in less than thirty seconds."

His voice was low, rough, and Lucy stilled, her heart hammering in sudden alarm as the image he described shimmered between them. She clearly imagined herself lying there on the chaise, Arden's firm body pressing her down, and her pulse gave a terrible, betraying jolt. The thought of a stranger putting her in that position was frightening, but the thought of *Arden* doing it was horribly enticing.

She'd dreamed of such shameful, wicked things before.

She was an idiot.

She sucked in a steadying lungful of air. "Stop trying to scare me off, Arden. I can handle myself perfectly well. Besides, the theater will be full. Help, if I need it, won't be far away." She plucked the letter from his hand and placed it neatly in the center of the velvet sofa. "What's tonight's performance? Do you know?"

He frowned at her apparent stubbornness. "It's Shakespeare. *Hamlet, Prince of Denmark*. It starts at seven o'clock."

"Excellent. I'll come then, and hope the Phantom's read my note. I don't suppose you get free entrance as one of the shareholders?"

He sent her a sardonic glance. "I do. But *you* can buy a ticket at the door, like everyone else. It's three shillings and sixpence for a seat in the pit, two shillings for a seat in the lower gallery, one shilling for a seat in the upper gallery, and seven shillings for a box. Like this one."

Lucy sent him a look of mock disappointment. She hadn't really thought he'd let her in for nothing. "Seven Shillings! I can see why there were riots about the prices a few years ago. And besides, why should I pay when you said the Phantom already paid *five hundred* pounds for the use of this box?"

"*Exclusive* use," Arden reminded her. "And since you've not been invited as his guest, you'll have to cough up the blunt."

Lucy gave a dramatic sigh. "Fine. I suppose I'll be getting that hundred pounds from Kit Hollingsworth soon enough. Seven shillings isn't too terrible to advance." She turned to leave. "I'd better get back to the carriage. Do *you* have plans for tonight, Arden?"

His sudden smile was so wolfish it made her pulse leap in her throat.

"Indeed I do. But telling you about them would make you blush. Suffice to say that I, too, will be in the vicinity."

Lucy bit her lip, certain she didn't want the details. A cad like himself would be up to no good, she was sure. The streets of Covent Garden were synonymous with pleasure and wickedness of all forms.

If only she could ignore the pang of jealousy for whoever he'd be getting up to no good *with*. It was foolish to wish it was her. She had a Phantom to unmask. She would forget about Arden and focus on her task; charming the 'ghost' into revealing his name.

CHAPTER 3

Two things made William Arden, Viscount Ware, extremely happy.

The first was increased ticket sales at the Theater Royal, Drury Lane, of which he was a part-owner.

The second was Lucy Jane Montgomery. A woman so vexing, so gorgeous, so infuriatingly *elusive* that she'd been the bane of his life—and most ardent desire—from the moment he'd laid eyes on her.

Not that he'd ever told *her* that, of course.

A man had his pride.

And a healthy dose of self-preservation.

Ten years ago, at eighteen, he'd been arrogantly convinced the world was his for the taking.

Lucy had been the irritatingly memorable little sister of his schoolfriend. In other words: untouchable. Completely off-limits. A Female Not To Be Trifled With Under Any Circumstances On Pain Of Death.

Will's heart, however, had blithely ignored the sensible edicts of his brain. Instead, it had made an unholy alliance with his cock, and the two of them had colluded to become alarmingly besotted with the girl.

Which was—obviously—a disaster.

He was young, handsome, titled, and rich. He couldn't possibly fall in love with the first girl he encountered. Especially since nothing could come of it. Girls like Lucy Montgomery weren't to be bedded then discarded, and he was far too young to even *consider* marrying.

He had adventures ahead. Drinking and gaming. Love affairs with wildly unsuitable women. Duels and capers and swashbuckling scrapes.

Will shook his head at the memory of his younger self.

God, he'd been such an ass.

Lucy's twin, Lenore, had enraptured every other male of their acquaintance, and while physically the two of them were almost identical, that was where the similarities ended. Lenore was bold and charming, and even at sixteen had been aware of the power she could wield over men with her looks and her sparkling wit.

Lucy had always been a tomboy, perplexed and somewhat irritated by the attention given to her beauty, always looking for a challenge, and for an explanation as to why the world was *just so*.

It had taken an extraordinary effort, but Will had managed to treat her with a credible amount of bored indifference and brotherly disdain whenever he'd encountered her—even as he dreamed of her with feverish intensity.

At university he'd distracted himself with other, more available women, but he'd still been plagued by thoughts of her pink lips and sly smile. He'd joined the fight against Bonaparte as soon as he graduated, cockily sure that he'd emerge unscathed from war. And despite the unfortunate incident in Sylvia Greenwood's gardens, he'd also naively believed that Lucy would still be within his reach when he returned.

He'd been wrong on both counts.

In France and Belgium, he'd found the adventure and excitement he'd craved. But he'd also found terror and misery and heartbreak. And while he'd been away, dreaming of her despite his fervent desire not to, she was off traveling the world with her intrepid family. Her father, a botanist, was the country's foremost expert on butterflies, and his work took them to some of the most far-flung corners of the globe.

At first Will had been glad that she wasn't back in London, where any man with half a brain might realize her brilliance and snatch her up for himself.

Then he'd been afraid for her, because he'd seen first-hand just how terrifyingly short and brutal life could be. He couldn't help imagining the myriad dangers that could befall a beautiful, inquisitive girl in the wilds of God-Knows-Where.

When a Frenchman's saber sliced his head open during the mayhem of Waterloo, and he'd fallen to the ground, stunned and barely conscious, his overriding emotions had been bitter self-recrimination and regret. Here he was, about to die a glorious, valiant, *stupid* death, without ever having told Lucy Montgomery that he loved her.

What a bloody waste.

He'd kissed her precisely once—and that had been by mistake—and his instinctive, panicked reaction on that occasion had been so forceful that he'd left her convinced that he hated her.

Nothing could be further from the truth.

As he'd clutched his bleeding face and crawled through the mud, with musket shots and cannonballs screeching all around him, he'd sworn to the Heavens that if he lived to see another sunrise, then he'd stop being such a stupid, stubborn bastard. He would go back to England, find Lucy Montgomery, and beg her to marry him.

He'd lived to see another sunrise. And he'd thought of her incessantly while his wound healed. But when he'd finally returned to London, it was to discover that while Lucy had returned from her trip to Brazil, she'd almost immediately set sail again, this time for the island of Madagascar, in the Indian Ocean. She was thousands of miles away again, and all Will could do was curb his miserable impatience and wait.

It hadn't taken him long to realize that instead of being repulsed by the scar that now curved across his eyebrow and cheekbone, ladies of every social level found it almost irresistibly attractive.

Before his injury, he'd have taken solace in a merry widow, or the practiced charms of the cyprians who frequented the clubs and brothels of Covent Garden. But the only woman he wanted now was Lucy, and despite the hunger and frustration humming through his veins, he hadn't been able to muster up the slightest interest in any of the tarts who approached him.

Subsequently, the only release he'd known for months had been provided by his own hand, which was a piss-poor substitute for the woman he ached to hold.

The thought that Lucy might reject him because of his physical imperfection didn't cross his mind. She'd never put any store into her own extraordinary good looks, nor been impressed by anyone else's beauty, and he was sure that she prized intelligence and wit over such superficial concerns.

There was, of course, the distinct possibility that she'd reject him for being too ill-read, or not amusing enough, or for lacking sufficient ambition and drive. All of those were true.

But not for his looks.

She'd always found him attractive. He had enough experience with women to know the signs. She sneaked glances at him whenever she thought he wasn't looking, and her reaction whenever he stood close to her was delightful. Her cheeks grew pink, her lips parted as she drew little panicked breaths, and her pulse beat in her throat in a way that made him want to press his lips there and inhale the heady perfume of her skin.

Will closed his eyes and took a deep breath as the memory of their one kiss rose up to haunt him.

It had been the best, most erotic moment of his entire life.

He'd been home on leave from the army, and they'd both attended Sylvia Greenwood's garden party.

Still in denial about his feelings for her, he'd avoided Lucy all evening and, as if to prove to himself that he didn't desire her, he'd agreed to meet Cressida Bonham in the maze at midnight.

Cressida was a well-known flirt, already widowed at twenty-five thanks to the death of her elderly husband, and Will had anticipated a brief, mutually pleasurable interlude before he left to rejoin his regiment.

He'd entered the maze, and a shadowy female arm had emerged from a side-path and tugged him into a leafy alcove. Assuming it was Cressida, he'd caught her in his arms and kissed her—forcefully—and been gratified when she moaned in immediate pleasure.

A second later he realized his mistake. The woman he was kissing was too small to be Cressida. She didn't smell like Cressida, either. She smelled better, *delicious*, a scent so familiar and yet at the same time so elusive that he struggled to place it.

Will stilled, his lips still on hers, as his confused brain tried to catch up with his hammering pulse.

The mystery woman gave a little sound of impatience and pushed herself up on tiptoe, silently encouraging him to continue. Her small hands slid over his shoulders and up the back of his neck, and it was at that moment Will realized exactly who he was kissing.

Lucy Bloody Montgomery.

For a split second his brain simply refused to believe it. Then desire surged through his bloodstream like hot lightning, obliterating logic and the need to know how this miracle had happened. Only one, irrefutable fact remained: Lucy was here, in his arms, *kissing him back*, and he might never get this chance again.

Did she think *he* was someone else, too? Had she agreed to meet another man out here in the gardens for a kiss? A stab of pure, possessive jealousy shot through him at the thought, but it vanished in the same instant. It didn't matter. Fate had put them here.

He had to keep kissing her.

He followed that instinct without any further ado. He slid his left arm around Lucy's waist, using it to tug her body completely against his, and her little gasp of shocked delight mirrored his own pleasure.

God she was perfect. Every dip and curve of her body fitted against the planes of his, and his cock hardened at the press of her breasts against his chest and the way she seemed to melt into him.

With his right hand he cupped the back of her head, tilting her face with a thumb under her chin so her lips were perfectly aligned with his.

In the distant part of his brain that still retained analytical ability, he marveled at the softness of the skin on her jaw, and the delicious warmth of her nape, and he stored the sensations away for future recall.

He kissed her again, more slowly this time, reining in his desire to give the moment the reverence it deserved. He grazed her lips with his own, savoring the sensation, marveling at the pillowy softness of her. She made a little humming sound of pleasure, a vibration against his mouth, and returned the pressure, tilting her head and parting her lips in silent, unknowing invitation.

She wanted him, even if she didn't *want* to want him.

His exultant heartbeat thundered in his ears.

When he ran his tongue across the seam of her lips, seeking entrance, she seemed initially confused, but when his tongue touched hers, she gave a little gasp and opened her mouth fully.

The kiss went wild.

Time lost all meaning. Will lost *himself* as their tongues slid and danced. The taste of her—champagne and strawberries—made his blood sing, and he devoured her, slanting his mouth over hers again and again, drinking deep, drawing her into a glorious, dizzying haze of passion.

Her perfume filled his lungs and he reminded himself to slow down, not to scare her with his ardency, when what he really wanted was to strip her naked and kiss every inch of her, to pleasure her with his hands and his mouth and his body until the two of them were sweaty and limp with satisfaction.

Glorious.

He almost groaned her name as he pressed a kiss to the skin beneath her ear, and he could hear her rapid, panting breaths as her fingers tightened in his hair, urging him on.

"Will."

His own name—a shivery, almost-inaudible sigh—escaped her and he froze in shock. Did she even know what she'd said?

Did she know she was kissing *him*? Or was she imagining him, while thinking she was kissing another?

Bloody Hell. This was madness.

Will's blood was pounding, urging him on, but the insistent, nagging voice of sanity refused to be silenced.

This was wrong. So wrong. What was he doing?

He absolutely should *not* be kissing Lucy Montgomery.

If the two of them were discovered there would be a scandal. The kind of scandal that would end with them hastily married to satisfy the gossips, or leave her ruined, and himself with a reputation as a shameless cad.

He wrenched himself from her arms, even though it almost pained him to do so. He caught her shoulders and thrust her away to arm's length. And then he said her name in the most shocked tone he could muster, as if he'd only just made the discovery that it was her.

"Lucy? What in God's name are you playing at?"

Her gasp was audible in the darkness.

He was glad that he couldn't see her face. He had to put a stop to this farce before he found himself on his knees at her feet, begging for her hand.

"Arden!" She staggered back, almost falling into the tall hedge behind her in her effort to escape. "I . . . you . . oh, God." Her voice was a strangled whisper.

"What are you doing out here?" he demanded, employing his best disapproving-older-brother tone. "You're supposed to be safe in the ballroom, not skulking about the gardens, kissing strange men in the shrubbery."

"I wasn't skulking. I was just getting some air when—"

"—you *grabbed* me," he interrupted, trying to sound outraged. "And kissed me. Most thoroughly."

"No," she countered hotly. "*You* kissed *me*."

"Because I thought you were Cressida Bonham!"

She sucked in a breath at his lie, and he forced himself to slide the knife home. "Why on earth would I want to kiss *you*?"

His own cruelty made him wince, but it was for the best. He was about to return to France; she needed to be free to pursue her own adventures. There could be nothing between them. Ever.

"Why indeed?" She sounded more mortified than haughty, and his stomach clenched at the thought of causing her pain. "Let's just agree that this was a terrible mistake and never mention it again. Agreed?"

"Agreed," he said solemnly.

She gave him a firm shove in the chest. "Stand aside, then."

He sidestepped with a sarcastic flourish. "With pleasure. Do you think you can make it back to the house without assaulting another innocent bystander, or do I need to accompany you?"

Her snort of disgust almost made him laugh. "I wouldn't dream of dragging you away from Cressida's superior charms. Goodnight."

Will shook his head at the memory. He hadn't kissed Cressida that night. Nor any other night. It had been Lucy's inexperienced, yet enthusiastic kisses that haunted his dreams. It had been the taste of her, the memory of her skin, that had dragged him from sleep on the brink of a full-body climax more times than he could count.

Bloody woman.

And now he was back, and so was she, so tantalizingly close that it took every ounce of his self-control not to simply push her up against the nearest wall and ravish her. To remind her how good it had been between them. To show her how good it could be again.

But Lucy would never believe that the Will Arden who'd rejected her so thoroughly ago could want her now. He'd done such a good job of appearing indifferent that she'd react with astonishment and suspicion if he confessed his love.

She needed seducing. Not just her body, but her mind, too. But there was too much history between them to allow that to happen. They needed a fresh start, so Will could woo her and win her as he should have done years ago.

As the Phantom, he'd have that chance.

He hadn't originally created the Phantom as a means to engage with her. When he'd first returned to London and realized he had months to wait for her return, he'd directed all his pent-up energy into making Drury Lane more profitable. Competition was always fierce, with countless playhouses vying for theater goers' attention, and he'd known that a mysterious figure haunting the boxes would drum up interest and fill seats.

His fellow directors had supported his plan, and it had worked, brilliantly. Covent Garden had been awash with gossip, and attendance had almost doubled as people began to come in the hopes of glimpsing the new 'theater ghost'.

But he'd become a victim of his own success. He'd had to use every one of Drury Lane's secret passages and alcoves to avoid detection, and he and the other directors had finally agreed that it was time for the Phantom to take his curtain call. Kit Hollingsworth's offer of a reward to whoever unmasked the Phantom had been a final attempt to create a buzz before Will disappeared as mysteriously as he'd come, banished into the realm of myths and legend.

The idea to challenge *Lucy* to expose the Phantom had just slipped off his tongue. She'd always loved a challenge, and he'd jumped at the excuse to spend time with her. But now he thought of it, it was the perfect opportunity for them to start again with a clean slate.

Not only could they indulge in some wicked flirtation, but he'd have the chance to become her friend, as well. Lucy would converse with the Phantom with a freedom and candidness that she'd never use when speaking to him as William Arden, Viscount Ware.

Yes, there was an element of subterfuge to the scheme, but all was fair in love and war, as they said. And Will would use any means necessary to win Lucy, body and soul.

She'd invited the Phantom to meet her, and he was only too happy to oblige.

CHAPTER 4

*L*ucy didn't usually pay much attention to her clothing, but she dressed with care to meet the Phantom. Her stomach fluttered as she stepped up to the booth and purchased a ticket for the evening's performance. Hamlet wasn't one of her favorites, but she wasn't there to enjoy the play.

Several people nodded to her in greeting as she ascended the stairs. Hopefully they'd assume she was on her way to the private box reserved for her brother-in-law, Max Cavendish, the Duke of Hayworth, who was married to her older sister Caro.

There was no-one in the hallway outside the fourth-tier box, and she held her breath as she pushed open the door. The chandelier above was unlit, as per the Phantom's demands, and the corners of the box were very dark—but empty. Just to be sure, she patted the drapery, but no-one was lurking there.

She quashed a wave of disappointment.

The letter she'd left was nowhere to be seen, but it could have been disposed of by someone cleaning the box, instead of being intercepted by the Phantom.

A bell rang, signaling the imminent start of the play, and an excited buzz rippled through the audience, followed by an expectant hush. Not wanting to be seen by those below, she settled herself in the darkest corner of the love seat as the curtain rose, and smiled at the familiar opening scene. Two actors playing night watchmen paced on the painted ramparts of 'Elsinore Castle in Denmark', discussing the sighting of a ghost.

If only *her* ghost would make an appearance.

Still, it had been so long since she'd had the pleasure of attending a play that she allowed herself to relax. Even if the Phantom didn't come, she would still enjoy the evening. She normally attended the theater with her twin, Lenore, who was the very worst companion; far more interested in peering into the audience and gossiping, than actually watching the performance. Lucy was constantly hissing at her to be quiet.

Act two was well underway when Lucy finally sensed a presence behind her. She spun around in her seat, then reared back with a gasp at the sight of the black-clad figure leaning casually against the back wall, arms folded across his chest, black mask covering the top half of his face.

The Phantom.

She cleared her throat and tried to calm her hammering pulse.

"Good evening, Sir. I suppose you got my letter?"

The man straightened, and a shiver of apprehension rippled through her. He was tall. Broad. Well-formed. She tightened her grip on the knife she'd placed in her lap.

"Your *summons*, you mean." His voice was low, a rough rasp that shivered across her nerve endings.

Lucy gulped. He did not sound overly welcoming.

He tilted his head and she tried to study his features in the faint glow from the stage. As Arden had said, he was dark-haired and clean-shaven, with a straight jaw and no sign of any scarring to his lips.

"I'm—" Lucy began.

"Trespassing," he finished with a growl that made her stomach somersault. "This box is reserved for my personal use."

"I'm sorry. Please, let me explain. I'm—"

"Lucy Montgomery," he finished again. "A woman accustomed to studying strange and fearsome creatures in the jungles of Brazil." He took a step forward and slid elegantly into the chair behind her. "Turn around and face the stage. Don't look at me."

Lucy did as he ordered, even though every instinct screamed at her to inspect him more closely. The back of her neck prickled in awareness as the movement of his body fanned the tendrils of hair at her nape. She clutched at her skirts, simultaneously thrilled and terrified.

"I hope you're not thinking that *I'm* some exotic creature you can examine, Miss Montgomery," he murmured. "I don't care to be prodded and poked for your entertainment."

Lucy shook her head. "That's not why I'm here. I came to see if you were a man, or a phantom."

His laugh rippled across the bare skin of her shoulder. "Oh, I'm not a ghost, despite the rumors. See."

His gloved finger gently skimmed the side of her neck and Lucy gasped at the contact. Her skin tingled.

"Flesh and blood, just like you."

She sucked in a deep breath. His scent filled her lungs and she closed her eyes, trying to identify the dark, delicious combination of ingredients, but it was completely unfamiliar.

She reopened her eyes and pretended to study the action on stage. "Why do you wear a mask?"

"Why do *you* ask so many questions?"

She relaxed a fraction at his gruff teasing. He didn't sound as if he was annoyed enough to throw her off the balcony. "Because I'm cursed with insatiable curiosity, I suppose. Always have been. Just ask anyone." She shrugged. "I would like to know your name."

He let out a soft huff of amusement. "You and the rest of London. Why do you think you'll be successful in getting me to spill my secrets when all the others have failed?"

"I could give you an incentive?" Lucy suggested. "Kit Hollingsworth's offering a hundred pounds to whoever reveals your name. What if we split the reward money?"

She saw the shake of his head from the corner of her eye. "I have enough money, thank you."

"Aha! So you're rich."

"Or lying," he pointed out. "Don't discount that."

Lucy pursed her lips at his playful evasiveness. "Hmmm. Is there something else I could offer you that would make you tell me? Perhaps you're in need of scintillating conversation? I've had some very unusual life experiences. I could provide you with some entertainment."

He tilted his chin toward the stage. "I come here for my entertainment. And not just to see what's happening on the stage. There's just as much drama happening in the audience. Men are foolish creatures, for the most part. Always quarreling and falling in love."

Her lips twitched at his dismissive opinion. She'd thought the same thing herself on a few occasions. "Wasn't it Shakespeare who said, 'All the world's a stage, and all the men and women merely players?'"

"Indeed, it was. Are you a fan of the bard?"

"I suppose I am. I took his Complete Works with me on my travels. When we were shipwrecked, off Madagascar, it was the only book I managed to salvage from the wreck."

Lucy realized she was babbling, but she couldn't seem to stop. She was supposed to be making *him* talk, but his presence seemed to be having the opposite effect on her.

"A surprising number of Shakespeare's plays feature shipwrecks, you know," she continued. "*The Tempest. The Comedy of Errors. Twelfth Night.*"

The Phantom shifted in his chair and leaned closer. His lips were beside her ear, his chin almost touching the side of her neck.

"I suppose that's because shipwrecks provide a fertile starting point for drama. Life and death situations. Or it can be a new beginning; a character can appear in a foreign land and reinvent themselves entirely. The slate of their past life can be wiped clean. They can be whoever they want to be."

"I never thought of it like that," Lucy murmured. "But yes, you're right."

"Is that what *you're* doing? Trying to reinvent yourself here in London after your travels?"

Lucy stared sightlessly down at the stage. The Phantom's voice was strangely hypnotic, and the semi-darkness created a sense of intimacy that made her want to share her deepest secrets. Up here, in the gods, they were in their own little world, removed from the hustle and bustle of the crowd. The shadowy box felt almost like the confessional booths she'd seen in Catholic churches, with the sinners conversing with a faceless priest from behind a concealing screen.

"Perhaps it is," she admitted wryly. "But it's not that easy. There are people here who've known me for years. People who refuse to see that I'm not the foolish, green girl I was when I left."

Like Arden, she added silently.

"You're beautiful," he said. "Perhaps that's all they see?"

She wrinkled her nose. "People put far too much store in beauty. The world would be a better place if we were judged on qualities like humor, and kindness, and bravery. Besides, the only man I ever *wanted* to find me beautiful has no interest in me at all."

She bit her lip, appalled that she'd let something so personal slip.

The phantom's lips curved upward. "A classic case of unrequited love, eh? How Shakespearean. At least you didn't drown yourself, like poor Ophelia."

Lucy shook her head. She was supposed to be unlocking the Phantom's secrets, not spilling her own.

"Are *you* trying to reinvent yourself by wearing that mask and haunting this theater?" she countered. "Here, you're exciting and mysterious. I bet in real life you're someone who writes tax law."

He chuckled, and her stomach contracted at the deep sound. How odd—Arden was the only man who'd ever produced such intense reactions in her before. And yet there was something about the Phantom's innate confidence that reminded her a little of him. Both were impossibly beguiling.

"I'm neither a banker, a lawyer, nor a clerk. You'll have to keep guessing."

Lucy suppressed a huff of frustration. She gestured at the actors playing Rosencrantz and Guildenstern on stage. Time for a different tack.

"So, what is it about the theater that you find so appealing?"

"It's an escape," he said, after a short pause. "There's something for everyone, a play for every mood. Tragedies and comedies, opera and farce. It's *life*, in all its messy glory, but in a neatly-rounded package, all wrapped up in a few hours."

Arden had said something very similar.

"There *is* something wonderfully predictable about a well-written play," Lucy agreed. "All the loose ends are tied up. Mistakes are rectified, lovers reunited, and villains are punished."

"Whereas in real life, good men die young, wicked men prosper, and virtue often goes unrewarded," he murmured drily.

"Too true." Lucy sighed. "Is the reason you're wearing a mask because you're wanted by Bow Street? Are you a highwayman? A cutpurse?"

"You seem to be blessed with a highly active imagination, Miss Montgomery." Amusement honeyed his tone. "And no. I'm not a fugitive from the law."

"Some say it's because you've been scarred," she persisted doggedly. "That you were once a soldier. Is *that* true?"

He stilled, and she cursed herself for pushing so hard.

"Yes, that's true," he said finally, and she let out a tiny, relieved breath that he wasn't leaving in a huff. "I was a soldier."

"And were you hurt?"

"I was. At Waterloo."

Lucy did some swift mental calculation. Napoleon's final defeat had happened two years ago. She'd been in Brazil at the time, and it had taken several weeks for the news to reach them.

"I'm lucky to be alive," the Phantom said softly. "I might have scars, but many of my friends were cut down in their prime. It's a privilege just to be here."

Lucy's heart squeezed in sympathy and she straightened her spine against the urge to turn around and comfort him. To cover his hand with her own.

"I know that feeling," she whispered. "I nearly drowned when our ship hit a reef. Luckily, most of us managed to reach a nearby island with the lifeboats. When the storm died down, we salvaged a few things from the wreck, like canvas, an axe, and a tinder box. It wasn't so terrible, in the end. We had fresh water, food, fire, and shelter. Those are the most important things."

A strangely companionable silence settled between them, an unspoken understanding of triumphing over adversity.

"People are far more necessary than *things*," Lucy continued softly. "One can live with relatively little in terms of possessions, but having your health, and people you love around you . . . those things are essential to happiness. To life."

"Was there no-one you missed when you were on that island?" The Phantom asked. "What about that fool who ignores you? Did you dream of him during the long, lonely nights?"

A telltale blush heated her skin, but she forced herself to answer. It was only fair. She ought to answer his questions if she expected him to answer hers.

"Truthfully? Yes. I dreamed of him." She gave a despairing, rueful laugh at her own foolishness. "Despite the fact that he did absolutely nothing to deserve it. I'm sure he never spared me a thought."

The Phantom stayed silent, and she shrugged. "I suppose I wanted a fairytale of my own, a happy ending like the ones that happen down there." She gestured toward the stage. "But as you've already observed, real life isn't like that. When I saw him again here in London, he treated me exactly as he'd always done, as his schoolfriend's hellion sister."

"You hoped he'd see you with fresh eyes. As a beautiful, fascinating woman."

"Well, yes," she laughed. "I suppose I did."

The Phantom tilted his head and she could sense his gaze on the side of her face almost like a physical touch.

"There is a man out there, Lucy Montgomery, who will love you until your dying day. You just have to find him."

"Easier said than done," Lucy said lightly, even though her heart warmed at the possibility. "But I appreciate your confidence."

"Oh, I suspect you're much closer to finding him than you think." There was laughter in his tone, and she was about to ask him what he meant when his gloved finger lightly stroked the side of her cheek.

It was a teasing touch, light enough to tickle, and her stomach did another strange little somersault. Apparently, matching wits with a mysterious, delicious-smelling stranger was something she'd been secretly craving.

"Will you tell me your name if I promise to give you my firstborn child?" she joked, a little breathless. "Like in the fairytale Rumpelstiltskin?"

"I've no need for a child. Firstborn or otherwise."

"What *do* you have need of then? There must be *something*. Tell me."

"Very well. I have need of . . . a kiss."

Lucy stilled, slightly shocked, yet also intrigued. "You'll tell me your name if I let you kiss me?" she clarified.

"Yes."

She blinked. Lord, it would be madness to agree. She'd be no better than a whore if she said yes only to win the hundred pounds.

But she was tempted.

She *wanted* to kiss him. Her body was humming and alive, and there was something about him that drew her, a strange familiarity, a kinship, as if they'd met before in another lifetime. How could she be attracted to mystery man whose name she didn't know and whose face she'd never seen? And yet there was no denying the thrill of excitement running through her veins.

"Agreed."

Before she could think better of it, she turned in her seat, leaned forward, and pressed her lips to his.

It was the briefest of kisses, a mere peck, and she pulled back, flustered and blushing at her own uncharacteristic daring before he could even move.

"There," she panted. "A kiss. Now tell me your name."

His laugh was deep and delighted. "Oh, sweet girl. That doesn't count. You agreed to let *me* kiss *you*, not the other way round."

A hot flush of mortification swept her cheeks. She felt tricked, foolish, but technically he was right. That *was* what he'd suggested.

Unable to look at him, she faced the stage again and braced herself as if preparing for the guillotine. "Fine. Then you have my permission to kiss me. Right now."

From the corner of her eye, she saw him shake his head. "I'm afraid I have to go. The house lights are about to come on for the intermission."

He stood, and a wave of disappointment crashed through her.

She twisted around on the love seat, gripping the back. "Wait! No! Don't leave."

He stepped back, easily blending into the shadows. Only the white of his evening shirt and cravat glowed pale in the darkness.

"Can we talk again?" Lucy pressed, strangely desperate for him to agree. "I'll come again tomorrow night."

He sketched her an elegant bow. "Then I shall be here. Goodnight."

Before she could say more, he slipped out of the door. She leapt to her feet and followed him just as the lights on the stage grew brighter, but when she stepped out into the hallway he'd already vanished.

Lucy cursed softly under her breath.

* * *

Will smiled in the darkness of the narrow passageway he'd entered to escape from Lucy. The entrance to this one was hidden behind a large gilt mirror on the lower landing of the stairwell, and he'd used it several times before to avoid detection.

He had little doubt that Lucy would be scowling down the empty staircase, her pert nose wrinkled in frustration that her quarry had eluded her. Her tenacity was just one of the many things he loved about her.

At least she hadn't seen through his disguise. He'd deliberately kept his voice low, and worn black leather gloves to hide a rather distinctive scar on his hand that eagle-eyed Lucy might notice.

He'd even applied a different cologne to alter his scent. According to Lucy's twin, Lenore, Lucy had once commented that 'the only good thing about Arden is that he smells nice.' It was still his most cherished compliment.

His pulse was pounding from their encounter, his blood simmering with desire. She'd looked so beautiful, sitting there in the darkness, her face illuminated by the footlights as she gazed, rapt, at the drama below. He'd watched her for several moments before she'd become aware of his presence, and his body had warmed at the way the light played on the upper curves of her breasts and danced along her collarbones.

He wanted to touch her, so badly he was almost shaking. He wanted to kiss those sweetly rounded curves and feast on her lips. Her impetuous kiss had been ridiculously brief, just the brush of skin. He'd fisted his hands in his lap to stop himself from reaching over the back of her chair, cupping the back of her neck, and kissing her *properly*, as ardently as he'd done in Sylvia Greenwood's garden all those years ago.

He'd left before temptation got the better of him.

Still, he would take the kiss she'd promised. . . tomorrow night.

CHAPTER 5

Lucy jolted forward on the seat as the Montgomery coach came to a rocking halt, and she leaned toward the window to call up to the driver.

"Is there a problem, Mister Cox?"

"I'm sorry, Miss. There's a crowd ahead, blocking the road."

"Can you turn around?"

"I'm afraid not. The street's too narrow. Woah there!" That last command was clearly directed at the horses, who had begun to fidget in agitation. "They're all coming this way."

Lucy sighed. She was keen to see the Phantom again, and this delay was irritating.

She'd dreamed of him last night. Strange, fitful dreams in which both the Phantom and Will Arden had made an appearance. Both men were with her in the steamy, humid jungles of the Amazon, playing hide-and-seek, flitting between the trees. She'd never been quite sure which man she was chasing. One moment it was Arden, the next it was the Phantom in his black mask. It had all been rather frustrating.

A shout snapped her back to the present.

"It's some sort of protest, Miss." The coachman said. "We'll have to stay right here and let them pass us by."

Chants and shouting filled the air as the crowd approached, and Lucy peered out of the window in sudden apprehension. The mood seemed angry, confrontational.

What were they protesting about?

The first people passed the carriage, and she saw that some had scarves pulled up over their noses, while others had their hats pulled down low in order to disguise their features. One brandished a banner that read; *'Feed the hungry! Protect the oppressed! Punish crimes!'* while another read, *'The brave soldiers are our brothers; treat them kindly.'*

A man in a dark green coat bellowed, "The fat Prince Regent gets a million a year in public money, but gives only five thousand to the poor!"

The crowd brayed and booed enthusiastically.

"The starving 'ave been abandoned!" another voice shouted. "The veterans ignored!"

The discontented noise swelled like a wave, and the carriage was suddenly surrounded on all sides by people slapping their hands on the wooden panels, and making it rock violently on its springs.

Outside, Cox cursed and bellowed at the protesters.

"Make way there. Hoi, stop that! This 'aint the Regent's coach, you numbskulls! Stand aside!"

The carriage gave a terrifying jolt as the horses reared in the traces and tossed their heads. Lucy made a grab for the handle by the door, missed, and was bounced off the seat and onto the floor. While she sat there, shaken, the door was forcibly wrenched open, and she screeched in alarm as a dark, unmistakably male arm reached into the carriage and grabbed her ankle.

She began to kick at the assailant as vigorously as she could. "Get off me, you cur!"

"Damn it, Lucy, stop that! It's me. Will!"

Lucy stilled in shock as she recognized the voice. "Arden?"

She peered at the indistinct figure in the doorway.

"Yes. You need to come with me. Quickly. This mob is getting out of hand. We're only a few streets away from the theater. We can take shelter there."

"What about Cox, and the coach?"

"Cox can handle himself, but he can't protect both you and the horses. We need to get out of here now."

"He's right, miss," Cox shouted down from above. He was struggling to keep the horses under control. "You go with Lord Ware. I'll wait this out and meet you at the theater after the performance."

Lucy shot a brief glance up the road; it was entirely filled with people, an unstoppable human tide.

Arden extended his hand, and she clasped it. He pulled her to her feet then looped his free arm around her waist and swung her down without bothering to let down the step.

The crowd engulfed them as soon as her feet touched the cobbles. She was crushed against Arden, stumbling against the hard wall of his chest, but he steadied her with his hands on her elbows.

"It's all right. I've got you."

He turned, craning his neck to peer over the crowd. "This way! Come on."

He took her hand in a grip that was almost painful, and Lucy ducked her head, following him blindly as he began to push his way through the crush. The throng was terrifyingly thick. There was barely any space to move, but he weaved his way expertly, jostling with his shoulders to forge a path.

Lucy almost gagged at the unpleasant odors surrounding them. The vast majority of the protesters were men, and the stench of unwashed bodies mingled with the oppressive smell of stale beer, pipe smoke, and coffee. They were all so tightly squeezed together that she couldn't even lift her arm to push herself away.

An elbow caught her in the ribs and she let out a cry, then she stumbled as someone else jostled her from behind. She would have fallen and been trampled underfoot, but Arden caught her, his firm grip never leaving hers.

"Careful!"

A crash of thunder directly overhead made several people shriek, and Lucy glanced upward just as the heavens opened and a torrent of raindrops was unleashed from the clouds.

She cursed soundly under her breath.

The mood of the crowd changed almost instantly from anger to desperation. People started to push in earnest, all keen to escape the sudden downpour, but the street was too narrow to allow such a large crowd to disperse quickly.

Just when Lucy didn't think things could get any worse, a troop of mounted soldiers appeared at the far end of the thoroughfare, and the air filled with cries of alarm.

"Bloody Hell!" Arden growled. "The militia. We need to go."

The soldiers began to push their horses forward, swinging what looked to be wooden truncheons or cudgels at whichever unfortunate beings happened to be in their way. Panicked protesters started to run, scattering down the narrow side streets and squeezing into shop doorways. One man climbed a lamp post to escape, and another pulled himself up and over a set of tall iron railings.

Arden tugged her hand and pulled her down an alleyway so narrow there was barely enough room for the two of them to stand side by side. They'd escaped the crowd, however, and Lucy took a relieved gasp of air as they stumbled forward.

"Where on earth are we?"

"Feather Lane," Arden panted, seemingly as out of breath as herself. "This way."

He still had hold of her hand, and they dashed forward

through the blinding rain. The buildings that loomed either side of them did little to shield them from the torrents. They turned a corner, but instead of carrying on, Arden stopped at the base of an unremarkable building and drew her down a set of slick stone steps, as if descending to a basement or scullery.

Lucy watched in interest as he pushed open a slim wooden door that was half-hidden in the shadows.

"What's this?"

His teeth flashed white as he smiled. "A secret way in to the theater. There's a passage that comes out beneath the stage."

Despite being desperate to get out of the rain, Lucy eyed the tunnel with deep suspicion. It was narrow and pitch black. "How often is this used, might I ask? It isn't going to be filled with spiders and cobwebs and rats, is it?"

"You're not afraid of a few spiders and rats, are you Montgomery? You must have encountered far worse on your travels."

"I have, but that doesn't mean I enjoyed the experience." Lucy pushed a dripping strand of hair from her face. "Fine. Lead on. At least it's dry."

Arden's shoulders were so broad they brushed the curved sides of the narrow tunnel as he pulled her forward, tugging inexorably on her hand. Lucy scowled at his back, even though he couldn't possibly see her in the fast-fading light.

After a few more steps the passage became completely dark, and she shuddered. She disliked enclosed spaces such as this, but she'd rather die than admit such a fear to Arden. He'd probably slow his steps, just to prolong her torment.

To distract herself, she focused her attention on her other senses, like the feel of her hand in Arden's much larger one. His fingers were warm and strong, curving around hers, and when she moved her thumb, she brushed the hard ridge of a scar that ran across his palm and curved up and over the back of his hand.

Her heart gave a funny little thump in her chest. She'd never imagined she'd ever be holding hands with him. It felt disturbingly pleasant.

"How long is this blasted tunnel?" she murmured.

"About a hundred yards or so." His disembodied voice sounded strange, bouncing off the walls. "It runs under White Hart Yard."

Lucy ducked her head and pressed closer to his back, praying that his taller form would sweep any spiders out of the way and leave the path clear for her. She was so intent on her task that when he slowed his pace unexpectedly, she barreled straight into him. Her nose bumped between his shoulder blades and she sucked in a shocked gasp.

"Oof! Sorry. I can't see a thing."

She cursed herself silently, and tried to ignore the way the delicious scent of his cologne wrapped around her, intensified by the rain and the enclosed space.

He gave a grunt that could have been either annoyance or amusement, and carried on.

Lucy frowned as a series of thoughts struck her. "Wait. What were you doing on Exeter Street? Were you taking part in that protest?"

"I happened to be in the area, and no, I wasn't taking part. Although I agree with the sentiments of the protestors. Veterans *should* get more help form the government, as should the poor."

"But how did you know I was in that coach?"

"The Montgomery crest is painted on the door."

"Oh." He'd probably envisaged a delightful evening visiting the taverns and brothels around Covent Garden. Instead, he'd turned into her knight in soaking wet armor. "Well, thank you for rescuing me. I'm sorry to have interrupted your night."

His grip on her hand tightened. "I hope you wouldn't have considered leaving the carriage if I hadn't been there. Covent Garden is no place for a woman alone, however intrepid."

Lucy rolled her eyes. "Of course not. I'm not completely dim-witted."

His answering snort sounded highly skeptical.

"This tunnel could be one of the ways the Phantom manages to get in and out of the theater without being seen," she mused aloud.

"Still hot on his trail? Is that where you were heading? Back to the Theater?"

Lucy nodded, then realized he couldn't see her in the dark. "Yes. In fact, I met him last night."

"You did? He obviously didn't throw you off the balcony. I applaud the man's restraint."

She debated how much to tell him. Not about the kiss, certainly. He'd probably be scandalized. "He was very polite, actually, although I didn't succeed in getting his name. I was hoping I'd have more luck this evening."

"You always were persistent."

"How do *you* know about this tunnel, Arden?"

"The architect, Benjamin Wyatt, is good friends with my father. He showed me the plans. This tunnel was already here when he redesigned the theater, though. I'm not sure when it was originally built. London has a whole warren of secret tunnels and passages below it. Ah, here we are."

Lucy bumped into him again as he stopped and finally released her hand. A crack of light entered the tunnel, outlining him as he pushed open what was presumably another door, and the sound of distant voices intruded.

They stepped out into a large, vaulted cellar, in which a single oil lamp illuminated another set of steps to their right. Arden straightened and pushed his wet hair back from his forehead. It settled into a perfect, albeit damp, wave, and she snorted to herself. The scoundrel *would* look handsome after a drenching. He'd probably look handsome after months trekking through the sweaty, muddy Amazon, damn him.

"There's a mezzanine floor above us, and above that is the stage," he whispered.

He turned, and his lips twitched as he noticed her bedraggled state. Lucy scowled at him, silently daring him to laugh.

He shook his head. "Dear God, you look like a drowned rat. You can't meet *anyone* like that, Lucia, not even a ghost."

"You're the one who pulled me out of the carriage," she growled.

He pressed his lips together, clearly trying to subdue his amusement. "Let's see if we can find you some dry clothes. We'll use the backstage route, don't worry."

CHAPTER 6

With a huff of resignation, Lucy followed him. Above them, the sound of shuffling feet and muffled voices indicated the evening's performance was well underway.

Arden led her to a set of narrow wooden stairs, which ascended to a small backstage room full of wigs and costumes.

"You can't use any of these," he said quietly. "They're for later in the play. We'll have to go up to the store rooms in the attic. That's where all the extra unused costumes and props are kept."

Lucy's shoes were so wet that she left dark footprints on the boards as they sneaked past the dressing rooms and started up another set of stairs. Her sodden skirts weighed twice as much as usual, and she bit back a complaint as she followed Arden upward.

"I suppose, between your months in the rainforest, and that shipwreck, you've spent an inordinate amount of time being wet." Arden's amused voice floated back at her down the stairs.

"It's not a sensation I enjoy," she grumbled. "Which is ironic, because it rains so much here in England that being damp is almost a permanent state. We should have settled somewhere warm and dry, like the Sahara."

"Ah, but then you'd be complaining about the heat," he chuckled. "If travel has taught me anything, it's to appreciate the comforts of home."

Lucy grunted.

After what seemed like an endless ascent, Arden stepped through a darkened doorway. The scrape of a flint was followed by a mellow glow as he lit an oil lamp, and she gazed around in wonder at the cavernous loft that was revealed.

Exposed wooden beams ran along either side of the vast room, where several distinct areas had been created; woodworking tools on one table, paints and brushes on another. An even larger area had been set aside for the storage of costumes and props.

"This is as big as a ballroom!" Lucy breathed. "I had no idea this existed."

Arden sent her an indulgent smile over his shoulder. "We're right above the auditorium and stage. The space runs almost the entire length of the building." He waved toward the far end. "Further back, over there, is above the flies—where the scenery is pulled out of sight by a series of ropes and pulleys."

The area was clearly a dumping-ground for all manner of unwanted items. Tall shelves overflowed with hats and canes, teapots, globes and vases. Larger items created a bizarre forest of obstacles; towering stacks of chairs, huge pillars painted to look like marble, cardboard trees, and rolled oriental carpets.

In the flickering shadows, everything seemed fantastical, like a bizarre dream world.

Arden beckoned her forward, and she skirted a gaudily-painted wooden carousel horse and dipped a mocking curtsey to a dressmaker's mannequin in a shimmering opera gown.

"Here you go. Take your pick." He swept his arm in a grand gesture to indicate row upon row of costumes, all hanging on rails. "We both need to get out of these wet clothes. I refuse to have survived four separate battles in France just to succumb to an ague here in England. That would be a paltry way to go."

He placed the lamp on a dressing chest, then peeled off his wet jacket to reveal a white shirt. The front section had not been spared the rain, and Lucy tried not to notice the way it had become almost transparent. When he untied his cravat, she hastily turned to inspect the numerous costumes on display.

"They're arranged by size," Arden said easily. "Small at this end. They should be about right for you."

Lucy bit back an instinctive retort about his ability to accurately guess a woman's garment size. No doubt he'd had plenty of practice. Still, the idea that he'd been thinking about *her* measurements, estimating the size of her breasts and hips and waist, made her skin heat in a way that chased away the lingering chill of the rain.

"What's your fancy?" he asked.

He moved closer, and she tensed, acutely aware of his proximity as his shoulder brushed hers as he browsed the row of costumes. "Come on, Lucia. Who's your favorite Shakespearean heroine? Let me guess. Cleopatra? Titania, queen of the Fairies?" He turned his head, assessing her, and his intent gaze made her even hotter. "Not Ophelia. She spends too much time in a river."

Lucy tried to ignore the fluttering sensation in her belly. The goosebumps on her arms were from the cold, not from the thrill of his closeness.

"What about Hermia from A *Midsummer Night's Dream*?" he pressed.

She scowled at him. "'*Though she be but little she is fierce*'?" she quoted. "You think that describes me?"

He sent her a cheeky smile. "It's a compliment! Fierceness is an excellent trait to have. But very well, what about Viola from *Twelfth Night*? She, too, survived a shipwreck."

"She also disguised herself as a boy."

Wicked amusement flashed in his eyes. "I can't say I'd object to seeing you in a pair of breeches."

Now Lucy was sure she was blushing. She'd worn loose-fitting trousers many times while traipsing through the jungle, but the thought of wearing them in front of Arden, with the curve of her hips and bottom immodestly displayed by the tight fabric made her a little lightheaded.

True, she'd ogled *his* derriere when he'd ascended the stairs. She had no doubt he'd do precisely the same to her, given the chance. Not because he fancied her, necessarily, but because she was a female, in his proximity, and he wouldn't be able to help himself. Flirting came as naturally to him as breathing.

"No breeches," she said sternly, "Stop teasing."

He gave an exaggerated sigh of disappointment. "Ah, but teasing you is one of my favorite activities."

Lucy snorted, and started browsing through the clothes.

There was an incredibly eclectic selection. She rejected a voluminous, ruffled dress that looked like it could have been worn by Marie Antoinette, a deep red velvet Medieval-style gown trimmed in gold lace, and a shimmery silver garment that looked to be almost sheer. Was that for a character like Salome or Delilah?

"This will do." The blue gown she chose was beautifully cut, with a scooped neckline and small puff sleeves. It would not look out of place in the Phantom's box. She turned, then let out a squeak as she found Arden tugging his shirt up and over his head.

"What are you doing? You can't undress here!"

He rolled his eyes. "Don't tell me you've never seen a shirtless man before, because I refuse to believe it."

He used the material to wipe the residual wetness from his skin and despite her every good intention, her eyes followed the movement of his hand.

In the lamp glow he was beautiful, a symphony of smooth skin and muscular curves, and for a moment she lost the ability to think. Broad shoulders were stacked above a tawny expanse of chest, and a series of muscles rippled down his stomach, terminating in an intriguing line of hair that disappeared into the top of his breeches.

Her mouth went dry, but she forced her gaze back up to his face, and discovered a devilish smile playing at the corners of his lips. He *knew* he was gorgeous, damn him. And he knew that *she* thought so, too.

Double damn.

She clutched the dress she'd chosen in front of her like a shield. "Stop that right now, William Arden. I forbid you to remove anything else."

He pushed his lower lip forward in a teasing pout. "Afraid you'll lose your head and ravish me? As you did in Sylvia Greenwood's garden?"

Lucy gasped. They'd agreed not to raise that subject. *Ever.*

"I didn't ravish you. You ravished me. And besides, you were fully clothed. We both were."

She'd felt his body, though, through their clothes. The delicious press of his chest against hers, the taut strength of those shoulders. The memory was etched into her brain. She tightened her fingers into the dress.

"I seem to remember you finding me irresistible," he grinned.

"I didn't know it was *you*."

Oh, she was such a liar. She'd overheard him making that assignation with Cressida Bonham. She'd deliberately stood on Cressida's hem so she'd have to go to the ladies' room to repair it, then sneaked out to meet Arden herself.

His snort indicated he had his doubts, but he let it drop. "Very well. I'll leave you to change in peace."

"Are you not going to choose something to wear?"

"Not from here. Florizel, the Stage Manager, keeps a change of clothes in his office down on the second floor. We're of a similar size. I'll borrow those."

"Fine."

"Need help untying your laces?"

His cheeky question brought another flush to her skin. "No, thank you. I've grown accustomed to undressing without the help of a maid. I don't require any assistance."

He sent her a theatrical bow. "In that case, I'll be back shortly. Try not to get into any more trouble in my absence. A protest and a rainstorm is quite enough excitement for one night, don't you think?"

CHAPTER 7

Lucy waited until she was sure Arden had gone before she began to remove her clothes.

She'd left her shawl back in the carriage, and her evening dress had taken the full force of the rain. The lilac silk was drenched, sticking to her body like a second skin, and she gasped in horror as she caught sight of herself in a huge gilt-framed mirror that had been propped against one wall.

Not only was the fabric covered in dark smudges and cobwebs from the tunnel, but the rain had rendered it practically transparent. The cut hadn't required a corset or stays, and her nipples were clearly visible through the silk and her thin chemise.

Dear God, it was a miracle Arden hadn't made some sarcastic comment.

Then again, he probably hadn't even noticed. He was doubtless more attracted to that headless mannequin than to *her*.

Feeling exposed in the huge space, and a little unnerved by the darkness beyond the circle of lamplight, she stepped behind a folding screen and stripped hastily. Cool air rippled over her naked skin, and she shivered as she slipped the dress she'd chosen over her head.

The gown, surprisingly, was a perfect fit, and she couldn't prevent a gasp of delight as she positioned herself in front of the mirror again. The scoop neckline was almost scandalously low, exposing the top curves of her breasts, and the midnight blue fabric shimmered in the lamplight like a raven's wing. The skirts were full, in the fashion of the previous century, and the way they swirled around her legs made her feel like a princess.

Would Arden think she looked pretty?

She gave herself a swift mental kick. She shouldn't care what he thought. Her goal was to meet the Phantom and discover his name.

She draped her ruined dress over the arm of a velvet chaise longue that had been placed next to the dressing screen, and turned her attention to her hair.

It was a disaster.

Most of the pins had fallen out of the upswept style, and rogue tendrils had started to curl around her face and neck as they began to dry. She'd been tempted to cut it all off a hundred times during her travels, purely for practicality, but had always changed her mind at the last minute. Her hair was one thing she liked about her appearance.

Pulling out the remaining pins, she gathered the wet mass in her hands and tried to pile it all back up on the top of her head, but it was impossible without assistance. She abandoned the task with a sigh, and let it drop back around her shoulders just as a shadow moved behind her in the mirror.

The Phantom stepped out of the darkness.

Lucy whirled around in alarm. How long had he been lurking in the shadows? Dear God, had he spied on her while she was naked? A hectic flush swept over her skin and she resisted the urge to fan herself.

"Heavens!" she gasped. "You gave me a shock, sir. I didn't hear you approach."

He took another step, into the circle of light, and his lips quirked below his mask as he casually lowered himself onto the chaise longue.

"I wouldn't be much of a phantom if I clomped about like a herd of elephants, would I? Stealth is an integral part of the job."

Lucy felt her own lips curve up, even though her heart was pounding against her ribs at his unexpected appearance. Her whole body seemed to hum with awareness, with excitement.

"True. Although I've heard of ghosts who make a terrible racket. Perhaps you should consider expanding your repertoire?"

"By rattling some chains? Groaning and shrieking? No, thank you. I'll leave the dramatics to the actors on the stage."

He was dressed as he had been the previous night, in black, with a white shirt and cravat. His hair was slicked back, off his forehead, and the familiar black mask covered the top half of his face.

"Arden—Lord Ware, will be back soon," Lucy warned, a little breathless.

A low chuckle escaped the Phantom. "I'm afraid not. He's been . . . waylaid."

"What do you mean? Have you done something to him?" Alarm made her voice quaver. As infuriating as Arden was, she'd never want anything *bad* to befall him.

"Nothing sinister. He's simply going to spend longer than expected in Mr. Holland's office."

"Because you've hurt him?"

"Locked him in, I'm afraid." The Phantom didn't sound the least bit repentant, and Lucy found herself rooted to the spot as he stood and moved closer. She couldn't step back without bumping into the huge mirror, and his knees pressed into the front of her full skirts.

This close, she could see the fine grain of the skin on his jaw, the hint of evening stubble.

She resisted the urge to reach out and touch it, and injected a scolding note into her voice instead. "That was rather wicked of you."

His shoulders lifted in a careless shrug. "I wanted you all to myself."

Her heart gave an irregular thump at the hint of possessiveness in his tone. She'd never had a man say something like that to her before. It was rather thrilling.

"What is Lord Ware to you?" the Phantom asked softly. "A suitor? A lover?"

A flush spread across her skin. "Neither of those. He's . . . we're . . ."

How *would* she describe their relationship? They weren't friends, exactly. Nor enemies. And saying *'He's just someone I kissed once, and can't seem to forget,'* seemed a little odd.

"He's a friend of the family," she said finally. "And he's not here for my company. He just happened to be in the right place at the right time to help me tonight." She bit her lip. "He has many disreputable qualities, but abandoning a damsel in distress is not one of them."

"I'm glad to hear it." The Phantom tilted his head and studied her. "Although any man who isn't interested in spending more time in your company must be a fool. That dress looks magnificent on you."

Flustered, Lucy turned back to face the mirror and smoothed her skirts with her hands. "Why, thank you."

The Phantom was so close behind her that she could feel the warmth of his body calling to hers, and when she sucked in a shaky breath the delicious scent of him made her stomach somersault.

In the mirror they made a striking couple, a symphony of dark and light. Her pale skin seemed to glow above the inky folds of her dress, and his white shirt stood out in bold contrast to the darkness all around them. His black mask seemed to hover above her shoulder.

Their eyes met in the mirror and her heart missed a beat as he lifted his hand and touched the side of her neck.

He wasn't wearing gloves.

The feel of his bare skin on hers was like a static shock, and her lips parted on a soft exhale. His fingers were warm, as gentle as a breeze, as he traced them across her bare shoulder, up the side of her neck, then ran his thumb beneath her ear and along the underside of her jaw.

Lucy couldn't move. It was as if he'd cast a spell on her, a sensual web that held her utterly in his thrall. Her blood pounded in her veins, and a strange recklessness filled her, a combination of excitement and trepidation.

"The last time we met you said you'd let me kiss you." His voice was low, beguiling.

"In exchange for your name," she countered.

"Does that offer still stand?"

Her breath caught. What should she say? She could feel the warmth of his body against her back, feel the dangerous tug of his allure. What was it about this man that tempted her so?

Kissing a stranger was beyond foolish, but Arden would be back at any moment to interrupt them. Even if he was trapped in Holland's office, he wouldn't be waylaid for long. Something as paltry as a locked door would pose little challenge to a man as resourceful as Arden. He'd pick the lock, or call for help, or simply kick the door down.

Which meant that Lucy had limited time to throw caution to the wind. She *needed* to know this man's name. Almost as much as she wanted him to kiss her. Other than Arden, this Phantom was the only man who'd ever had this fascinating effect on her, and she knew she'd regret it forever if she didn't explore the possibility now.

"Yes," she whispered. "The offer still stands."

The Phantom stilled, almost as if she'd surprised him. Then he let out a low, pleased sound. "You'll have to turn around, then."

Before she could move, his arm snaked around her waist, and she gasped as he spun her round in a swirl of skirts. Her hands came up to brace against his chest, and her heart fluttered as she looked up into his masked face.

However scarred he might be beneath the fabric, there were no imperfections to the lower half of his face. His lips were beautiful.

A flash of panic seized her. She'd only been kissed once before, by Will, in the garden. Would this be the same? It had been so long ago. What if she'd forgotten what to do?

And damn it all, why was she thinking of *Arden*, now?

"Close your eyes."

Lucy did as he commanded. She slid her hands up, over his lapels and onto his broad shoulders . . . . and held her breath.

She'd expected the kiss to be forceful—maybe even a little desperate—but instead, it was gentle, tentative, as if he was holding back for fear of scaring her.

Her heart squeezed in sympathy. Did he expect her to reject him?

His lips were warm, and surprisingly soft, and she stilled, enchanted. His hand came up to cup her jaw, and when he started to lift his head, to end the contact, she went up on tiptoe, following him when he would have pulled away.

She pressed her lips to his again, silently urging him to deepen the kiss, and with a groan that sounded like surrender, he gave her what she wanted. He pulled her closer, hard against his chest, slanting his mouth over hers as his tongue slipped between her lips to taste.

Yes!

Familiarity, so strong it was almost like relief, flooded her.

This was how it had felt to kiss Arden. This swooning, swooping sensation. This delicious dance of breath and lips and teeth.

In fact, it was *exactly* like she remembered. In the darkness behind her eyelids, images of Arden overlaid themselves with those of the Phantom. Past and present merged in a confusing swirl.

Almost without thought, Lucy slid her hands up to the nape of his neck to stroke the hair that curled over his cravat, and felt the Phantom tense against her.

Did he think she was trying to remove his mask?

She was about to murmur a reassurance when she realized his hair was... damp. As if he, too had been out in the rain.

She stilled, confused by the discovery, just as he lifted his head.

"I'm . . . sorry." He panted. His voice was even deeper than before. "That was . . . more than just one kiss."

His breath tickled her lips and she deliberately kept her eyes closed, trying to ignore the niggling feeling of recognition she was experiencing, the bizarre sense of *dèja-vu.*

The Phantom's cologne was stronger than it had been last night—almost as if it had recently been applied—but she could detect a trace of Arden's scent, too. It was more subtle, but definitely there, like a faint echo.

His hand was still cupping her jaw. With dawning suspicion, she put her own hand up to cover his, and stroked her thumb over the back of his hand.

Her heart missed a beat.

Arden's scar. The one she'd felt in the darkness of the tunnels. There, on the Phantom's hand. What were the odds of two men having exactly the same injury?

Impossibly slim.

A host of conflicting emotions bombarded her. She snapped open her eyes and took a good, hard look at his lips.

They were the exact same lips that had haunted her dreams from half the world away.

She gazed up, trying to determine the exact color of his eyes behind the mask, and even though they was shadowed, she was sure they were the laughing slate-blue she'd known for years.

Suspicion coalesced into certainty. How could she have missed something so obvious? How had she been so blind?

Will was the Phantom.

And she'd just kissed him.

Again.

But why? Why would he disguise himself so? Was this some elaborate game to provide entertainment for himself and to humiliate her?

Her skin heated in mortification as she remembered how they'd talked last night. How much she'd revealed. *God, she'd admitted to missing him, to dreaming of him.*

Was he playing with her? Mocking her? Did he think her so lonely and pathetic, so in need of diversion, that he'd concocted this subterfuge out of *pity?* She should throw *herself* off the nearest balcony if that was the case.

Or had he seduced other women in this same way? Was she just one in a long line of similar conquests, all seduced by the thrill of a striking, mysterious stranger promising to fulfill their secret desires?

God, she was a fool.

Lucy bit her lip, her thoughts a whirl.

On the other hand, he'd *chosen* to kiss her.

Her, Lucy Montgomery.

He knew exactly who he was kissing.

Was he waiting to see how far she'd let him go, then planning to rip off his mask and laugh at her for being so desperate for the touch of a man that she'd let a stranger fondle her in the darkness?

Anger heated her blood, but her heart was still pounding with desire, and the recklessness that had seized her earlier still simmered beneath her skin.

What did it matter? She'd wanted to kiss him.

She *still* wanted to, damn it.

She'd wanted to for years.

And now she had the chance.

Who cared what his reasons were? She was here, now, in his arms, and she would take whatever he would give her.

Whatever she could get.

CHAPTER 8

"*I* suppose I owe you my name."

The Phantom's low murmur snapped Lucy from her whirling thoughts, and she shook her head, decision made. "No, you don't."

"But I kissed you."

"Yes, I noticed."

She sensed his frown, even under his mask. His lips compressed. "You *don't* want to know who I am?"

Lucy sent him a serene smile. "I've changed my mind. Some things are better left a secret, don't you think?"

"But you'll lose your hundred pounds." He sounded shocked, even a little indignant.

"I don't care. If you tell me your name it'll make this *real*, somehow. And to tell you the truth, I'm rather enjoying the fantasy."

His lips parted on a surprised exhale that made her stifle a delighted giggle. *Oh, it was glorious to have the upper hand for once. To have turned the tables so neatly.*

He was amusing himself at her expense—why shouldn't she do the same? After all, he didn't know that she'd guessed his identity. Why shouldn't she see how far *he'd* go? With any luck, it would include more than kisses.

Arden was a scoundrel, no doubt about it. He knew women, how to please them, and this might be her only chance to be seduced by a man like him. She was too independent to tempt most men, and she'd long ago resigned herself to a lifetime of spinsterhood. But that didn't mean she intended to die a virgin.

She sent him a sultry look from beneath her lashes, as she'd seen her twin Lenore do on countless occasions, and curled her fingers into the lapels of his jacket. "I was hoping you'd kiss me again."

Will—the Phantom—pulled back, just a fraction. "What is this? Pity? A charity kiss for the poor, scarred Phantom?" His tone was scathing, suspicious.

Lucy gave an amused snort. "No. This is *desire*. You're an excellent kisser, and I enjoy being kissed. I'm taking advantage of your expertise."

"You haven't seen my face. I *am* scarred beneath this mask."

"I don't doubt it," she said evenly. "But scars don't bother me."

"Your friend Lord Ware will be back—"

Lucy hid a smile. "I thought you locked him in an office?"

"He's a resourceful man. He'll manage to get out sooner or later—"

"Then you'd better get on with kissing me, don't you think? Unless you don't *want* to, in which case—"

"I want to kiss you." he growled. "I've wanted to kiss you since the very first moment I saw you."

The absolute conviction in his voice left no room for doubt, and Lucy's stomach gave another delighted somersault.

"Then do it."

* * *

WILL'S HEAD WAS SPINNING.

Bloody Hell, he should have expected something like this. No interaction with Lucy Montgomery *ever* went the way he expected it to.

What on earth was she playing at? Inviting a stranger to kiss her.

A part of him was a little outraged at her taking such a risk, but another part was proud of her for chasing her own desires. She'd always been a woman who forged her own path. He could hardly blame her for seizing the opportunity now, and he could only be grateful that *he* was the lucky recipient.

Still, he'd never intended for things to go this far. He'd thought to give her a brief kiss—as she'd given him in the box last night—then tell her his name. He would push off his mask, reveal himself as Will Arden, and declare his love for her in no uncertain terms.

She would be annoyed by his deception, of course, but she'd forgive him once he convinced her was in earnest and begged for her hand in marriage.

This particular situation, however—with her inviting the Phantom to seduce her— was not one he'd anticipated.

And yet it opened up a whole host of intriguing possibilities.

As the Phantom he could do what Will Arden could not. He could kiss her, touch her in ways he'd only dreamed about. He could take his time, worship her, show her a glimpse of how wonderful lovemaking between them could be.

And God, he wanted to. He was practically vibrating with need.

His resolve was crumbling with every breath he took, but he made one last attempt to do the honorable thing.

"You're so perfect. So beautiful." He shook his head. "You don't want a scarred monster like me."

Her clear gaze didn't waver. "Yes, I do."

"But there are hundreds of other men you could kiss," he argued. "What about Arden? He just saved you from an angry mob. Isn't that the kind of heroic behavior women are supposed to appreciate? Why don't you throw yourself into his arms?"

Her lips quirked. "He did save me, that's true, but he doesn't want to kiss me."

Will clenched his fists against the need to grab her shoulders and show her just how wrong that was.

"Are you sure about that? I saw the way he was looking at you earlier, before he left. He couldn't take his eyes off you."

She gave a soft feminine snort. "That's because my dress was practically see-through. Arden's a man who appreciates the female form. He was just enjoying the free show. The fact is, I could strip naked in front of him and he wouldn't be interested."

Will sucked in an outraged breath at this falsehood. "No man in his right mind would refuse to make love with you."

"Then Arden is clearly deranged, because he didn't even like kissing me. The one time he did so, he was disgusted."

"Will Arden is an idiot," Will muttered.

Her smile widened. "Indeed."

"Maybe he regrets his mistake? Men change, after all. You should give him a second chance. I bet he'd jump at the offer to kiss you now."

She gave another shrug. "You might be right, but unfortunately for Arden, he's not here. And you are." She put her hands on her hips. "Now, are you going to kiss me or not?"

Will couldn't bear it any longer. Irritation and desire, a disastrous combination, were coursing through his bloodstream, urging him on. "Fine, I'll kiss you. But remember, you asked for this."

She gave a solemn little nod at his warning. "Understood."

He didn't give her another chance to change her mind. He simply caught her face between his palms, pulled her toward him, and captured her lips with his.

This kiss was nothing like the first.

Will abandoned all restraint. He captured her mouth and

plunged his tongue inside, tasting her with a rhythm that made his blood sing in his ears. When she clasped his shoulders and kissed him back, little lights exploded behind his eyelids. He slanted his head and kissed her deeply, drawing her scent into his lungs like a drowning man gasping for air.

He couldn't get enough. His hands slid over her body, molding her curves to his larger frame, loving the way she fit so perfectly into all his hollow spaces. Her breasts against his chest, her legs between his.

His damned mask was an annoyance. Her nose pushed against the bottom edge of it, knocking it askew, and he made a grab for the ties that secured it as her hands swept up into his hair.

She dragged her lips from his. "Turn out the light."

His brain took a moment to process the request. His throbbing cock was claiming most of his attention.

"What? Why?"

"I want to kiss you without your mask. You can take it off when it's dark."

Will frowned. "Why? So you can pretend I'm someone else?"

She was panting, just as he was. Her gorgeous breasts were rising and falling against the neckline of her bodice. She opened her mouth to reply, but he shook his head.

"No, actually, don't answer that. I don't want to know."

This whole situation was beyond ridiculous. If he had a rival for her affections, some stupid fool who didn't appreciate her, then he'd deal with that obstacle later. He wasn't ready to reveal himself just yet. If he could steal a few more kisses, even under false pretenses, then he would do it.

With a growl of frustration, he reached out and extinguished the lamp, plunging them both into a darkness so profound he could barely make out her faint outline in front of him.

And then he felt her small hands cupping the back of his head as she untied the ribbon that held his mask in place. She pitched it to the side; he heard it drop to the floor with a soft thud.

His hands found her waist and he pulled her back against him just as she gave a happy little sigh against his lips.

"That's much better."

She threaded her fingers through his hair and pulled his mouth down to hers, and without thought he slid his hands around her hips to grasp her bottom.

This. This woman. He'd dreamed of having her in his arms like this for eons.

He bent, lifting her against him, and she jumped up, wrapping her legs around his hips, her full skirts filling his arms as she clung to him like a monkey.

Thank God she'd chosen such an antiquated dress. The long, straight skirts of her fashionable gown would never have allowed such freedom of movement.

His cock was like an iron bar, pressed against her stomach between them, and he staggered back until his calves hit the chaise longue. He lowered them both, turning her so she lay beneath him.

His mouth barely left hers. He kissed her with all the pent-up longing in his soul, trying to make up for all the times he'd awoken without her, alone and aching. Craving this: her body next to his, her skin beneath his hands.

In the darkness all he could do was feel, and he kissed his way blindly down her throat and along her collarbone as his hand cupped her breast over her bodice. She surged restlessly against him, arching her back to press herself more firmly into his hand, and Will went a little mad.

He caught her lips again and slid his hand inside her dress, catching her gasp of shock on his tongue as his palm cupped her bare breast.

"Oh! Oh goodness!"

He gave her a gentle squeeze, felt her nipple harden against the center of his palm. "Nice?" he panted. "More?"

She tightened her fingers in his hair. "Yes!"

A wave of desire swamped him, a need to show her the incredible things her body was capable of. He pushed down the fabric and fastened his mouth over her nipple, flicking it with his tongue, then sucking it hard.

She gave a little shriek. "Oh, God, . . . that's . . . don't stop!"

He had no intention of stopping. Her perfume filled his head, drowning his senses. The entire world narrowed to the feel of her beneath him. So small, and yet so strong. So delicate that a wave of protectiveness swamped him. He wanted to keep on doing this, keep on pleasuring her forever. He wanted her in his arms until he died.

"There's more," he groaned. He pressed a kiss to the uppermost curve of her breast, then gave a teasing nip to her shoulder with his teeth. "Want me to show you?"

He thought she'd say no. Thought she'd tell him to relight the lamp.

But Lucy Montgomery had never done what he expected.

She caught his face between her hands, stroking her fingers over the scar that slashed across his skin. Her thumb found the notch where it bisected his eyebrow, her fingers traced the furrow that curved over his cheekbone like a sickle moon back up toward his temple.

And in the darkness, she leaned up and pressed her lips to his skin, kissing his wounds as if they were the most beautiful thing about him.

Will forgot to breathe as she leaned close to his ear and whispered, "Yes. Show me now."

CHAPTER 9

*L*ucy didn't give Will time to think. This was no time for logic, for reason. If he started thinking he'd probably stop *doing*, and that was the last thing she wanted him to do.

So she tugged his shirt from the waistband of his breeches and slid her hands up, under his shirt, greedily absorbing the feel of his muscles bunching beneath her palms, just as she'd dreamed of doing a thousand times in her imagination.

He let out a groan against her temple and she sent a silent, incredulous, *thank you* to the universe for finally gifting her the opportunity to touch him as she'd always dreamed of doing.

The darkness made her bold. She kissed his throat, his jaw, breathing in the delicious scent of his skin, and her heart leapt in delight as his hand slid down her leg and burrowed beneath her skirts. His fingers curled around her ankle, and then his palm was sliding up, over her stockinged calf and garter.

"I . . . God, it's been too long since I've had a woman." His voice was almost a growl, and her stomach fluttered at his anguished confession. He sounded delirious. As if he'd lost his senses.

Good. She wanted to befuddle him as much as he befuddled her.

He was half-lying on top of her, but she welcomed his crushing weight. She writhed against him as his hand found the bare skin above her knee, then moved higher, squeezing the top of her thigh before sliding around to caress her bare buttock.

A heavy, insistent throb pulsed between her legs.

"Lucia," he groaned. "You're killing me."

Lucy bit back a laugh in the darkness. If she'd needed further confirmation, that was it.

Loo-chee-ah. Three syllables, the Italian way. As only he said it.

She fisted his hair and put her mouth next to his ear. "I need to tell you a secret."

A distracted grunt was his only reply.

"The man I've been in love with for years? It's Will Arden."

His entire body stiffened, and she held her breath, afraid she'd miscalculated. Would he reveal himself? Laugh at her? Pull away?

His fingers tightened on her thigh. "Say that again. Did you just say you *love* Will Arden?"

She nodded in the darkness, wishing she could see the look on his face. "I did."

"Is *he* the man you dreamed of on your island?" he rasped.

"I'm afraid so."

His breath tickled her lips as he pressed his forehead against hers. "Is he the man you're thinking of when I touch you? Are you wishing he was here instead of me?"

"Yes," Lucy whispered.

He gave a soft, disbelieving laugh, as if he was on the verge of madness. As if he'd just realized his only competition was *himself*. "Will Arden is the luckiest bastard in London."

"And also the stupidest," Lucy couldn't resist adding. "After all, he doesn't love me back."

He paused for the space of three heartbeats.

"What if he does?" The question was barely audible, as if the thought were so delicate it would break if voiced too loudly. "What if he's loved you for even longer than you've loved him?"

Lucy's heart was thundering against her breastbone, but she managed to inject a note of skepticism into her tone.

"I'd find that hard to believe. He didn't want to kiss me four years ago."

He hissed out a tortured breath. "What if he wanted to kiss you so badly, he was shaking with it? What if he was seconds away from pulling you deeper into the gardens and ruining you completely?"

"I—"

He didn't let her finish. "What if he was cocky, and arrogant, and thought he was too young to get married? What if he was scared by the strength of his own feelings? What if—" his voice held an ache that brought a lump to her throat. "What if he's realized how stupid he's been?"

Lucy sucked in a breath. This was more than she'd ever expected. More than she'd ever dreamed.

"That's a lot of 'ifs,'" she managed.

His nose brushed hers in the darkness. "I have another. What if he was here with you right now?"

Lucy grazed her lips across his, a deliberate, provocative challenge. "Then I'd tell him to put on the light."

All the breath seemed to leave her lungs as she waited to see what he would do.

For a terrible moment he didn't move.

And then his weight lifted off her. The chaise creaked as he shifted his position and she almost protested as his hand slid from beneath her skirts. The air moved as he stood, and she heard the scrape of something metallic as his hand swept the top of the dressing chest in search of the tinder box.

She pushed herself upright on the chaise just as he struck the flint and lit the wick on the oil lamp. In the sudden flare of light, she saw his face, unmasked, and her stomach clenched with a terrible mixture of excitement and trepidation.

He leaned back, resting his hips against the dressing chest, and met her gaze. "Lucia."

She raised her brows and matched his solemn tone. "William."

How could turning on the light have made it so difficult to speak? It was as if they were suddenly strangers, with a yawning gulf between them.

But her lips were still tingling from his kisses, her skin still hot from his touch.

He gave a helpless little shrug and gestured to the scrap of black fabric she'd discarded on the floor. "No mask." He raked his hand through his hair, only adding to its disorder, then touched the pale ridge that marked his cheek and temple. "I told you I was scarred."

"And I told you, I don't care."

"How long have you known I was the Phantom?"

A smile curved her lips. "I suspected when I smelled your cologne, but I was certain when I felt that scar on your hand."

He turned his palm down and frowned at the offending evidence. "I forgot my gloves," he said, as if chiding himself. "I was too desperate to get back to you."

She tilted her head and tried to calm her pounding pulse. "Is that true?"

He sank onto the end of the chaise but made no move to reach for her. "I'm afraid so." His lips quirked as he realized he'd repeated her own words from earlier.

"You aren't teasing me?" she pressed. "I'm not just one of a hundred women you've brought up here and seduced?"

His brows lowered. "No! God, no. You're the only one I've ever brought here." He stared deeply into her eyes. "You have to believe me. I was so stupid four years ago. I wanted you, but I didn't *want* to want you. I fought it with everything I had. I told myself I was about to leave for war, that I was in no position to offer for you. But it's different now. *I'm* different now. And not just because I've got this scar." He touched his left hand to his head. "I know exactly what I want, and I'm not afraid to go after it. I want y*ou*, Lucy Jane Montgomery. Now and forever. Will you marry me?"

Lucy bit her lip and pretended to give the matter serious thought. A warm glow of happiness was building in her chest, but he deserved to be punished, just a little bit.

"Only if you prove that you love me."

He gave a groan of dismay. "How? Please don't say you've thought of some ridiculous, heroic quest for me to undertake, like tramping through a snake infested jungle, or finding the source of the Nile."

"Would you do something like that for me?" she asked, genuinely curious.

"God, yes, if you asked me to."

She threaded her fingers through his. "I don't think I need anything quite so dramatic."

"Then what can I do?"

"Make love to me. Here. With the lamp lit."

A wicked spark of interest flared in his eyes. "What, now?"

She nodded, astonished by her own daring, certain that her cheeks were a hectic shade of pink, and his lips curved upward in that devilish grin she knew so well.

"Lucia Jane Montgomery," he chided, mock-sternly.

She raised her brows in faint challenge and leaned back against the arm of the chaise longue. Her pulse beat a frantic tattoo in her throat as he moved over her, sleek as a jungle cat, caging her with his hands on either side of her head.

"Are you sure?" he asked softly. "We can wait for a bed. Do this properly." His grey-blue eyes bored into hers. "I want this to be perfect for you."

"It will be."

He shook his head, sending his disordered hair falling over

his brow. "But it's been so long, and I want you so much. I don't think I can go slowly. What if I'm too rough? What if I hurt you?"

"I'm pretty sure I've survived worse."

"You deserve better for your first time. You deserve candles and cushions and—"

A smile curved her lips. "I deserve *you*, Will Arden. Right now."

"No going back from this." He traced her lips with his thumb, watching the movement as if mesmerized. "This is the point of no return."

Acting on pure instinct, Lucy sucked the tip of his thumb into her mouth, then gave it a gentle bite, and his guttural growl sent a thrill of feminine satisfaction through her.

She sent him a mocking look. "Oh no, I'm about to be ravished. What a terrible fate."

He narrowed his eyes at her sarcasm. "You, Lucy Montgomery, are a hellion."

"Yes, but I'm yours."

His eyes darkened. "Mine."

He kissed her, pressing her back into the velvet, and Lucy bit back a triumphant smile as he lowered himself on top of her again. His hands roved her body, stroking and squeezing as if he was trying to memorize the shape of her, and she shifted restlessly as he slid his hand back under her skirts.

Yes!

When his fingers slipped between her legs, she closed her eyes in scandalized delight. Her skin was hot, aching for his touch. His tongue delved into her mouth while his wicked fingers slid between her folds, teasing the entrance to her body, and she arched up into his touch, desperate for more.

"*Mine*," he breathed again.

He pressed a fevered kiss to the hollow at the base of her throat just as his finger slipped inside her, and she let out a soft groan of shock, of pleasure. Every muscle in her body seemed taut, quivering.

"You like that?" He swirled his finger in a devilish figure of eight pattern that made stars twinkle behind her closed eyelids.

"Yes!" she managed to gasp. "More."

His low chuckle made her clench around him. "Beautiful girl."

Her entire body was throbbing, poised on the edge of some momentous abyss, and she groaned in protest as he suddenly withdrew his hand. She opened her eyes to find him unbuttoning his falls, then his weight was back on top of her and she felt him position himself between her legs. The hot flesh of his cock pressed against her, and she wriggled in nervous excitement. Of all the adventures she'd ever been on, this, surely, was going to be the most life-changing.

He straightened his arms on either side of her, raising the top half of his body from hers to relieve her of some of his weight, and held her gaze, refusing to let her look away as he rolled his hips and slowly, slowly, pressed into her.

Lucy caught her breath at the intensity of it all. She felt a stretch, an aching sting, and she bit her lip, a little uncomfortable.

"Relax," he breathed shakily. "Let me in. Please, Lucia."

He drew back and she shuddered, feeling her own wetness between them, and when he pressed forward again, she lifted her hips, hot and desperate to feel his body fully joined with hers.

"Slowly," he chided. "It's all right. You'll get used to me. You just need to—"

He slid deeper, still holding her gaze, and she absorbed the new feeling of fullness with a dizzy sense of amazement.

She'd never been this close to another person, *ever*, and the way he was staring at her, as if she were some sort of goddess, caused a strange, heavy ache in her chest.

"God, do you know how many times I've dreamed of this?" He shook his head, as if he couldn't believe what he was seeing. "Of you. Of being *inside* you, Lucia. I—"

He couldn't seem to finish the thought. He rocked his hips, just a fraction, and a shimmer of sensation raced through her, the possibility of pleasure.

He slid his hand down her thigh. "Lift your knee. Wrap your legs around me."

Lucy did as he commanded, and gasped as the new angle slid him deeper still.

How had she lived so long without experiencing something so incredible?

He let out a long, shuddering breath. "You—I can't—" His cheeks were flushed, his breathing choppy. "Next time, we'll take hours, I swear. I'll strip you naked and worship you. But right now, I *have* to move. Please, God, or I'll die."

She almost smiled at his desperation, but his mouth found hers and his palm cupped the nape of her neck and this time, when he pumped his hips, he nudged a spot somewhere deep inside her that made her shiver in delight.

Lucy closed her eyes and abandoned herself to sensation, to *him*. Every slide of his body created a wicked friction inside that sent her higher, closer to the edge.

His movements became faster, more frantic, and she held her breath, loving his urgency, reaching for that promise that seemed just out of reach.

Jumbled words fell from his mouth, incoherent murmurs and pleas that matched her own.

Yes.

Please.

More.

Perfect, so perfect.

Don't stop!

Her body was burning up, so taut she felt like she would snap, and then with a gasp he sent her hurtling over the precipice, falling into a smothering ocean of pleasure. Her body convulsed, wave after wave of glorious release.

"Will!"

His big body surged against her and he let out a groan that reverberated from his chest into her own. With one last thrust, he pulled out of her, and Lucy held him as he shuddered and bucked, spending himself in the rumpled fabric of her skirts.

It seemed to take forever for her breathing to return to normal. Will lay sprawled, completely boneless, on top of her, and she relished the feel of his weight, pressing her down. She stroked his nape, playing with the hair that curled above his cravat, and with a spurt of amusement she realized that they were both still fully clothed.

Will finally pushed himself upright with a satisfied groan. He tucked his shirt back into his breeches, buttoning his falls with the ease of long practice, then took her damp dress from the back of the chaise and used it to wipe the evidence of his climax from her skirts.

A smile curved his lips as he glanced up at her, and he reached out and flicked her flushed cheek with his fingertip.

"I love it when you blush, Lucia. It makes me think of all the things I can do to make you even pinker."

Lucy let out a shaky exhale and pressed her hand to her bodice where her heart still hammered against her breastbone. "I'm not sure that's possible."

His low chuckle liquefied her insides. "Oh, challenge accepted." His eyes held hers, and his expression sobered as he lowered himself to one knee beside the chaise. He reached out and took her hand.

"You, Lucy Montgomery, have been the bane of my life—and my greatest desire—from the first moment I ever set eyes on you."

Lucy opened her mouth to speak, but he held up a silencing hand.

"I know that's hard to believe, considering my past behavior, and I'm no good at making pretty speeches. I'm a soldier, not a poet. But there's a bit from Hamlet that says it far better than I ever could; *Doubt thou the stars are fire; Doubt that the sun doth move; Doubt truth to be a liar; But never doubt I love.*"

"Polonius says that," Lucy said softly. "In act two."

"I know how much you love Shakespeare," he said. "But it can't possibly be as much as I love you. Please say you'll marry me."

Lucy sat up and straightened her skirts. "Yes, I'll marry you, you scoundrel."

His smile warmed her from the inside out. "Because you love me too?"

She rolled her eyes at his persistence. "Yes, my Lord Phantom. I love you too. With or without your mask."

CHAPTER 10

The Phantom of Drury Lane's last public appearance occurred during the final performance of Hamlet.

People were already gossiping about the fact that the chandelier above box number four had been lit—in clear contravention of his orders—and many were hoping he'd make a dramatic protest, when his tall, masked figure stepped to the front of the box.

A ripple of speculation fluttered through the crowd. A few people slipped out of the auditorium and headed for the stairs to the upper boxes, hoping to claim the hundred pounds reward, but the majority simply craned their necks and waited with bated breath to see what, if anything, the Phantom would do.

Even the actors on the stage paused mid-fight scene, and squinted upwards.

Those seated in the closest rows saw the Phantom's lips curve into a smile beneath his mask, and there was a collective intake of breath as he stretched his arm behind him, toward the back of the box, as if summoning someone.

An audible gasp echoed around the theater as a *female* figure stepped forward and took the Phantom's hand.

The mystery lady wore white, the perfect foil for his darkness, a shimmering, ethereal dress that looked like it could have belonged to the tragic French Queen Marie Antoinette. A matching white mask covered the top half of her face, obscuring her features from the rapt and speculative gazes, and her upswept hair was powdered white and threaded with pearls.

No sound emerged from the box, but the entire audience watched, spellbound, as the Phantom lowered himself to one knee and pressed a kiss to the back of his lady's hand in a silent, but very obvious, proposal.

For one suspended moment, they were a couple out of time. A shadowed Hades proposing to a sunlit Persephone. A highwayman begging for the hand of a fairy princess.

Fans fluttered in breathless anticipation as the lady in white pressed her free hand to her chest, to cover her racing heart. Then she reached forward to caress the Phantom's clean-shaven jaw in a gesture of loving affection.

The Phantom rested his cheek in her palm, his adoration plain, and when she nodded her acceptance, he stood in one graceful movement and took her in his arms.

An enormous cheer erupted from the stalls as the Phantom swept his lady into a lusty kiss. Cries of *"Bravo!"* and *"Encore!"* accompanied a thunderous round of applause as the entire theater rose to its feet and began stamping and shouting their approval.

The Phantom released his love with every indication of reluctance, and with hands still clasped, they both turned to face the audience. The phantom gave an elegant bow. The lady made a deep curtsey.

And then, to the delight of all, they stepped back into the shadows and simply . . . disappeared.

The audience cheered even louder.

Some said they were hiding in the curtains at the back of the box. Others speculated a secret trap door, or even a complicated series of mirrors.

Whatever the truth, when the door to the box burst open mere moments later, those seeking to claim a hundred pounds were disappointed to find it empty, save for one black mask and one white mask left lying on the red velvet seats.

And so the Phantom of Drury Lane and his ghostly bride took their place amongst the many other myths and legends that swirled around London's Covent Garden. Their happy ending was deemed to be suitably satisfying, even if the Phantom's identity had never been revealed.

* * *

HIGH UP, in the vast room that stored the myriad props and costumes of the theater, a breathless Lucy Montgomery and a laughing William Arden emerged from yet another hidden passageway. Lucy brushed some cobwebs from her skirts, while Will stepped around a fake cannon and pushed aside part of a splintered section of ship's decking that had last been used on a production of *The Tempest*.

Lucy sank onto a pretty floral armchair with a satisfied sigh.

"There. The Phantom's made his final curtain call."

"Without being caught," Will added with a grin. "You were magnificent, my love. I couldn't have done it without you. People will be talking about it for weeks." He slid into the seat opposite her, an enormous gilded throne with blue damask cushions and padded arm rests, and crooked his finger at her. "What are you doing over there? Come sit in my lap."

Lucy tried and failed to look scandalized. "Lord Ware, we're not even married!"

"We're engaged," he countered. "And there's only a week to go before I can call you my wife. I say that's close enough."

Lucy flicked a laughing glance at his lap. The bulging front of his breeches clearly showed how much he'd enjoyed kissing her in the box.

"Have I told you you're a wicked man?" she said, rising to her feet.

"On multiple occasions." His gaze heated as she stepped toward him. "Most recently when I kissed your beautiful—"

"Shhh!" She pressed her hand over his mouth to stop his scandalous words, but knew her cheeks were scarlet.

In the weeks since she'd accepted his proposal, they'd been forced to act with the utmost propriety in public, but they'd still managed to meet a few times here, at the very top of the theater. Will had shown her just how much he loved to make her blush—and also how much he loved *her*.

She couldn't wait to say her vows.

"Here, I have a present for you." Will dug into the pocket of his black jacket and handed her a small, leather-covered box.

Lucy sat on his lap and opened the hinged lid. Inside was a golden bracelet, and when she held it up in the flickering lamplight she saw letters inscribed on the inner surface, a secret message intended only for the wearer.

"Doubt thou the stars are fire," Will quoted softly, pressing a kiss to her jaw. "Doubt that the sun doth move." He kissed her again, below her ear. "Doubt truth to be a liar." A kiss on the corner of her lips. "But never doubt I love."

Lucy turned her head and pressed her lips to his. "Thank you." She pulled back and sent him a saucy smile. "Do you think Kit Hollingsworth will still give me a hundred pounds if I tell him your name?"

Will shook his head. "He already knows it's me. He's one of the directors of the theater. That bet was just a way of getting more ticket sales."

She let out a good-natured huff. "You are a scoundrel."

"Yes, but I'm yours."

She tilted her head. "I don't suppose we can leave here for a good hour at least, in case someone sees us."

"You're right. No sense in risking discovery now." His smile grew wicked and his gaze fastened hungrily on her lips. "What could we possibly do to pass the time until it's safe to leave?"

Lucy wound her arms around his neck and laughed, her heart impossibly light.

"Oh, I have a few ideas."

"Reading Shakespeare aloud?" he teased. "Comparing tales of danger and adversity?"

"Even better than that. Let me show you. . ."

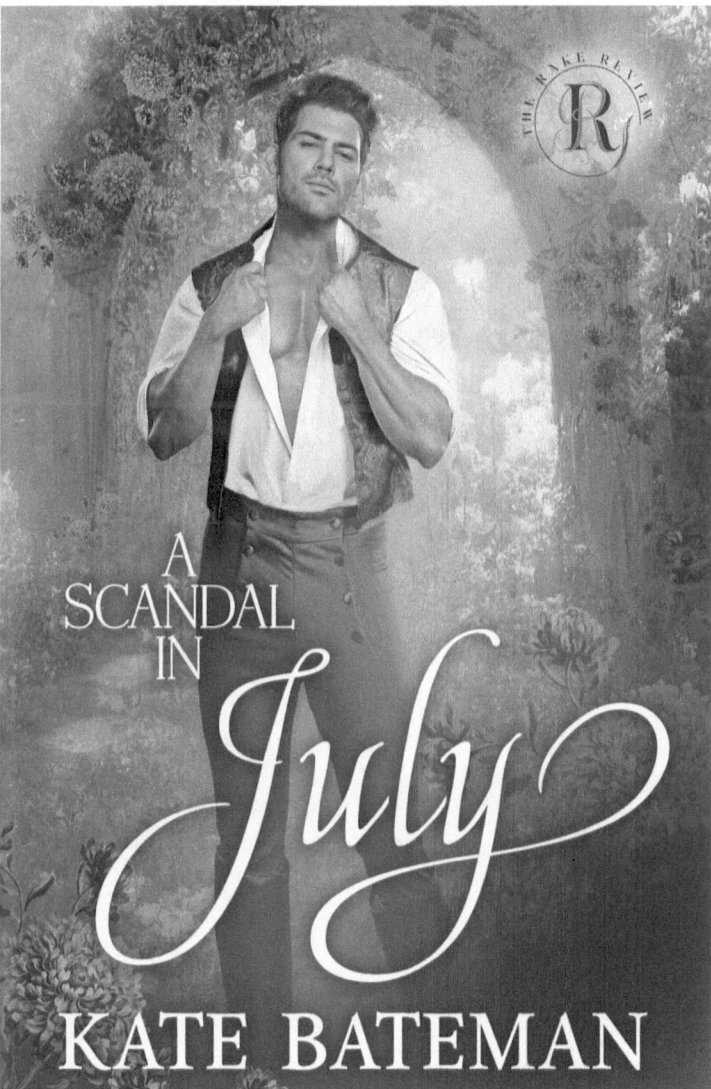

THE BRAZEN BELLE

JULY, 1820.

Dearest reader,

It is often said that there is no justice in the world, but those who have had the pleasure of making the acquaintance of a certain Mr. R— D— will disagree. It would have been an injustice, indeed, for Fate to have provided a man so handsome and charming with a fortune and a lofty title to boot.

Luckily for those gentlemen with plumper pockets, or calling themselves Marquis, Earl, or Duke, Mr. R— D— is a mere second son, with neither fortune nor title to recommend him.

While this unfortunate state of affairs has scarcely diminished his female admirers, Mr. D— remains stubbornly unattached. But will the imminent arrival of three young ladies with the surname M— make this handsome bachelor reconsider his single state?

The rivalry between these two prominent families is legendary, after all, and there's nothing so irresistible as forbidden fruit...

Your bold and brazen friend,

   The Belle

CHAPTER 1

ondon, 1820.

Lenore Montgomery had faced many challenges in her twenty-three years. She'd wrestled a giant water snake in Brazil, chased a panther with a shoe, and survived an unfortunate shipwreck off the coast of Madagascar.

None of those things had been as difficult as seducing Rhys Trevelyan Davies.

The rivalry between her family and their wild Welsh neighbors, the Davies, had been the stuff of legend for centuries, but the mutual antagonism had been tempered in recent years by a series of scandalous marriages between the two sides.

First, her cousin Maddie had married Gryff Davies, the current Earl of Powys, then Maddie's brother Tristan had fallen for the red-haired Davies hellion, Carys. Shortly after that, her *other* cousin, sensible mapmaker Harriet, had succumbed to the seductive pull of captain Morgan Davies.

Clearly, the combination of a Davies and a Montgomery led

to all manner of exciting possibilities, and for someone with an adventurous spirit like Lenore, that was thoroughly irresistible. She'd determined to meet one of the dreadful Davies for herself as soon as she returned to London with her globe-trotting family, and her wish had been granted at Lady Carrington's summer ball.

Unfortunately, she'd taken one look at Rhys Davies, and promptly lost her heart. And her wits.

It had not been the stuff of fairytales. Their eyes hadn't met across a crowded ballroom. He hadn't begged her to dance, or even saved her from being run over by a carriage.

She'd found him, quite by accident, in the garden. The unmistakable sounds of an altercation had been coming from the shrubbery; raised male voices, the scrape of gravel, a shout, and then a splash. Being naturally curious, Lenore had peered around a hedge to find Rhys Davies coolly straightening his cravat, and another man floundering about in the fountain.

She'd known it was Rhys from the unmistakable likeness between all three Davies brothers. She'd already been introduced to Gryff and Morgan earlier in the evening, and they'd had the same dark hair, sharp jaw, and sinfully full lips as their sibling. Neither of *them*, however, had made her heart feel like it was trying to beat out of her chest.

"When a lady tells you no, Burton, she bloody well means no!" Davies growled at the man in the water. "And if I *ever* hear you've mistreated a woman again, I'll do more than just ruin your coat. I'll fucking bury you. Understand?"

The man in the fountain wiped some pond weed off his cheek and sent him a surly scowl. "Yes."

Lenore stepped back, intending to withdraw unobtrusively, but her shoe crunched on the gravel and Davies's head whipped round.

His hair was wildly disordered, his lower lip bleeding from where his opponent had obviously managed to land a punch before he'd been vanquished, and his eyes, when he caught sight of Lenore standing in the path, had been glittering with fury.

Until they'd widened in astonishment.

Lenore didn't believe in love at first sight. At least, she *hadn't*, until that very moment. But the combination of outrageously handsome features and a noble urge to protect the innocent had done something funny to her brain.

"I'm sorry, I didn't mean to interrupt," she said stiffly, ignoring the way her pulse was hammering in her throat.

Davies took a step toward her, his eyes roaming over her face as if she were some sort of apparition.

"Who are you?"

His voice was deep, a gravelly growl that made her knees go weak and her stomach somersault in the most outrageous way.

Lenore tossed her head and studied him back with equal intensity. "I'm Lenore."

He stilled, and his eyes narrowed in sudden suspicion. "Not Lenore *Montgomery*?"

She sent him her widest smile, the one her father said could charm the birds from the trees. "The very same."

Davies's expression changed from guarded to horrified in an instant, and he raised his hands up in front of him as if to ward off a blow. She thought she heard him mutter *Oh, Shit,* under his breath, but she couldn't be sure.

Lenore paused. She was used to rendering men speechless. She'd been told she was beautiful ever since she was a girl, and while she found people's fascination with her appearance quite ridiculous—really, it was just luck that she'd been blessed with a combination of green eyes, straight nose, and pink lips that people generally found attractive—there was no denying that the ability to wind men around her little finger was a useful tool to have.

To date, she'd received six marriage proposals, and countless more indecent ones, but Rhys Davies was looking at her as if she'd just told him she was carrying the bubonic plague.

A mortified blush heated her cheeks, even as a bubble of hysterical laughter threatened to escape her chest.

Oh, God, had she finally found the man of her dreams, only to discover he was the one man she'd ever encountered *not* to find her attractive?

The universe had a wicked sense of humor.

Davies was still staring at her with a combination of annoyance and dismay, but the cad in the fountain had managed to extricate himself and now leaned, dripping, on the curved stone rim.

"I say, you're a sight for sore eyes. Don't think we've been introduced. I'm Gordon Burton."

He extended his hand, as if he expected her to shake it, and Lenore sent him a scathing glance.

"I'm not interested in making the acquaintance of a man who takes advantage of women," she said crossly. "Go away."

Burton's face fell, and he limped off into the bushes, leaving a trail of water in his wake.

Davies still didn't seem in the mood to introduce himself, so Lenore twitched her skirts and straightened her elbow-length gloves. "Well, then. I suppose I'll go back inside. Goodnight, Mister Davies. You've certainly lived up to expectations."

With that parting shot, she withdrew, hurrying back inside to the safety of her family, but the image of Rhys Davies's face had been imprinted on her brain. And her heart.

CHAPTER 2

*R*hys Davies was excellent at evading things, especially punches and marriage.

He'd learned to dodge the punches at his twice-weekly boxing sessions, not merely because he didn't enjoy pain, but because the ladies seemed to love his face just the way it was. Not ruining it with a broken nose was reason enough to stay sharp as the blows flew his way.

He'd avoided marriage because the idea of settling down with just one woman had seemed extremely restrictive, despite the obvious happiness of his three siblings, who'd all tied the knot in the past few years.

Rhys was a rational man. He put no store in the ridiculous idea that some mystical force kept throwing Davies and Montgomerys together. The fact that both his brothers and his sister had ended up with members of the rival clan was purely incidental—an interesting anomaly, but one that could easily be explained by the inherently perverse, stubborn and competitive natures of both families.

If someone told a Davies not to do something, it—naturally—became the very thing that Davies most desired to do. Rebellion was in their blood, and had been since some distant ancestor Davies had fought by the side of Llewellyn ap Gruffud, the last Prince of Gwynned, in his unsuccessful quest to drive the invading English from Welsh soil, back in the twelve-hundreds.

Now, six hundred years later, it was clear the English weren't going anywhere, and since killing each other with swords was frowned on in a civilized society, both families had relished coming up with less violent but ever-more-sneaky ways to annoy the other.

Ergo, if a Davies knew the last thing they should do was to provoke a Montgomery, it became an irresistible quest, a source of both enjoyment and deep satisfaction.

The Montgomery family felt precisely the same way, and it was no surprise to Rhys that conquering their rivals on the field of love had surpassed beating them on the battlefield. Sleeping with the enemy was the ultimate forbidden fruit, and it wasn't at all incredible that all the years of mutual taunting had produced several successful marriages, those of his three siblings included.

Rhys had been adamant that *he* wouldn't succumb to the fatal charms of some Montgomery siren, however. Even so, he'd been feeling oddly relieved at Morgan's wedding, believing all the available Montgomery girls had been taken.

He was in the clear. The Davies Curse, as he'd started to call it, couldn't touch him.

And then he'd spoken to the two meddling Montgomery great aunts, Constance and Prudence, who'd gleefully informed him that three *more* Montgomery chits were sailing back from Madagascar.

That news had been enough to make Rhys break out into a cold sweat, even though he'd told himself quite firmly that there could be a *dozen* Montgomery women in London and he wouldn't fall for any of them. It was not pre-ordained. It wasn't his destiny. Such thinking was ridiculous.

But when their ship had been wrecked off the coast of Madagascar (and once he'd heard that nobody had died), he'd actually laughed in relief, knowing their arrival would be delayed.

And when Aunt Prudence casually mentioned that they'd finally docked in London, he'd breathed another sigh of relief to learn that the eldest of the three sisters, Caro, had already married one of their fellow castaways, his old school friend Max Cavendish, the Duke of Hayworth, on board the ship.

That still left the twins, Lucy and Lenore, and Rhys knew he'd feel a lot better once the two of them were taken out of commission, too.

Not that he put any store in the idea that he was in danger from falling for a Montgomery. Of course not.

But better safe than sorry.

He'd deliberately stayed away from London for the first few months after their arrival, lurking about at Trellech Court in Wales, but he'd been bored and lonely and itching to get back to town and the many diversions of the city during the social season.

News that Lucy, one of the twins, had married Will Arden, one of the aristocratic investors of the Drury Lane Theater, had been music to Rhys's ears, and he'd decided to throw caution to the wind and return to the capital.

How hard could it be to avoid Lenore, the last remaining twin? He'd just make sure their paths didn't cross until she was safely engaged to someone else, and then he'd be home and dry.

His plan had worked splendidly for several weeks, mainly due to the fact that Lenore was, apparently, spending most of her time down at Kew Gardens, advising on setting up a new hothouse for tropical plants and butterflies, her specialty.

He'd been introduced to both Caro and Lucy, and while he'd found them remarkably attractive females, there had been no lightning strike of infatuation, no hint that he was in any danger.

The fact that Lucy was Lenore's twin gave him great confidence, even though it was impressed upon him that they weren't identical, and that men usually found Lenore to be the most striking of the two.

Still Rhys hadn't been worried. He'd met scores of fabulously beautiful women, and had affairs with several of them, and he was no callow youth to be blinded by a pair of fine eyes and a well-turned ankle. Beauty was more than skin deep, and it usually didn't take him long to see past the outer layers of a woman to their innate character. If they were mean, or bitchy, or avaricious, then he was immediately repelled, no matter how pretty the outer packaging.

And then had come the fateful night he'd encountered Lenore Montgomery.

He'd been in Lady Carrington's rose garden, teaching a salutary lesson in manners to the boorish Gordon Burton, who'd tried to grope Carys's friend Annabelle on the terrace. He'd just pushed the ill-mannered sod into the fountain, when he'd turned and lost his mind.

At first, he'd thought she was a hallucination, the result of Burton's one lucky punch that had caught him on the jaw and split his lip, but when she didn't disappear in a dramatic puff of smoke, he'd realized that the most beautiful woman he'd ever seen in his life really *was* just standing there, just a few paces away.

The moonlight had been bright enough for Rhys to see the utter perfection of her features; wide eyes fringed with long lashes, a small, straight nose, and a slightly-too-wide mouth with the most kissable lips he'd ever seen. Her brown hair had been styled half up, half down, and the single curl that trailed over her shoulder made his fingers itch to trace it down over the snowy perfection of her breasts, which rose and fell beneath the deliciously low-cut neckline of her gown.

"Who are you?"

The question had slipped out of his mouth without conscious

thought, and he'd almost been too lost in her eyes to listen to her answer.

And then he'd heard, "I'm Lenore," and his stomach had dropped in absolute dread.

His next question was almost pointless, since his body already knew what his brain was frantically trying to deny, but he asked it anyway.

"Not Lenore *Montgomery*?"

"The very same."

Oh, shit.

His heart was pummeling his ribs as if he was being punched from the inside, and a horrific feeling of inevitability was sweeping over him, a sense of soul-deep recognition, as if he'd been waiting his whole life for this woman, without even being aware of it. That thought was immediately followed by another; that nothing was ever going to be the same, ever again.

Bollocks.

Rhys had never imagined he'd be thankful for Burton's presence, but his timely interruption had been most welcome. Rhys's mouth seemed to have forgotten how to frame words. Even when Lenore dismissed Gordon, he still hadn't been able to think of anything to say. He'd just gazed at her like a simpleton, his usual quick-wits gone begging as she'd muttered something about getting back to the party.

His knuckles were still stinging from the punches he'd thrown at Gordon, but Rhys had clenched his fists against the ridiculous urge to catch her wrist and stop her leaving. To keep her there so he could . . . what?

He shook his head. He had no idea what. Gaze at her some more? Demand to know where she'd been his whole life? Kiss her, right there in the moonlight? Cave to the inevitable, get down on one knee, and just say, "Marry me?"

God, no. There was no such thing as Fate. He was concussed. That would explain it.

Except Gordon had caught his lip, not his temple.

Rhys chose to ignore that pertinent piece of logic.

No. His reaction had been a momentary aberration. He'd been taken unawares. Hadn't had time to brace himself. Now that she'd gone, he could be reasonable and admit that Lenore Montgomery was a remarkably beautiful woman. In fact, if she'd been anyone other than a Montgomery, he'd have been striding back toward the house intent on making her his next conquest. He knew how to charm, how to flirt. How to seduce.

Bloody Hell.

Why couldn't she have been one of the scores of merry widows looking for a lover, or a courtesan seeking a new protector? Why did she have to be the very thing he'd absolutely promised himself he wouldn't have?

He would not be a cliché, the reason society laughed and whispered behind their fans because *another* Davies had been conquered. He hadn't survived three years in the Hussars, fighting Napoleon's finest, only to be vanquished on home turf by a pair of flashing eyes and the most splendid bosom he'd ever—

Not the point.

She might be gorgeous, but she was probably vain and shallow along with it, and no doubt desperate to marry a title now that she was back in civilization. With looks like hers, she'd have her pick of suitors. She'd be a duchess or a countess in no time.

In fact, Rhys's lack of title would exclude him from consideration. He might have a handsome face, but his fortune, thanks to his remarkable success on the stock market, was something only his family was aware of. Lenore wouldn't be interested in him. Not when she could accept a duke or a marquis.

He had nothing to worry about. All he had to do was stay away from her until she'd chosen someone else. He had too much honor to dally with someone else's wife and she'd be regretfully, but firmly, out of his reach.

It had been an excellent plan, except for the fact that Rhys hadn't been able to stay away from her.

He'd tried. He really had. But London society was surprisingly small, and the intermingling of their two families meant that he and Lenore regularly attended the same party or fete.

Even then, Rhys had attempted to keep his distance, spending hours in the card rooms instead of watching her with hungry eyes as she swirled around the dance floor with any number of besotted partners.

But every time he tried to avoid her, there she would be, inflaming his senses with her laughing green eyes and her coppery-brown curls. Making some sly, teasing comment that showed she was not just pretty, but witty and clever as well.

She was a natural seductress, charming men without even meaning to, and by the end of her first season she'd left a trail of broken hearts in her wake.

Rhys had ignored the gnawing feeling in his gut when he'd heard that the Duke of Andover had offered for her. She'd already turned down eight other suitors, including three earls, but Andover was the most eligible bachelor on the market. He was rich, affable, and almost as handsome as Rhys himself, and Rhys had been absolutely certain that Lenore would accept his suit.

She did not.

Rhys had drunk himself into a stupor in frustration. The girl clearly wasn't right in the head. Maybe she'd spent too much time in the sun on her travels and fried her brain. Who refused a duke? Didn't every girl dream of being a duchess? Andover wasn't even old. Or ugly. Or bankrupt. What possible other criteria could she have for choosing a husband?

The answer, when he'd grumpily posed that same question to

his sister, Carys, had made his heart stop in his chest. Lenore Montgomery had determined to marry for *love.*

She'd stated as much in public, apparently, and instead of mocking her aspirations as foolish and unrealistic, society had wholeheartedly agreed that a woman as beautiful as Lenore Montgomery *should* be allowed such a radical view.

Ordinary girls should be glad of whatever offers they received, but a diamond of the first water, like Lenore, could apparently indulge in whatever romantic notions she liked.

Rhys's brain hadn't stopped burning for a week.

Lenore wasn't holding out for a title. She didn't want a duke. She wanted a man who loved her. A man she could love in return.

The solution settled in his chest with an absolute sense of rightness.

That man could be *him.*

The past few months had been torture, holding himself back, pretending he had no interest in her. Enough was enough. He was interested. Drawn like a moth to the flame. The idea of marriage, so unappealing before, was perfectly palatable if it was with a woman like Lenore. In fact, she was the *only* woman he could ever imagine committing himself to.

It was time to take action. To see if there could be more between them just scorching attraction.

CHAPTER 3

Great Aunt Prudence's eightieth birthday celebrations at Newstead Park—the Montgomery mansion adjacent to the monstrous Davies Welsh castle, Trellech Court—provided Lenore with the perfect opportunity to put her plan to capture Rhys Davies's heart into action.

He might have done his best to avoid her for almost an entire social season, but he would definitely be attending the week-long party. Almost all of his Davies relatives would be there, and Lenore had decided enough was enough.

Something had to be done.

She'd spent months trying to get the stupid man to notice her, but even her most unsubtle attempts had met with failure. She'd been sure that once he saw how many other men desired her—including a duke!—that the well-documented competitive nature of the Davies male would kick in, and he'd start trying to win her affections, just to prove to everyone that he could.

He hadn't even asked her to dance.

She'd dressed in the most heart-stoppingly gorgeous gowns she could find, ones made by the infamous French seamstress

Madame LeFèvre on Bond Street, known for her skill in creating dresses that brought men to their knees.

All Rhys had done was glare at her from across the room, as if she was being deliberately provoking.

Which she was. So why didn't he do something about it?

He clearly desired her. His brown eyes darkened to almost black whenever they met hers, and a thrilling jolt of excitement flashed over her skin. She'd smiled at him, but instead of shoving every man in his path aside, stomping across the room, and dragging her out into the gardens for a thoroughly welcome ravishing, he'd merely clenched his jaw and turned away as if the sight of her was more than he could bear.

Lenore was reaching the limits of her patience. Her stupid heart was fixed on Rhys, despite how little he'd done to deserve it, but she had her pride. If, after a week in her company at the party, he still showed no signs of returning her affections, then she would abandon her pursuit of him.

Every sense urged that he was the perfect man for her, but perhaps she was being blinded by a healthy dose of infatuation. He was, after all, the most physically attractive man she'd ever met, so maybe she was just suffering from a case of unrequited lust, and not love?

She almost hoped that was the case. If Rhys rejected her, she'd be heartbroken, but at least she'd know she'd have to settle for one of her many other suitors, or remain a lifelong spinster, like her great aunts Constance and Pru.

This party was her last chance to either capture his attention, or assure herself of his indifference.

Luckily, Aunts Constance and Prudence were some of England's finest meddlers. They loved nothing more than poking their noses into other people's business, *especially* if that business included a Davies, and they both nodded with gleeful enthusiasm when Lenore told them of her predicament.

"Well of course we'll help you, darling," Prudence had smiled.

"Although are you sure he's the one? He's outrageously handsome, I'll give you that, but the man must be blind not to have noticed how wonderful you are."

Lenore wrinkled her nose. "Oh, he's noticed me. He just does an excellent job of pretending *not* to whenever we're in the same room. And when he does deign to look my way, he acts as though my looks are an annoyance, not an attraction."

"That's still an excellent start." Constance grinned up from her knitting. "At least you're arousing a primitive reaction. Anger is still passion, after all. If he were indifferent, that would be far worse."

"I suppose," Lenore shrugged. "But I need to show him there's more to me than just a pretty face. I am funny and clever and resourceful."

"You just have to spend some time with him, alone," Pru said. "If he deserves you, then he'll come to appreciate your excellent qualities. And he'll show you his own."

"There will be plenty of opportunities to be alone with him this week." Constance nodded. "Especially if we make them happen."

Lenore smiled. "What are you thinking?"

"Well, you and Rhys are the only ones who aren't married, which means the others will naturally form their own couples whenever it comes to playing games. And you know how much we all love a little friendly Davies-Montgomery rivalry."

Pru grinned. "Connie and I had the marvelous idea of doing a treasure hunt of some sort. It's going to take place here, in the Newstead grounds, and on Davies land, around Trellech Court. That way there can be no claims of an unfair advantage for either side."

"We'll put everyone in teams of two, of course," Constance chuckled. "One Davies and one Montgomery."

Lenore chuckled. "Genius."

"We have at least four Davies-Montgomery couples already.

Gryff and Maddie, Carys and Tristan, Morgan and Harriet, and you and Rhys."

"What about Caro and Lucy? Neither of them succumbed to the dreaded Davies curse."

"Their husbands will be honorary Davies. Just for this week."

"I love it," Lenore laughed.

Prudence gave a satisfied nod. "Knowing how ridiculously competitive you all are, I predict all manner of amusing skullduggery. I can't wait."

"And with you teamed up with Rhys, we'll make sure to send you to the most remote locations to find clues." Constance gave a wicked wink, her eyes twinkling with mischief. "Nothing like having to work together through adversity to really find out what the other person's made of."

Prudence nodded. "You might find him completely obnoxious and unbearable."

"It might be a blessing," Lenore said wryly. "At least I'd be cured of this ridiculous infatuation."

"Or you might discover he's been harboring exactly the same infatuation," Constance snorted. "And he's been too stubborn to do anything about it. I think that's far more likely. Either way, you'll have your answer by the end of the week. You'll either love him, or be free of him."

Lenore nodded. "Let the games begin."

CHAPTER 4

"Montgomery."

Lenore smiled at Rhys's typically dry greeting as he strode across the lower lawn towards her. She tried, unsuccessfully, not to notice the divine way his pale buckskin breeches molded to his thighs, nor the careless disorder of his hair that made her fingers itch to stroke it.

"Morning, Davies. It seems we've been paired together for this challenge."

Rhys's lips gave a cynical twitch. "Indeed. I see you've dressed for the occasion." He sent her pretty lavender day dress a disapproving frown.

Lenore hid a grin. The dress might not be the most practical outfit for a treasure hunt, to be sure, but it did wonders for her figure and the color was the perfect foil for her coppery-brown hair and green eyes.

"We'll be searching the grounds, not paddling up the Amazon." She sent him a challenging, sideways look. "Which I've done, by the way."

A muscle twitched in his jaw. "Yes, I know. Your sister Caro told me all about your intrepid adventures when we were seated together at dinner last night."

Lenore bit her lip. She'd been unreasonably jealous of Caro when she'd glanced down the long table and seen her chatting so effortlessly with Rhys. He seemed to smile and charm with every other woman except her. What was wrong with her?

Both Davies and Montgomery families were amply represented this morning. Cousin Tristan, the architect, stood with his arm around his wife, red-haired Carys. They'd come over after breakfast from their house just over the hill.

Gryff, Rhys's eldest brother, was whispering something in Maddie's ear that made her blush, while cousin Harriet was arguing with her Davies husband Morgan about an alternative way to read the compass she'd pulled from her pocket.

Lenore's sisters, Lucy and Caro, were also there, each with their respective partners. It was going to be an exciting morning.

Aunt Prudence cleared her throat to get everyone's attention. "Ahem! I hope you're ready to begin." She held up a bundle of folded papers. "The aim of this treasure hunt is to find the ten colored flags, like this one Connie is waving about, that have been hidden around the place. They could be on either Davies or Montgomery property, and they could be high or low, indoors or out."

"And don't think that because neither myself nor Prudence are particularly nimble, that they'll all be hidden in easy-to-reach places." Constance said. "We employed several wonderfully athletic footmen to place the flags where we wanted them."

Lenore grinned at the sparkle in her aunts' eyes. They'd probably relished the opportunity to ogle the young men while they worked; they were bawdy old crones.

"There is one clue for each flag." Prudence handed one folded paper to each team, winking at Lenore as she took hers. "When I say go, you may open the papers and read the clues. The team that finds the most flags, and brings them back here to us, will be declared the winner."

"What's the prize?" Gryff demanded, earning him a laughing glance from his wife, Maddie.

"The glory of being the victors, of course." Aunt Prudence said. "And bragging rights over your siblings."

"The very best kind of prize," Morgan chuckled.

Aunt Constance pulled out a silver pocket watch and squinted at the time. "The day will be split into two sessions. You may search this morning until lunch, which can be partaken either here or at Trellech at one o'clock. The afternoon session will start at two, and you'll have until dinner—that's nine o'clock—to find as many flags as you can. Now... go!"

Rhys leaned over Lenore's shoulder as she fumbled to open the paper, and the delicious scent of his cologne made it hard to concentrate on the handwritten lines in front of her.

"What's the first clue?"

"I'm a handsome male, a sight to be seen. All eyes are on me when I preen." Lenore read.

Rhys wrinkled his nose. "What on earth does that mean?"

Carys and Tristan were already hurrying away across the grass.

"It's a peacock," Lenore smiled. "Don't the males have hundreds of 'eyes' on their tails?"

Rhys nodded. "Of course. Well done. There are scores of 'em over at Trellech, all wandering around, screeching at people."

"How are we supposed to know which one has the flag?" Lenore asked. "Do they have a cage where they go at night?"

"No. They just roam free. But knowing your great Aunts, and their penchant for making things difficult, I bet it's somewhere near Geoffrey." Rhys said darkly.

"Geoffrey's a peacock?"

"To all outward appearances, yes. But I sincerely believe he's the devil in avian form. I've lost count of the number of times I've wanted to strangle him for waking me up at dawn."

Lenore bit back a smile at how aggrieved he sounded. "Perhaps the Trellech menagerie would be a good place to start?"

"Probably. In fact, I bet that's where Carys and Tristan are headed right now."

Lenore turned to start across the lawn, but Rhys's hand shot out and he caught her wrist. She glanced down at it, surprised by the contact—and by the flash of heat that skittered over her skin—and he released her as if she burned him.

"Don't go haring off to Trellech just yet," he said. "We need to be clever about this if we're going to win." He sent her a sideways glance. "You do *want* to win, don't you?"

"Of course."

"Right, then. There might be other flags, closer to here, that we can find. Let's read the rest of the clues then make a plan for the most efficient route to get to them. No point running back and forth between here and Trellech and wearing ourselves out."

"You can tell you were in the army," she teased. "That's very organized."

He inclined his head at the compliment. "As an officer, having my men conserve their energy was of vital importance."

"Very well, clue two is: *I'm part of a ship, a game with cards, I link two houses with a shaking of hands.*"

"Ships?" Rhys grumbled. "Morgan's bound to get this one. He's the only one of us who joined the navy." He bit his lip and leaned closer, apparently unaware of the fluttering his proximity created in her belly. Or perhaps he knew only too well, and he was determined to torture her until she died of unrequited lust.

That was far more likely.

"One Davies and one Montgomery have to meet and shake hands on the spring equinox every year to keep the peace," Lenore mused. "Perhaps it's a reference to that?"

"Of course. The answer's *bridge*. That's where the captain

stands on a ship, and it's a card game, like whist. The flag must be must be on the bridge over the river that marks the border between our lands."

Lenore glanced across the lawn and saw that Gryff and Maddie were already headed in the opposite direction to Carys and Tristan, no doubt on their way to the bridge.

"That's not too far from here," she said. "But there still might be somewhere closer."

Rhys nodded and read. "Clue three is: *I have jackets but I'm not a wardrobe. I have thousands of leaves, but I'm not a forest."*

"A library!" Lenore chuckled. "Books have dust jackets and leaves, don't they? But which library should we search? There's one here, but I'm sure you have one over at Trellech, too."

"We do," Rhys nodded. "It's where Tristan proposed to Carys after they'd been chasing that wretched bear all over the county."

"I heard about that. It sounded very exciting."

"Not nearly as exciting as the story Caro told me last night about you chasing off a panther." His brown eyes sparkled with interest.

Lenore fought a blush. "It's wasn't as impressive as it sounds. It was when we were in Brazil, in the rainforest. I was in my tent one evening, and I heard a strange sound, almost like a cough, then a growl. I opened the flap, and there was a black jaguar, just slinking through the camp, not five feet from me. I panicked. I picked up the closest thing to hand, which happened to be my shoe, and threw it at him with a shout. It hit him on the tail, and he ran off into the forest."

She shook her head in recollection. "He was such a beautiful creature. His fur wasn't completely black, but dappled, and his eyes were the most incredible yellow. I'm glad I got to see him."

She glanced up at the man next to her. Rhys reminded her of that panther. Dark and muscled, with a sinuous, athletic grace. And yet his comment about taking care of the men under his command showed there was more to him than just his outward appearance. He was responsible, compassionate. Kind.

"So, we'll check the library here first, and if there's no flag, we'll head over to Trellech. Next clue?"

"Clue four: *Red or white, the ancients say there's truth in me.*" Lenore read.

"That's easy. Wine. *In vino Veritas*, and all that."

"So, a wine bottle? Wine cellar? Both houses have those, too."

Rhys shrugged, an elegant lift of his muscular shoulders. "We'll have to look in both, I suppose."

"Right. Next clue. Number 5. *A foolish ruin.*" Lenore thought for a moment. "Oh, that's *folly*. There's one on the Montgomery side of the river, in the woods. Our great grandfather had it built when things like that were all the rage."

"Excellent. Clue six?"

"*A healthy source of water.*"

They both frowned. "What could that be? A water source could be a spring, a river, a stream. But why healthy?"

"What's another word for healthy?" Rhys asked. "Hale. Hearty?" His brow cleared. "I have it – well! As in, not sick. And somewhere you can get water."

Lenore nodded enthusiastically. "They must mean the wishing well, near the western border. That's about halfway between here and Trellech. So is the folly. We should go to them one after the other."

"Agreed."

Lenore smiled, her heart beating in satisfaction at how well they were working together. They made an excellent team.

"Clue seven is: *I'm surrounded by water, but I'm not a fish. No man is this, according to John Donne.*"

Rhys chuckled. "That one is for you and your sisters. You've spent time on several of them. The answer's an island."

Lenore gave a good-natured groan. "One flag's on an island?"

She sent a mock-furious glare over at Constance and Prudence, and the two of them erupted into fits of giggles.

"Figured out clue number seven?" Pru chuckled. "We thought you'd appreciate that one, my love."

"And you'll need number eight to get there," Constance added.

"Hush!" Pru scolded her. "Don't help them. No favoritism, remember?"

Lenore glanced back down. Clue eight read, *I can have gravy in me or water under me.* "A boat," she groaned. "I thought I'd seen the last of boats when we docked in England."

"What's clue number nine?" Rhys asked.

"*I have hands but no arms, a face but no eyes.* That's a clock." Lenore hit her lip. "But there must be hundreds of clocks between this house and Trellech. There's one in almost every room."

Rhys glanced over at Prudence and Constance, who were watching them with undisguised interest.

"That's true, but knowing how much your Aunts love excitement and entertainment, I doubt it's going to be hidden behind some nondescript mantel clock. It's going to be something big and bold. Maybe even somewhere dangerous." He thought for a moment. "The most visible clock—and the most difficult one to get to—is the one in the highest tower at Trellech. I bet it's somewhere like that."

"You're right," Lenore nodded. "They did say they weren't going to make it easy for us."

"Very well. What's the last clue?"

"*I could be an admiral, a monarch, an emperor, or a painted lady.*"

"Another naval question," Rhys grumbled. "They're clearly favoring Morgan again. What have an admiral, a king or queen, and a courtesan have in common?"

Lenore laughed. "They're not people. Those are all species of butterfly. I bet my father helped them write that clue. The flag must be somewhere in the butterfly house. That's at the far end of the gardens, behind those trees over there."

She gestured past the edge of the formal lawns, toward the walled garden.

"Right. So, by the sounds of it, there are three or four flags here near Newstead, three in the land between the two houses, and another three over at Trellech. Let's check the closest ones first, like the library, the wine cellar, and the butterfly house, then head further afield. Agreed?"

Lenore nodded. She'd spent ample time with men who simply told her what to do without asking for her agreement or her opinion, but Rhys had seemed pleased at her cleverness in deciphering some of the clues, and keen to work with her as an equal.

"Agreed."

CHAPTER 5

While a few of the other couples disappeared into the gardens, Lenore led Rhys back into the house. The Newstead library was a handsome room, with shelves of leather-bound volumes lining the walls and Uncle William's desk, piled high with various papers and correspondence.

They made a thorough search, but no colored flag could be found, and Rhys finally turned to her with a sigh.

"Either someone's already beaten us to it, or the flag is in the library at Trellech, not here."

"Let's move on to the clue about wine instead, then. Should we check the pantry? There might be some cooking wine in there. Or the wine cellar?"

"Cellar first."

They stepped out into the hallway just as Lenore's older sister Caro emerged, giggling, from the steps up from the wine cellar. Max, her husband, was tickling her as she ascended the stairs.

"There's no flag down there," Caro laughed as she caught sight of Lenore, and batted Max's hands away so she could catch a breath. "We've already looked."

"Nothing in the library, either," Lenore said, ignoring the way

Rhys elbowed her in the ribs and hissed, "Don't tell them anything. They're the enemy!"

Lenore rolled her eyes and went to follow Caro back out into the garden, but Rhys caught her waist and turned her gently in the opposite direction.

She ignored the swooping sensation in her stomach at his casual touch.

"Don't let them see where we're going, either!" he scolded. "They might not have cracked the clue about the butterfly house yet. We need to use a different exit. Where?"

"This way." Lenore led him through the music room, then the drawing room, and together they slipped out of the tall French windows and onto the terrace.

She lifted her skirts so she could move more quickly, and they hurried across the narrow patch of lawn and ducked behind a tall yew hedge.

"It's this way, through the orchard."

Lenore told herself she was breathless because of the pace, and not because she was suddenly alone with Rhys Davies.

A few laughs and shouts from the other couples could still be heard as they weaved between the apple trees, but they became fainter as their distance from the house increased.

"Let's hope we're the first to crack this particular clue," Lenore said, silently impressed by the way Rhys matched her steps by shortening his naturally longer strides.

Sunlight glinted off the hundreds of glass panes that made up her father's pride and joy; the glazed butterfly house he'd commissioned while they were over in Brazil.

Rhys let out a whistle when he saw it. "Impressive."

Lenore smiled. Her father, Rollo, was one of England's foremost lepidopterists, and he'd dragged his long-suffering wife and children all around the world to study his beloved butterflies. Lenore wouldn't have changed a thing about her slightly unorthodox upbringing, but she was glad to be back in England now, after so many years abroad. It was lovely to have creature comforts like baths, cake shops and modistes so easily accessible.

She'd also been getting restless, keen to start pursuing her own passions, instead of taking part in someone else's. And now she had her chance.

Rhys looked around in interest as they reached the glazed door. The structure was huge, with hundreds of panes of glass supported by an elegant framework of cast iron. The inner surfaces of the panes were foggy with condensation.

"Prepare yourself," Lenore warned. "It's going to be extremely hot and steamy in here thanks to all the tropical plants. In fact, you might want to remove your jacket."

Rhys raised his brows and sent her a cheeky grin. "Trying to undress me, Montgomery? How scandalous."

Lenore fought a blush. "Not at all. I'm only thinking of your health. I'm used to the oppressive heat of the tropics, whereas you might find it overwhelming. I'm not likely to catch you if you suddenly faint on me."

"We'd both end up on the floor in a tangle of limbs," he agreed, and the twinkle in his eye proved how much he was enjoying the double-entendre. "Can't have that."

He shrugged out of his jacket and hung it on a nearby bush, and Lenore drank in the sight of him in shirt sleeves and cravat. In the *ton*, a gentleman would never remove his jacket in the presence of a lady, and she sent up a silent thanks to her aunts for engineering this more relaxed atmosphere.

She pushed open the door and stepped inside, and the blast of hot air was still a shock, even though she was expecting it.

"I have an interest in tropical plants," she said over her shoulder. "I sent Uncle William a detailed lists of all the ones that would be good to grow in here to help the butterflies flourish."

She started along one of the brick paths, then turned to see Rhys's reaction. Hundreds of brightly colored butterflies were flitting about, or sunning themselves on the foliage.

"Amazing!" Rhys said, his tone genuinely awed.

"Most naturalists and collectors simply pin dead specimens to a card." Lenore wrinkled her nose at the thought. "But a dead butterfly doesn't give a sense of the living beauty of the creature—the way they flutter and glide and flap. Father's made it his mission to breed as many of these exotic species as he can, and to educate people about them. He disagrees with capturing them just to put them in a collection. And I agree. They should be allowed to live a full life."

"These are all butterflies you brought back from Brazil?"

Lenore nodded. "And a few from Madagascar, too."

"How did you get them back here? On a ship?"

"We brought almost five hundred caterpillars, from around fifty different species, and hundreds more caterpillar eggs. It's quite skill to rear butterflies from eggs. Father's writing a paper on it."

Rhys tipped his head back to admire the ones flitting above their heads, and the sight of his strong throat and angled jaw made her feel even more light-headed. What would his cheek feel like under her fingers? Would the slight dark stubble she could see there be rough? Or smooth?

She cleared her throat and forced herself to concentrate on less incendiary topics.

"There are butterflies in the Amazon that camouflage themselves so well they look just like dead leaves. And others, like the huge Caligo butterflies, that have markings on their wings that look like the eyes of an owl."

She pointed. "Do you see that bright yellow one? That's the cloudless sulphur. Phoebis sennae. And that red one is called a postman."

"What do they all eat?" Rhys asked.

"Nectar from flowers mainly, or the juice from rotting fruit. Each species has their own particular favorite. The Heliconius feed on passion flowers, which makes them mildly poisonous to predators. The bright coloring of their wings acts as a visual warning that they will be horrid to taste."

She lifted her fingers toward an enormous turquoise-blue butterfly that had settled on a nearby leaf. It was almost the size of her hand, its wings tipped in black.

"This is one of my favorites. A blue morpho, Morpho peleides. From the family Nymphalidae. Isn't he beautiful?"

"Yes. Very."

Rhys's voice was rough, almost raspy, and when she shot a look at him, she found him looking at her, not at the butterfly. Her skin heated even more, but the butterfly took off, breaking the moment, and they both watched it sail up toward the roof.

"See how he floats in the air? He hardly needs to flap its wings at all."

Lenore started along the path again, keeping an eye out for a colored flag. But every flash of red or yellow turned out to be another butterfly. The Aunts had chosen an excellent place to hide the prize.

"How did you know that butterfly was a male?" Rhys asked suddenly. "You called it a he."

"Only the male morphos are that lovely bright blue color. The females are camouflaged, a mottled brown and white. They're very dull in comparison."

"Like peacocks, then," Rhys said. "Do you think it's nature's way of letting the men show off? Or is it a clever ploy to put the more expendable males in danger by creating a distraction, so the predators attack them instead of the females?"

"I wouldn't say you men were expendable," Lenore said. "But that's effectively what you soldiers did, when you were fighting Napoleon. You put yourselves in harm's way to protect the rest of us. The country owes men like you an enormous debt."

"It was our duty. I'm just glad I lived through it, to tell you the truth."

Rhys ran a hand through his hair and looked charmingly

uncomfortable with her admiration, and she turned away with a smile. His modesty was just another aspect of him that she liked.

"Morpho caterpillars defend themselves by producing a repellent smell." She said, mainly to lighten the mood.

It worked. Rhys chuckled. "I know a few members of the *ton* who use the same principle. I swear Lord Ashwood doesn't bathe more than once a year."

She loved his humor, too.

"I helped collect most of these caterpillars."

"You don't have a disgust of them?"

"No. Some are rather sweet, actually. And they come in all shapes and sizes. My favorite ones are hairy, like little wooly bears. They're very comical." She pointed to another butterfly. "That's a glass-wing, Haetera piera. Its wings are almost entirely transparent."

Rhys snorted. "Much like Lord Bollingbrook's motivation for proposing to Violet Brand. He's sixty-two, with a crumbling estate and debts up to his eyeballs, and she's the beloved only child of a textile magnate. Unsurprisingly, Violet's father doubted his insistence that it was 'true love'."

Lenore chuckled at his dry, cynical tone. "That's the *ton* for you. Violet might not have accepted him, but there are plenty of other society marriages that have been based on such a principle. Rich merchants ally themselves with impoverished aristocrats all the time; a fortune in exchange for a noble title."

"Alas, I have no noble title to tempt a lady," Rhys grinned, his eyes sparkling. "I am but a lowly second son, with no hope of acceding to the title unless something dreadful befalls Gryff. And knowing what a stubborn, perverse sod he is, he'll live to be a hundred, just to thwart me."

Lenore laughed. The bond between the Davies siblings was as strong as that between herself and her sisters, and she knew he'd be devastated if anything really did happen to his brother.

He glanced over at her. "But perhaps a lofty title isn't the most important criteria for a lady? You, for example, turned down the chance to be a duchess."

He raised his brows in question, and she glanced away, flustered by his probing. She didn't want to discuss her reasoning with the very man who'd brought about the decision. Not yet, anyway.

A flash of red in her peripheral vision provided a welcome distraction, and she let out a shout of triumph. "There's a flag! Up there. Look!"

Rhys followed the direction she indicated and let out a groan. The flag had been lodged high up in the fronds of a huge palm tree.

"That's at least twenty feet up! How are we supposed to get up there?"

"There was a butterfly net by the door. We could use that."

Rhys dutifully went to retrieve it, but even when he stood on tiptoe, and waved the net, the flag was still out of reach. They both looked around for something they could use as a step, but there was none to be found.

"Could you climb the tree?" Lenore suggested.

"Not easily," he said, hands on his hips as he surveyed the problem. "Is there a ladder somewhere? In one of the gardener's sheds?"

"We don't have time for that. One of the other teams could come at any moment. What if I lift you up?" She threaded her fingers together to make a step. "I can give you a leg up, as if you were mounting a horse."

He sent her a scoffing glance. "You wouldn't be able to take my weight. I might hurt you."

"Well then, why don't you lift *me* up?"

"That wouldn't be much use. We'd only gain a few inches. Unless you sit on my shoulders."

"Let's do that then," Lenore said.

Rhys's eyes widened as if she'd said the most scandalous thing in Christendom. "You're wearing skirts, Montgomery. To sit on my shoulders, you'd have to wrap your thighs around my head."

Lenore rolled her eyes, even though the very thought of doing something so shocking made every cell in her body tingle.

"I know that. Breeches would be better, but it can't be helped. I'm game if you are. Don't you want that flag, Davies?"

The challenge was the perfect goad to poke him into action, but her cheeks heated as she waited for his response. Was she being too daring? Would he be disgusted by her wanton suggestion and call her a terrible hoyden?

And then his lips parted in a wicked grin, and her spirits lifted in relief. She'd always suspected he was as ready for an adventure as herself. A kindred spirit.

He crossed to stand directly under the tree, and bent down on one knee.

"Come here then."

Lenore's heart was pounding as she put her hand on his shoulder and looked down at him. If only he'd adopt this position to propose marriage to her.

"Right, now, put one foot on my bent leg, then hook your other knee over my shoulder." His tone was one he'd doubtless used to command his troops, but all she could think about was that without his jacket, only the fine cotton of his shirt separated her palm from his skin.

His muscles twitched beneath her hand as he shifted his weight, and her mouth went dry.

"I've done this a hundred times," she said, trying to focus. "On Caro or Lucy's shoulders. How do you think we picked bananas and green coconuts when we were in the jungle?"

Rhys nodded. "Fair enough. Up you go."

Her pulse rocketed as she bent her right leg over his broad shoulder. Her skirts hitched up, gathering in lilac pleats behind his neck and flowing down his back, and he grasped the front of her shin to hold her steady. The heat of his strong fingers bled through the silk of her stocking.

She placed her right hand on his head and threw her other leg over his left shoulder, then let out a little shriek as she wobbled. His left hand caught her left shin, and he rose from his kneel with a fluid movement that was undeniably impressive.

He was *much* stronger that either Caro or Lucy—one of them usually had to help the other to stand with Lenore on their shoulders.

His hair was delightfully soft beneath her fingers, but her cheeks burned at the feel of his head nestled between her legs, so close to her womanly core.

The fabric of her skirts had ruched up to knee-height, and her stockings were only visible to the knee—not even high enough for him to see her garters—but the knowledge that she was wearing nothing except her chemise and petticoats beneath her dress, that only a few layers of fabric lay between the skin of his jaw and the inside of her naked thigh, made her stomach somersault in dark delight.

A deep pulse of pleasure clenched her core.

"Reach up and grab the flag."

His voice brought her back to the task at hand. She carefully released her grip on his hair and tightened her thighs around his ears to steady herself, as he handed her the butterfly net.

He gave a soft grunt of exertion. She reached up, pushing her heels against his chest as leverage to lift herself, and finally managed to scoop the little red pennant into the net.

"Got it! First flag for us!"

She kept her balance as he slowly lowered himself back down, and climbed off his shoulders with the most elegant dismount she could manage. She stepped back and twitched her skirts back into place as he stood and turned to face her. His cheeks were slightly pink, but he wasn't sweating in the heat. Perhaps he'd become accustomed to working in such warmer temperatures when he'd been in Portugal and Spain?

"Good job!" He grinned, and Lenore had to force herself not to throw herself into his arms for a celebratory hug. She handed him the flag instead.

"You hold this. Now, let's get out of here. I'm rather hot."

She fanned her pink cheeks, hoping he'd ascribe the humid conditions to her flustered state, and not to the thrilling excitement of his presence.

CHAPTER 6

Rhys took a deep, welcome breath of cool air as he stepped out of the butterfly house behind Lenore.

He felt slightly dizzy, and while it would be tempting to blame the oppressive heat inside, he knew the real reason was the outrageously provoking woman in front of him.

His blood was still pounding at the memory of having his head between her thighs. The delicious, perfumed scent of her had filled his nose as her skirts had billowed round him, and it had taken all his willpower to concentrate on lifting her up to get the flag.

The temptation to run his hands up the front of her shins, over her knees and then higher, to the soft feminine skin he knew lurked just above her garters, had been almost too much to bear.

His cock had hardened to the point of pain, and as soon as she'd climbed off him, he'd turned away and pretended to admire a swallowtail butterfly while subtly rearranging himself in his breeches.

He'd let her precede him out of the glasshouse.

Lenore had surprised him with her cheeky suggestion. He'd

known she had the reputation as someone who put little store in the tedious formalities of social convention, and he was delighted to find she had a naughty, rebellious streak.

He couldn't have planned things better himself. They'd already skipped the traditional, dull first steps of courtship, like exchanging longing glances and holding hands, and progressed straight to more intimate physical contact.

And Lenore hadn't seemed to mind it one bit. In fact, she'd been the one to suggest it.

Rhys's heart swelled with hope. Perhaps she might not be so averse to him as he'd thought.

Lenore handed him his jacket from where it had been dangling from a bush, and he shrugged it back on with a smile of thanks. Her cheeks were a becoming shade of pink, and a few wisps of her coppery-brown hair had sprung free from her upswept hairstyle and curled in the heat. She looked deliciously tousled, and his stomach clenched at the thought of all the other ways he'd like to tousle her even more. He wanted her positively disheveled.

But not yet. He had to know that she was willing. And that she knew his intentions were honorable. He wasn't some cad who would ravish her and then leave her. He wouldn't touch her unless he was certain she understood that it was marriage, not merely seduction, he had in mind.

Lenore pointed at the flag he still held in his hand. "Should we take this straight to the aunts, or go after the next flag?"

"Next flag, of course. The sooner we get there, the better chance we'll have of getting it. Which is the next nearest clue?"

"The wishing well. It's that way, through the woods. We can either walk, or go back to the stables and get horses."

"Saddling horses will take a bit of time. If there's a chance of beating the others to it on foot, then we should go."

"I'm perfectly happy to walk. I'm not some idle miss who's never done more than amble around Hyde Park. I can trek for miles." She gave her skirts a dismissive twitch. "I'd do much better in breeches, of course, but never mind. Let's go."

Rhys bit the inside of his cheek to distract himself from the mental image of Lenore's delicious curves encased in a pair of breeches. God, that was something he'd give half his fortune to see.

She was already heading off through the trees, so he started after her, enjoying the seductive sway of her pert bottom as she strode along in front of him.

They walked for a good ten minutes, following a barely-visible path, and Rhys found his senses soothed by the dappled greens of the ancient woodland. Mossy oaks and lichen-covered boulders were bordered by an outrageous number of ferns and flowering plants, and he took a moment to appreciate the joy of being home.

When he'd been in Spain and Portugal, exhausted after a day of fighting or scouting, trying to sleep on some dusty, uncomfortable cot and cursing the dry heat that seemed to suck every drop of moisture from his bones, he'd closed his eyes and dreamed of this place.

Of Wales, and Trellech, and this soul-calming green. Of this profound feeling of contentment and rest. Of some unknown woman who was out there, somewhere, waiting for him. A woman he'd yet to meet, but one he knew, deep in his gut, that he *would* meet, one day.

That wishful yearning had a face now, and a name. And eyes the same green of this forest. He wanted to drown in them.

"Here we are."

Lenore stopped, and Rhys almost bumped into her back. He peered over her shoulder and saw a clearing up ahead, with a low circular stone wall in the center.

"The Virtuous Well." Lenore said reverently.

Rhys snorted. "That's the English name for it. We Welsh call it Ffynnon Pen Rhys—Pen Rhys's well."

She gave him a playful nudge in the ribs with her elbow. "Of course you'd prefer that. It's got your name in it."

He puffed his chest out with mock pride. "I'll have you know that Rhys is an ancient Welsh name. One given to princes and kings. Like Rhys ap Gruffud, the ruler of southern Wales in the twelfth century."

He leaned closer, loving the way her eyes widened slightly. "It means ardor or passion."

Her lips parted as she sucked in a breath, and he quashed the almost overwhelming urge to kiss her.

"Passion?" Her lips curved up at the corners and her gaze held his. "Really? How interesting."

It was on the tip of his tongue to ask if she wanted him to demonstrate said passion, but instead he turned his head and broke the sizzling contact between them.

Patience.

"I've never come at it from this direction before," he said easily, brushing past her and into the clearing. "I've always ridden over here from Trellech." He cocked his head and listened. "Doesn't sound as if anyone else is here. We might be the first."

The curved stone wall that protected the well was scarcely knee-high, but Rhys descended the set of shallow steps about six feet down into the earth and stepped into the tiny stone-flagged 'courtyard', open to the sky. The well itself was housed in a small, arched enclave at one end, surrounded by a lip of flat stones.

"Local tradition has it that if you toss a coin, or some other metal offering, into the water, your wish will come true." Lenore said, following him down.

"*Might* come true," Rhys corrected. "That's what Carys told me, anyway. She said if the bubbles that form on the object rise quickly, then the wish will be granted with equal speed. If they're slow to rise, the wish will take longer to come true. And if there are no bubbles at all, your wish won't be granted. Nothing's guaranteed."

Lenore thrust her hand into a side slit in her skirts and rummaged around in the pocket beneath. She pulled out a bent hairpin. "Might as well try my luck."

She stepped to his side and tossed it into the waters with a splash, and they both leaned forward to watch it sink to the bottom. The shaft was very deep—fed by an underground system of caves that his older brother Gryff had stumbled upon one day with Maddie, Lenore's cousin—but it was so clear that it was easy to see the rapid stream of bubbles coming off the bent metal as it sank.

Lenore gave a pleased little hum.

"Whatever you wished for, it's going to come true very soon," he said.

She sent him an enigmatic smile. "Oh, I certainly hope so. It's something I've been wanting for almost a year now. I'm getting rather impatient."

CHAPTER 7

Lenore was delighted to see the bubbles rising from her hairpin as it sank. She'd wished for Rhys to kiss her, and even though she put little faith in superstition, there was no denying the tingle of excitement at the possibility that it might actually happen soon.

There was no sign of a flag, however, and she climbed back up the narrow steps and back into the clearing, hotly aware of Rhys following her, his head level with her bottom.

"We should check the cave entrance, too. Just in case the flag's been hidden in there." She strode over to another, far newer, set of steps in a hollow of the valley just beyond the well.

Her cousin Maddie had accidentally discovered an enormous underground cave system here only a few years ago, which in turn had led to the discovery of a rich seam of gold. Since ownership of this particular section of land was shared equally between the Davies and the Montgomerys, both families had profited from the unexpected windfall.

"Maddie took us to see the mine a few days ago," Lenore said. "It was fascinating. Our ancestors would be shocked to the core to find Davies and Montgomerys working together in such a joint collaboration."

Rhys grinned. "I like to think we've finally evolved. Although it's taken a few hundred years. We both come from families who are particularly resistant to change. Wait, watch your step."

He reached out and took her hand to help her down the stairs, and her fingers tingled at the contact.

In truth, the steps were perfectly safe. Gryff had ordered them to be built to allow easy access to the tunnel system, to replace the steep pile of rubble that had been created when Maddie had fallen through the roof of the cave. But Lenore was glad of the excuse to touch Rhys again.

The light faded as they reached the bottom, and a cool blast of air raised the hairs at her nape. She reluctantly dropped Rhys's hand.

He pointed to one of the lanterns that had been left by the entrance. "Want to go and explore?"

The cavern extended for some distance, some sections leading all the way to the coast, but Lenore shook her head.

"No, although I don't mind caves. We explored a huge one in Brazil, once. The only thing I didn't like was the bats. Or rather, the smell of the bat droppings." She wrinkled her nose in memory. "I can't tell you how vile it was."

"I can imagine," Rhys chuckled. "Probably as bad as the smell of a regiment of sweaty, unwashed men and their equally sweaty horses, after weeks traipsing around Portugal."

Lenore nodded, struck by the fact that they had much in common. They'd both suffered hardships and difficult situations abroad.

"I can't tell you how much I appreciate being able to have a bath whenever the mood takes me," Rhys said lightly. "It makes up for all the times I dreamed of having one when I couldn't. I promised myself that if I made it back from the war, I'd never take something so wonderful for granted ever again."

"I know exactly what you mean. I used to fantasize about Gunter's ices when we were shipwrecked. I'd imagine entire six-course dinners, the most comfortable feather bed with silk sheets and velvet covers. All the things I couldn't have."

Including him.

She'd dreamed of him. Well, not him specifically, but a tall, dark, handsome mystery man who would capture her heart and sweep her off her feet. He'd kept her company at night and featured in her most lurid daydreams.

She had an *excellent* imagination.

Lenore bit her lip to hide her smile. Rhys had, technically, already swept her off her feet when he'd lifted her up on his shoulders. But if she was honest, he'd stolen her heart long before that, the first night she'd ever laid eyes on him.

"I don't think even Prudence and Constance would have ordered a flag hidden down here," she said. "Besides, the clue was for a well, not a cave. One of the other couples must have already been here and found it, while we were in the butterfly house."

"On to the next clue, then," Rhys sighed. "Which is closer, the folly, or the bridge?"

"The bridge." Lenore ascended the steps without his help and pointed to a tree-lined path. "That leads to the track between Newstead and Trellech. The bridge is over the river that marks the border."

"Let's go then."

The sun fell in dappled patches on the ground as they walked together beneath the trees, and a companionable silence settled between them. Lenore was constantly aware of him, but she felt entirely at ease in his company. She'd spent a great deal of time around men, porters who carried their equipment, sailors with whom she'd been shipwrecked, and a few of them had made her distinctly uncomfortable in the way their eyes had lingered on her body.

Rhys was a physically impressive specimen, but she felt safe with him. He was a man who'd provide protection, not a threat.

When they came to the road—little more than a well-used track—they turned and followed it until they reached the bridge that separated England from Wales.

Thanks to an ancient kingly decree, one member of the Davies clan and one member of the Montgomery family had to meet on this bridge on the day of the summer equinox and shake hands in a show of amity. Gryff, as the current Earl of Powys, and Maddie, Lenore's cousin, had represented the two families a few years ago, and subsequently fallen in love.

Lenore had always thought the little stone bridge very pretty, and she stuck out her hand toward Rhys as they set foot upon it.

"What's that for?" He glanced down at her palm with a frown.

"I know it's not the equinox, but we should shake hands anyway. Just in case the universe needs more convincing that we Davies and Montgomerys really have set down our weapons."

She sent him her most teasing, challenging look.

His dark eyes studied her face for a long, thrilling moment, then his large fingers wrapped around hers.

"What if shaking hands isn't enough?" he murmured. "Perhaps we should kiss, to be really convincing."

His gaze dropped to her lips and Lenore's heart began to pound, but she forced herself to pull away. However much she *wanted* to kiss Rhys Davies, she refused to be an easy conquest, and showing her hand too early in the game would be foolish.

If there was one thing she'd learned while stranded on that blasted island, it was that waiting for something was the perfect way to increase desire.

"After three weddings between our families in the last few years, how much more evidence do you think the universe needs?"

She turned away and made a great show of bending over the low stone wall to look for a flag. Rhys muttered something under his breath—hopefully a disappointed curse—and stalked to the opposite end of the bridge.

"We've been beaten to it," he said. "Look."

He bent and picked up something from the ferns. It was a purple silk flower.

"That's from Harriet's hat," Lenore frowned. "It's covered in flowers like that. She must have pulled it off and left it here as a sign that she and Morgan have already been here."

"And presumably claimed the flag," Rhys growled. "Ugh."

"We'd better hurry to the next clue. It must be getting close to lunch time."

He checked his pocket watch. "You're right. It's already past noon. But we still have time to get to the folly before one o'clock. Come on."

Rhys clearly knew the direction of the folly, because he started to follow the riverbank south, and Lenore smiled at the suspicion that he'd trespassed on Montgomery land on more than one occasion.

She trailed after him, enjoying the way the sun glinted off the rippling water and the swish of cornflowers and buttercups against her skirts.

After half a mile or so they branched off into the trees again, and the cool shade was a welcome relief. She was no stranger to walking miles on foot, but perhaps they should have gone back for horses after all. She felt hot and sweaty, which probably wasn't the best way to attract the man of her dreams.

With his handsome face, Rhys had always been inundated with female attention, and while she knew she was reasonably pretty, she was also wild and alarmingly self-sufficient. Her skin was unfashionably tanned after months beneath a harsh tropical sun, and she had a regrettable number of freckles that no amount of powder could conceal.

Many men, she knew, preferred cool, serene beauties who

looked like they needed rescuing. She was perfectly capable of rescuing herself and refused to pretend otherwise.

She didn't want a man who would sweep in and save her from the perils of the world. She wanted a fellow adventurer who would toss her an oar and pitch in if they were headed towards the reef. Someone who would treat her as an intellectual, if not a physical, equal.

Rhys was like that. And she wanted him by her side.

The folly's single crenellated tower and artfully crumbling walls came into view just then, peeking through the wild tangle of ivy and moss that threatened to engulf them completely.

It had never been a complete building. Lenore's great grandfather, Sir Lionel Montgomery, had commissioned it, back when no self-respecting landowner was content without a dilapidated temple somewhere on the grounds. Family legend had it that he'd employed a live-in hermit to wander about whenever he had guests.

Four classical marble statues guarded the ruin, each one representing one of the four elements; water, fire, earth and air, and Rhys paused as they neared the one depicting water.

He held his hand up for quiet and Lenore stilled at his back, then heard what he had: a distinctly feminine giggle.

"Tristan, no! Someone might come!"

Rhys's lips curved upward. "That's Carys!" he whispered. "Come on."

No-one was in sight, so he bent low and pushed through the undergrowth. Lenore followed, trying to stay quiet, and together they crept around the curved outer wall of the turret and peered through the remains of a gothic-arched window.

Rhys's sister Carys was enjoying a scandalously thorough kiss with her husband, Lenore's eldest cousin Tristan.

Rhys's eyes gleamed with amusement as Lenore's cheeks heated. He gestured upward, pointing to a fluttering green flag nestled in a giant fern sprouting from the stonework directly above Tristan's head.

There was no chance the couple hadn't seen it—they were clearly celebrating their victory prematurely.

Rhys put his fingers to his lips, then silently gestured his intent to circle around behind them, climb the wall from the opposite side, and attempt to grab the flag while they were otherwise engaged. Lenore nodded and watched him sneak away, and decided to help by creating a distraction.

She backed up a few paces, then said in her most peevish tones, "Oh, *come on* Davies! I've seen three-legged donkeys move faster than you. I thought you soldiers were good at marching?"

She swished her skirts and batted some ferns, making as much noise as possible, and heard Carys utter a frustrated curse just before her coppery-red hair appeared in the window embrasure.

"Oh, hello Carys!" Lenore called, waving madly. "Is Tristan there with you? Or have you split up to cover more ground?"

Tristan's face appeared next to his wife's and his expression was one of a man who'd been interrupted in the most unwelcome manner. His hair, usually so ordered, was definitely ruffled, and his once-perfect cravat was decidedly askew.

Lenore bit back a chuckle.

"Ah, there you are Tristan. Have you found any flags yet?"

"Just the one," Tristan growled. His eyes narrowed in sudden suspicion. "Where's Rhys?"

Lenore tried to look innocent, but the sound of scraping stone gave Rhys away. Tristan's head whipped back round, and he rushed back toward the flag, jumping up and grabbing it moments before Rhys could seize it from his precarious position astride the top of the wall.

Lenore let out a disappointed groan. "No!"

"Ha!" Carys crowed in delight and flung her arms around

Tristan's neck. "Well done, my love! And bad luck, brother. Better luck next time!"

She stuck her tongue out at a glowering Rhys, who shook his head in frustration.

"Bloody hell, I was *this* close," he grumbled, holding his finger and thumb an inch apart to demonstrate.

Carys sent a cheeky glance up at her husband. "I've always been extremely lucky here."

Tristan swatted her playfully on the bottom. "Enough, hoyden. It's time to head back to Trellech for lunch."

Rhys disappeared as he climbed back down the wall, then reappeared beside Carys. He glanced over at Lenore. "Do you want to go back to Newstead Park for lunch, or are you brave enough to risk potential poisoning with the Dastardly Davies over at Trellech?"

Lenore chuckled. Logically, it made sense for them both to go to Trellech, since that was where they needed to be for the final clues, but Rhys obviously didn't want to say that out loud, in case Tristan and Carys hadn't solved all the riddles.

Besides, she'd never actually seen the infamous Davies stronghold, and she'd been dying to get a look at it for months.

"I'd love to join you at Trellech," she said regally. "If Tristan's brave enough, then so am I."

CHAPTER 8

Lenore's first sight of the sprawling architectural monstrosity that was Trellech Court produced much the same reaction as her first sight of Rhys: instant infatuation.

If someone had given her ten-year-old self a paper and pencil and told her to draw a fairytale castle, a Tudor manor house, and a Palladian villa, all mixed up together, Trellech would have been the result.

The outer ramparts were fifteen feet high, complete with a drawbridge and moat, but inside that, the main structure was an astonishing cluster of styles all cobbled together as if by some mad, drunken architect.

Every generation of Davies had tacked on their own section, just to leave their mark, and the overall effect was quite extraordinary.

A crumbling Medieval clock tower butted up against a half-timbered, red brick section that didn't have a straight line on it anywhere. Another wing, sprouting from the other side, was pure Neo-Classicism, all elegant cornices, huge windows, and pillars.

Lenore almost clapped her hands in delight. After the elegant perfection of Newstead Park, the haphazard charm of Trellech was irresistible. It was perfect in its imperfections.

"Not quite as orderly as Newstead," Rhys muttered as they strode across the courtyard and in through a vast, metal-studded door that looked like it could have withstood a horde of Viking marauders without any difficulty whatsoever.

"It's certainly... eclectic," Lenore whispered back.

"I don't blame Tristan for building his own place on the other side of the valley. As an architect, this place probably gives him an attack of the vapors. There's not a straight line or a right-angle anywhere."

He guided Lenore past an imposing suit of armor, and into a dining room with an enormous oak table that could have easily seated twenty people. A cold collation had been set out on the top, and she accepted a plate and indicated to one of the hovering servants which of the dozens of dishes she'd like to try.

She'd dreamed of such lavish spreads while she'd been shipwrecked, and she felt absolutely no guilt for accepting a little of almost everything. She needed to keep up her strength for the afternoon's flag hunting, after all.

"I've told Gryff he should just burn the place to the ground and start again," Rhys continued with a sideways look at Carys that made Lenore certain he was only saying such a thing to get a rise out of his sister. "He's got more than enough money, after all. Why can't we have a nice, orderly place like Newstead Park, eh?"

Carys sent him a laughing look. "Stop trying to make me quarrel with you. You love this place just as much as I do, warts and all. Anywhere else wouldn't have dungeons and priest holes, secret tunnels and trapdoors. It wouldn't be half as much fun."

"True," Rhys conceded with a smile. "And I must confess, growing up here was never dull. There was always some mischief to be made or new place to explore."

Lenore could just imagine him as a cheeky, tousle-haired rascal. Her heart gave an odd little squeeze.

Morgan and Harriet arrived just then, and they all sat down to eat in a jovial mood. The other couples, Gryff and Maddie, Caro and Max, and Lucy and Will, must have all decided to have lunch at Newstead.

Harriet admitted to finding the flag at the bridge—and to leaving a flower from her hat as a taunt to any future visitors—although she claimed it was all Morgan's idea.

Rhys showed the flag they'd found, but refused to say where they'd found it, presumably to make the other couples waste extra time looking for it at the butterfly house once they deciphered the riddle. Lenore silently applauded his sneakiness.

He wasn't the only one trying to mislead the competition, either. When Tristan held up his flag and baldly declared that he and Carys had found it in the wine cellar at Newstead, Lenore bit her up and tried not to laugh, knowing it to be a shameless falsehood.

Carys caught her eye and sent her a stern warning glare, and Lenore kicked Rhys's ankle under the table to make sure he didn't say anything either.

He shot her a mock-offended look at her for daring to suggest —even silently—that he was too stupid not to keep his mouth shut.

When lunch was over, they all watched the clock and the minute it struck two o'clock everyone raced for the doors. Rhys caught Lenore's hand as she stepped out into the hallway and gave it a gentle tug to stop her heading for the exit.

"This way, come on."

He pulled her down the hall, then, with a glance to make sure none of their siblings were still about, he pushed on a section of the dark wooden paneling on the wall. It swung open and Lenore's eyes widened in excitement.

"A secret door!"

"It leads to the stables." He stepped through, into the darkness beyond, his shoulders barely fitting through the narrow opening.

"I swear this gap was much bigger when I was a lad," he grumbled.

Lenore hitched up her skirts and followed him, pulling the door almost completely shut behind her, enclosing them in near total darkness.

"Wait here," he whispered. "I'll go and open the other door."

He stepped away, and could hear him scrabbling around, and then a shaft of light illuminated the tunnel as he opened another small door ahead of him. He climbed out, and Lenore followed, accepting his hand as she straightened.

The scent of fresh straw and the contented whicker of horses indicated he'd been right about where the tunnel led—they were in the empty last stall in the large Trellech stables—but Lenore sent him a confused look.

"Why are we here? There weren't any clues about horses or stables."

Rhys grinned, his teeth flashing white. "One should always take the opportunity to harass the opposition. In the army, we used to do all sorts of things to disrupt the French supply lines. We'd steal their artillery, pilfer their food, and bribe the locals to give them false directions. If we knew they were following us, we'd remove all the road signs to make it harder for them to figure out where they were on a map."

"Brilliant! But I'm assuming your siblings already know their way around here without any kind of signage."

"They do, but if they were planning to make their way to the lake and the boat house on horseback, we can slow them down." He peered over the wooden stall divider to make sure no grooms were loitering about, then strode over to the wall that contained the tack, including saddles, bridles and reins.

"Quick, come and help me."

He hefted a saddle from its hook and placed it on the floor, next to a huge mound of clean hay. "We'll put some of these under this hay, and hide all the bridles in the tunnel. They won't know where to look."

Lenore grinned as she scooped up an armful of hay and used it to conceal the saddles he placed on the straw-covered ground.

She loved being his partner in crime. She'd pulled equally silly tricks on Caro and Lucy in her time, and the fact that Rhys obviously had a mischievous streak of his own was delightful.

A sense of humor was an absolute necessity in a man, in her opinion, and one of the reasons she'd rejected so many suitors over the years was because most men she'd encountered were either sadly lacking in any kind of light-heartedness, or, on the other end of the scale, found humor in the most childish of things, like passing wind in public places, and pushing people into puddles.

"There." Rhys brushed his hands together, then lifted an assortment of bridles and reins from the hooks and gestured to her to re-enter the secret passageway. She did so, lifting her skirts so they wouldn't get too dusty, and he closed the door behind him—not a moment too soon.

Morgan and Harriet entered the stables with one of the Trellech grooms, and Rhys let out a gleeful little snort as he placed the leather straps on the ground at his feet, then followed Lenore back out into the paneled hallway and shut the little door with a click.

"Mission accomplished!" he crowed. "Now, let's get some flags. I think we should forget about trying to find Geoffrey and the other peacocks. Carys always has much better luck in finding her animals, because they actually *like* her. Geoffrey's given me a wide berth ever since I chased him off with a broomstick a few years ago. We could waste hours looking for him, and the other peacocks could be anywhere on the grounds."

"Agreed. We'd be better to concentrate on the flags we have a decent chance of finding. There was that clue about a clock. How do we get up to that clock-tower you mentioned?"

"There's a trap door in the east wing, but first we should try the library, since we didn't find anything in the one at Newstead."

He led her along the hall, past a billiard room, and into a library with a huge, vaulted ceiling and a fireplace big enough to roast an ox.

"Right. Get to work."

They both searched high and low, with Lenore even looking under the large celestial globes and Rhys climbing up the rolling ladders to peer along the top of the uppermost shelves, but there was no sign of a flag.

"Someone's found it," Rhys grumbled, dusting his hands. "Either that, or it was in the library back at Newstead and someone else beat us to it."

Lenore shrugged. "Caro might have been lying when she said it wasn't there. That's more likely, now I think about it. She's a devious little thing. The clock, then?"

"This way."

CHAPTER 9

*L*enore looked around with undisguised interest as Rhys led her up an impressive carved wooden staircase, with snarling lions guarding the newel posts at the bottom of each banister.

Ancient tapestries and suits of armor vied for position with gorgeous paintings and elegant gilt furniture, none of which matched, but which somehow managed to give the impression of being the perfect eclectic combination.

The place was a hodgepodge of at least six centuries, with sections built on top of one another, and little thought to aesthetic harmony. One draughty stone corridor had glazed arrow slits for windows, while another, far more comfortable, had huge panes of leaded glass giving picture-prefect views over the rolling green hills beyond the walls.

Lenore had seen all manner of interesting architectural styles in her travels and she'd stayed in everything from mud huts to royal palaces, but nowhere had been quite so eccentric nor as interesting as Trellech. It made her glad that Rhys's childhood here had been just as chaotic as her own.

She'd *love* to live somewhere like this.

They passed a whole wing of bedrooms—she spied an ancient four-poster through a door that had been left ajar—and her heart leapt at the thought that one of them might be Rhys's.

Had he ever brought a woman back to his chambers here? Would *she* ever get the chance to see inside?

They finally came to the entrance to a circular turret, with a winding staircase that got gradually narrower as they ascended. Rhys went up first, and she took the opportunity to appreciate the strong curves of his buttocks and the way the muscles of his thighs rippled under the soft buckskin of his breeches.

"This reminds me of that fairytale about the girl with the golden hair. Rapunzel." Lenore panted, a little out of breath from climbing all the stairs.

She'd asked Caro to lace her stays quite tightly that morning, to accentuate her breasts, but now she was regretting it. She hated blasted stays. She'd gone months without them in the jungle, and the first time she'd had to put on a corset again, back in London, had made her long for the freedom she'd once had.

"I prefer getting to the top this way," Rhys said. "Climbing up the outside is a lot more work."

"That sounds as if you've actually attempted it," she joked.

"Oh, I have. Several times, much to my father's annoyance. I once got all the way up to the third floor, almost up to the gargoyles, then my boot slipped."

She gasped. "Dear God! That's so dangerous. You could have fallen and broken your neck!"

His chuckle echoed down the spiral stair. "I didn't fall. Not far, anyway. I'd tied a rope around my waist, and Gryff was up here in the tower holding the other end. He looped it over the beam that holds the bell, so it would take my weight if I slipped. It worked a treat."

Lenore shook her head, still feeling a little queasy over the idea of him being injured, or worse.

Rhys stopped on the steps and reached up above his head.

"Three years in the army's cured me of such recklessness. I wouldn't try something so idiotic now. At fifteen you think you're invincible. By the time you reach twenty-five, you realize life's far too precious, too easily lost, to tempt fate that way."

Lenore nodded, even though he couldn't see her in the darkness. She'd had quite a few close shaves, herself.

"Here's the trapdoor, I hope you're not afraid of heights."

"I don't think I am," Lenore said truthfully. "But then again, I haven't been up very many places like this."

The hatch fell flat with a bang, and sunlight flooded the stairwell as she followed Rhys up and out into the bell tower.

Instead of having windows, the sides were open to the elements, and two black ravens, startled by the noise, took flight through the open arches, cawing loudly.

"That was Huginn and Muninn, Carys's pet Ravens," Rhys pointed after them. "She named them after Odin's ravens in Norse mythology. They're an absolute menace. Always stealing things, and mimicking the sound of gunfire."

"We had a ship's parrot that could make sounds," Lenore chuckled in recollection. "It could whistle God Save The King, but mainly the sailors had taught it rude words and to demand extra rations of rum."

The floor of the parapet was made from wooden planks, and a circular wall, barely waist high, encircled the tower. Lenore's breath caught in her chest. Her knees felt decidedly wobbly, and she had no desire to go any nearer the edge.

A cool breeze fanned her hair back from her face as she steadied herself on a huge wooden crossbeam from which hung a large brass bell.

"That bell's been there for hundreds of years to warn of impending Montgomery invasions," Rhys said with a smile. "I wonder how many times it's been rung?"

"Almost as many times as the one in the tower at Newstead Park," Lenore countered pertly. "Designed to let everyone know when the Wild Welsh Davies were on the rampage with their torches and pitchforks."

"Ah, the good old days," Rhys chuckled. He gestured over the countryside which spread out before them in all directions like a verdant green patchwork quilt. "Isn't that an excellent view?"

It was undoubtedly worth the climb. Far below, the small figures of Morgan and Harriet could be seen crossing toward the woods, and further away Lenore caught a flash of Caro's pink skirts near the Davies menagerie.

The glint of sunlight on water in the distance made her squint.

"That's the lake," Rhys pointed, noting the direction of her gaze. "There's a boat house too, by the water's edge. We'll need to head there in a bit for the boat and island clues."

Lenore turned west. "Can you see Newstead Park from here?"

"Not even with a telescope," Rhys grinned. "And believe me, we all tried spying on you Mad Montgomerys." He pointed upward, toward the roof. "There's a flagpole up there, where Gryff once hung Maddie's shawl as a war trophy. That was years ago, but taunting you lot never seems to get old."

Lenore bit back a smile, then a blur of movement below caught her eye, and a shrill avian screech filled the air.

"Oh! Morgan's chasing that peacock!"

Rhys leaned over the parapet for a better look, apparently unafraid of the monstrous drop, and Lenore bit back the urge to grab the back of his jacket to steady him. His younger brother was indeed racing across the lawn after an aggrieved peacock.

"I wonder if it's Geoffrey?"

"Look!" Lenore pointed. "Carys is hiding behind the hedge. Morgan's chasing him toward her without even realizing it!"

Rhys squinted downward. "There's a red flag attached to one of its tail feathers."

"Who knew peacocks could run so fast?" Lenore marveled.

Rhys cupped his hands around his mouth. "Run, Geoffrey! Run!" he bellowed.

Morgan glanced up at the shout, spied them in the tower, and sent his brother a very ungentlemanly hand signal.

"That's not one they officially recommend in the army," Rhys chuckled.

Turning back to the pursuit, Morgan increased his speed. He made a valiant dive for the flag but missed as the clever bird changed direction at the very last second, zig-zagging away from him with a cry that definitely sounded gloating.

Morgan rolled down a grassy embankment and only just managed to stop himself from falling in the moat.

Rhys let out a whoop of delight.

Carys, meanwhile, stepped out from behind the hedge and gave a shrill whistle. Geoffrey slowed his pace and turned toward her, obviously recognizing the sound, and Carys crouched down and moved her hand in a shallow arc.

"Clever bugger," Rhys growled. "She's bribing him with seeds. Geoffrey never misses the chance for a second lunch."

Sure enough, the peacock strutted eagerly towards Carys, then started pecking at the grass at her feet. With a grin, Carys reached down and gently tugged the flag from where it was nestled among his tail feathers.

"If I'd done that, he'd have pecked my eyes out," Rhys grumbled, his voice tinged with reluctant brotherly admiration.

Carys's grin was visible even from up in the tower as she waved the flag over her head in a victory dance. Tristan emerged from behind her and gave her a congratulatory hug from behind.

"It's a miracle anyone other than Carys managed to get close enough to Geoffrey to set the flag in the first place. I wonder if they did it while he was asleep? Or maybe they gave him fermented apples to eat. It gets them drunk, you know." Rhys shrugged at the mystery. "Either way, that's two flags for Carys and Tristan now. We need to improve our game."

Lenore made a quick circle of the tower. "Where's the clock?"

Rhys lifted his arms toward the wooden planks and beams above them and took hold of an iron ring in the ceiling that Lenore hadn't noticed before.

"Up here."

He pulled, and another, smaller, hinged door swung down to reveal the inner workings of a clock, its pendulum swinging with heart-beat precision back and forth.

"Yes!" Lenore cried.

There, tied to one of the cylindrical lead weights was a cheerful yellow flag. Rhys went up on his tiptoes and untied it, then tucked it safely in the inside pocket of his jacket.

"Two for us, as well. We're still in the running."

"Wine cellar next," Lenore said, the excitement of the game adding a catch to her breath almost as much as the sight of Rhys's handsome face and carelessly windblown hair. "Let's hope Caro wasn't lying about it not being at Newstead."

CHAPTER 10

*L*enore was glad to climb down from the tower, and she and Rhys sneaked along the corridors, keeping an ear out for the other teams. When they reached the ground floor again, he led her through Trellech's enormous medieval great hall, complete with minstrel's gallery, and an astonishing assortment of gruesome-looking weaponry displayed on the walls.

"The four of us used to play with those all the time," he said, noting the direction of her fascinated gaze. "We had our own tournaments. We'd dress up in the suits of armor and batter each other with swords and pikes and hatchets until one of us yielded, or until Nanny Maude called us to go wash our hands for tea. Whichever came first."

"Didn't Nanny Maude scold you for fighting?"

"Not at all. She thinks exercising the body is as important as exercising the mind. In fact, she even taught me a few moves. She's a wily old bird. Much like your aunts Constance and Prudence."

Rhys shook his head in wry recollection and Lenore smiled. It was clear he held the old retainer in high regard.

His smile faded a little. "I sometimes wonder if those innocent childish battles gave me an edge when it came to fighting in earnest."

Lenore placed her hand on his arm, distressed by the sudden bleak look his eyes. "If they did, then I'm glad. Who would have given Gordon Burton a lesson in manners if you hadn't made it back from France?"

His eyes flashed at the implication that she didn't wish his demise, and he smiled again. Her spirits soared.

She dropped her hand, and they moved into what was clearly the oldest part of the castle.

"The wine cellar wasn't originally built for wine," he said, glancing over his shoulder. "It used to be the dungeons."

He pushed open a heavy oak door studded with iron spikes, and a blast of cool air from below raised goosebumps on her arms.

Rhys took one of the lanterns that were hanging on a hook on the wall, lit it with a tinderbox he produced from his jacket pocket, and held it high.

The steps led down to a dark hallway lined with a row of cells, each with a metal grille set in the door and a tiny, barred window near the ceiling to let in a sliver of fresh air and sunlight. Lenore shivered, clearly able to imagine how miserable it would have been to be locked up somewhere so inhospitable.

"Instead of storing Montgomery hostages down here," Rhys said, a laugh in his voice, "now we've realized these cool, dank conditions are perfect for storing wine."

The cellar opened out into a vast space, far larger than the feeble circle of light cast by the lamp, and Lenore sucked in an awed breath.

A network of arched, vaulted stone was supported by a series of thick pillars, and between the pillars were rows upon rows of wine bottles, all stacked in tall, latticed shelves, stretching out into the darkness as far as she could see.

"That is a *lot* of wine," she breathed. "I don't think I've ever seen so much in one place. This is ten times bigger than the cellar at Newstead."

"Well, we Davies have always been fond of a tipple, historically. If the family annals are to be believed, we had one ancestor who was known as Owen the Unsteady, thanks to his love of the grape. But this isn't all to be drunk. Not yet, anyway. Most of it's been bought as an investment."

Lenore did some swift mental calculation. "This must be worth a fortune!"

His lips twitched at her obvious astonishment—and at her inability to disguise her unseemly curiosity.

"It is," he said mildly.

Lenore frowned. She'd known the Davies weren't badly off; certainly, they were richer than her Montgomery relatives, who'd only been saved from penury a few years ago by the fortuitous discovery of the gold seam that stretched across their jointly-held lands.

But while the income from the mine was steady, it certainly wasn't enough to fund this level of extravagance. Were the Dastardly Davies living up to their name and taking *more* than their fair share of half the profits?

"Did your family buy all this with money from the gold mine?"

Rhys grinned, as if fully aware of her suspicions. "No. We have a few other sources of income. Even ones that don't include pillaging with our pitchforks."

He clearly wasn't going to say any more on the subject, and while Lenore was desperate to interrogate him, it would be the height of rudeness to pry into his financial affairs.

Besides, this probably all belonged to his older brother Gryff, as the Earl of Powys. As far as she could tell, since he'd left the army, Rhys had no profession, except semi-professional brawler and general libertine-about-town.

If she was a sensible woman, she'd have made sure to fall in love with a man like the Duke of Andover, who possessed both money and a lofty title. Instead, she was hopelessly drawn to Rhys. A handsome second son with neither title nor fortune to his name.

Shakespeare was right when he said that 'reason and love keep little company together.'

Unaware of her inner turmoil, Rhys stepped up to read the labels on some of the dust-covered bottles that lay stored on their side, each with the cork facing outward.

"Not a good year, that one. Here, take this."

He thrust the lantern forward and she took it automatically, then followed in his wake as he strode off into the gloom as confidently as a cat in the dark.

The rows of racking passed by in a blur, the lantern light glinting off the glass bottles as they followed one long row to the end, then turned a corner and followed another section deeper into the shadows.

Lenore's heart was pounding at the slightly oppressive sensation of the thousands of bottles looming around her. She felt like Theseus, sneaking through the corridors of the labyrinth, terrified of turning a corner and encountering the minotaur. She hoped Rhys wasn't getting them lost.

He finally stopped and she skidded to a stop next to him, peering around to see if they'd finally found one of the elusive flags.

Instead, he pulled two bottles from the shelves, and held them up to her.

"Let's have a drink."

"To celebrate finding another flag?" she asked doubtfully.

"No. Something more important. To celebrate being *alive*. Here. Now."

His dark eyes glittered in the lamplight, and the angles of his cheeks and chin cast intriguing shadows on his face, making him look both wicked and playful at once.

"Being alive is the very best thing to celebrate, don't you think?" His deep voice curled around her. "Surviving the war made me look at things from a new perspective. Before, I took everything for granted. I put value in all the wrong things. Now, I'm just grateful to wake up every morning. I've learned to appreciate things like the warmth of sunlight on my face, the first sip of an excellent bottle of wine, and the company of friends."

"Would you call us friends?" Lenore's heart seemed to pause as she waited for his response.

"Why not?" he said easily. "We're not enemies, are we?"

She held his gaze. "No, we're not."

He glanced down at the labels. "Shame we had to fight the French. Hopefully now the war is over, they can go back to doing what they do best, which is making excellent wine." He held the two bottles aloft. "Now, Chateaux Margaux, or Haut Brion? Both are fabulous Bordeaux, if you like red wine. Any preference?"

"I do like red wine, but I'll bow to your superior knowledge over which one to choose."

He peered at a label to read the date. "Well, Haut Brion is best to drink between twelve and twenty years of aging, so this one should be perfect."

"How will we open a bottle? Don't tell me you always carry a corkscrew with you."

"Sadly not. But there are other ways. One is to push the cork in, instead of pulling it out. But you need the handle of a wooden spoon, or something like that. And it runs the risk of the cork disintegrating and ruining the wine."

"Sacrilege!" she said, with light mockery. He was clearly a man who knew and loved his wine. "What's another way then?"

"You can heat up the air in the neck of the bottle, just under the cork. When it expands, it pushes the cork out."

"We can use the lamp flame, if we take the glass protector off." Lenore said.

He nodded, and she held the flickering flame of the oil lamp steady while he kept the bottle in exactly the right spot. To her surprise, the cork began inching out of the bottle neck.

"It's working!"

He sent her a dry, mocking look. "O ye of little faith."

"Wait. We don't have any glasses," Lenore groaned.

"We'll just have to drink from the bottle."

She sent him a mock-horrified look. "How terribly uncouth. What would the *ton* say?"

"I've never really cared for what the *ton* thinks of me," Rhys shrugged. "And I'm fairly sure *you* don't care, either. Besides, I won't tell anyone if you don't."

"Deal," she grinned.

He pulled the cork the final way out of the bottle with a satisfying pop, the muscles on the back of his hand rippling most intriguingly as he did so. He held the bottle out to her.

"Ladies first."

CHAPTER 11

Sensing the challenge in Rhys's eyes, Lenore set the lantern safely on a shelf, then tilted the bottle up against her lips. She took a ladylike sip, then handed it back.

The near-darkness seemed to have heightened her senses, and her skin prickled with awareness of his proximity; the warmth of his body was a delicious contrast to the chill, damp air around them.

His swig was much deeper, and her stomach clenched at the realization that his lips were touching the same place hers had just been. It seemed oddly intimate.

His lips were positively sinful, too; full and firm, and when he tipped the bottle higher and swallowed again, his throat moved in a way that made her want to feel the muscles rippling against her fingers.

She took the bottle back and took a longer drink, desperate to cool the heat that was rising in her cheeks, and the liquid slid down her own throat, smooth and rich. When she lowered the bottle, she found him looking at her expectantly, as if waiting for her reaction.

"So? What do you think?" His voice was a little rougher than it had been. "What does it taste like to you?"

"Wine?" She teased, certain such a bland response would infuriate him.

He shook his head in mock horror. "Is that the best you can do? Try again." He pushed the bottle back toward her and she took another long swallow. It settled in her belly with a lovely warming sensation.

"Close your eyes," he ordered, "and concentrate on identifying the flavors in your mouth."

She did so, and he took another sip himself.

"This wine is beautifully complex," he murmured. "There are hints of smoke and tar, earth and leather. Maybe a little bit of spice at the back of your throat."

Lenore's skin felt flushed. His voice was as delicious as the wine, sliding over her like a velvet caress.

"I *can* detect a bit of smoky flavor," she admitted. "But I'm afraid I don't have your extensive experience."

"Have you ever been drunk before?" he asked, sounding genuinely curious. "And don't lie. I bet you have."

She opened her eyes. "A few times," she admitted wryly.

She took another drink. The wine seemed to be improving the more she tried it. "When we were shipwrecked, off Madagascar, we were able to rescue most of the stores from the ship, because it didn't sink, it just got stuck on a reef. Some of the men rowed out in lifeboats and brought all the wine back to shore. We drank most of it while waiting for rescue."

"That sounds like the perfect shipwreck," he smiled.

"The first—and worst—time was when Lucy and I stole a bottle of our father's special brandy. We were about sixteen, I think. Lucy was sick in the window box outside our room, and I decided to give myself a haircut with a pair of crimping shears. I woke up with one side of my hair three inches shorter than the other, and the worst headache I've ever encountered in my life."

Rhys snorted in amusement. "I once rode a donkey backwards

through White's, because Gryff bet me ten shillings I was too drunk to stay seated."

"Did you fall off?"

"Absolutely," he grinned. "But only because Morgan was pelting me with fruit to make me lose my balance."

"You make me quite glad I never had brothers," she smiled.

"You're welcome to one of mine."

His dark eyes glittered in the flickering light as he leaned closer. "I must admit, I'm intrigued to find out what *kind* of drunk you are. Some fellows become quarrelsome and want a fight. Others get sad and start crying. A few even get amorous and try to compose love poetry."

"I'm think I'm a happy drunk," she said.

He waggled his eyebrows with a comical leer. "Scared I'll reveal my true Davies nature and steal a kiss while you're tipsy?"

She laughed. "You wouldn't. You might be a dastardly Davies, but you'd never take advantage of a woman like that."

"How do you know?"

"You were defending a woman against just such an offence the night we met. Gordon had insulted her or tried to kiss her—I didn't quite catch what—but you were the one who was administering his punishment for being so ungentlemanly."

"Ah." He looked a little embarrassed as he took another long pull from the bottle. "Well, Annabelle is one of Carys's friends, and she doesn't have any brothers of her own so I—"

"—punched him into a fountain on her behalf?" Lenore chuckled.

"Something like that." His lips quirked.

"A knight in shining armor, then," she teased. "Or rather, evening clothes."

Her gaze seemed to have become fixed on his lips. The wine was giving her a warm, fuzzy feeling. He had the most beautiful lips.

A surge of recklessness filled her and she leaned towards him, as if to impart a great secret. "Just so you know," she whispered. "I am *not* drunk right now."

Her heart was thundering with excitement, but she'd bided her time long enough. It was time to take a risk.

He leaned closer, too, trapping her against the bottles of wine stacked in the shelves. "No?"

She shook her head. The air between them was heavy, almost throbbing with anticipation.

His eyes bored into hers. "So, if I kissed you, for example, that wouldn't be taking advantage?"

"Definitely not," she breathed.

His face remained impassive, there was a twinkle in his eye that made her blood sing.

"Maybe I should try it, then."

He leaned in, and his warm breath stirred the tendrils of hair by her ear. A nervous thrill of anticipation twisted low in her belly.

His lips brushed her temple, and she heard him inhale softly, as if he were drawing in her scent, her essence, into his lungs. Her knees went weak, and she breathed in the delicious masculine smell of *him*; musky woods and clean sheets.

His lips danced along her cheekbone, deliberately teasing out the moment, and then his fingers cupped her jaw, then slid around the back of her head to tangle in her hair.

Her whole body tingled.

The pad of his thumb brushed her lower lip, sliding across it, dragging it down, and she tilted her face up to his, desperate for him to close the distance and put her out of her misery.

When his lips finally pressed hers, she gave a little groan of relief and went up on her tiptoes to meet him. His tongue traced the seam of her lips, and when she opened her mouth to his insistent pressure, his tongue slid inside to tangle with her own.

Lenore closed her eyes in scandalized delight. She was kissing

Rhys Davies! And it was *glorious*. Even better than her feverish imaginings.

He tasted of wine; smoky, rich, delicious. The lazy swirl of his tongue against hers was a slow, delicious seduction, fogging her brain, and making her knees weak.

He groaned, deep in his throat, a thrilling, masculine sound of torment and need, and her stomach clenched at the sound. She abandoned herself to the kiss, returning what he gave, silently urging him on. She pressed herself against him, full-length, feeling the warmth of his chest as it rested against hers, the strong columns of his legs.

Giving in to temptation, she ran her hands up his chest and over his shoulders, then up to touch the warm skin of his cheek. The slightly rough hint of stubble beneath her fingertips made her heart jolt, and she kissed him again and again, loving the swirling vortex of darkness and pleasure he conjured.

She'd never kissed *anyone* like this before, never dreamed it was possible, but it also felt incredibly *right*. As if her body recognized this man, this feeling of being home.

She wanted to do this forever.

The sudden scrape of feet on the stairs and the muffled echo of voices only vaguely intruded on her consciousness, but Rhys dragged his lips from hers with a groan that sounded almost pained.

"Bloody Hell. Someone's coming."

Lenore opened her eyes in sudden panic as she came back to earth with an unwelcome jolt.

"What?"

Rhys stepped back, releasing her, and she reluctantly dropped her hands from his face. Her soul felt as though it was being ripped from her chest.

Her lips were tingling, her cheeks flushed, and a strange swirling sensation gnawed in her belly. She knew what it was: lust. Desire. Need.

Oh, hell.

She glanced up at Rhys and found his gaze fixed on her lips, his chest rising and falling in rapid, panting breaths, and a surge of feminine satisfaction rushed through her. At least he looked as shaken as she felt.

He blinked, then shook his head, as if coming out of a trance, and cocked his head to listen for the unwelcome intruders.

"It's Lucy," Lenore whispered, easily recognizing the tones of her twin, despite the dark and distance. "And Will."

Rhys grabbed the lantern with his left hand and threaded the fingers of his right hand through hers. Lenore smiled at the gesture.

He bent to whisper in her ear. "You, Miss Montgomery, are the very *worst* distraction."

She grinned up at him, her heart strangely buoyant at the feeling they'd got away with something naughty.

Lucy and Will were traversing the left side of the room, and although Lenore and Rhys tried to sneak along their row, the light from their lantern gave them away.

"Hoi!" Will shouted. "Who's there?"

Rhys rolled his eyes in comical despair and shouted back. "It's Rhys. And Lenore."

"Lenore?" Lucy called over the racking. "Have you found the flag?"

Rhys shook his head just as Lenore shouted, "Not yet."

"Race you for it!" Will called, and Lenore could hear the rapid pounding of their footsteps as they started along their row.

"Quick!" she gasped, tugging Rhys's hand and pulling him along.

He held his lantern aloft, and they both looked frantically for the flag, moving as quickly as they could while making sure they didn't miss it. They turned into another aisle, then another, as Lucy and Will's lantern glow on the ceiling revealed the rows they were exploring.

"Found it!"

Lucy's triumphant shout echoed along the rows and Lenore let out a growl of frustration.

"Best twin wins!" Lucy taunted loudly.

"Luckiest twin wins," Lenore grumbled.

In truth, she didn't mind too much. She was feeling rather lucky herself, and she'd happily give up the chance of finding the other flags if it meant Rhys would kiss her again.

He released her hand as they reached the end of their row and found Lucy and Will beaming with happiness near the bottom of the steps.

"Well done," Lenore managed, praying the darkness would conceal her flushed cheeks and well-kissed lips.

The other couple started back up the stairs and Lenore smoothed her skirts and took a steadying breath as she prepared to follow them.

Kissing someone in the shadows was one thing, a wicked secret buried deep beneath the earth, but how was she going to face Rhys in the harsh light of day?

Did he regret what they'd done? Would he dismiss it as something trivial, a lark not to be taken too seriously?

Lenore was almost afraid to find out.

CHAPTER 12

Lucy and Will were already hurrying toward the open front door by the time Lenore and Rhys emerged from the cellar.

Lenore didn't regret their kiss one bit, but she was a little shaken to imagine what would have happened if they hadn't been interrupted. Would Rhys have stopped kissing her of his own free will? Because *she* wouldn't have had the fortitude to do it.

And would he have taken things further? She would have allowed it, willingly, but what would he have thought of her if she'd given herself to him fully? She was still a virgin, although she'd read enough books and seen enough erotic drawings to know exactly what it meant when a man and a woman made love. Her blood heated at the thought of Rhys touching her body so intimately.

She slid a glance over at him as they headed out into the courtyard, half afraid he'd apologize and call it an impetuous mistake.

"Only two clues left to find," he said brightly, clearly determined to act as if nothing had happened. "Island, and boat. I say we try the boat shed first."

Lenore fanned her warm cheeks and nodded, just as a shout of annoyance emerged from the direction of the stables.

Rhys sent her a conspiratorial smile. "Sounds like someone else just discovered there's no tack to saddle their horses."

Lenore couldn't help but smirk. That had been an excellent idea.

"What's the shortest way to get to the boat house from here?"

"Through the formal gardens, then a short walk through the paddock. Follow me."

Rhys led her away from the main house and through a small wooden door set in the outer wall of the courtyard. Lenore had glimpsed these formal gardens from up in the turret, but there was no time to admire the flowers and box hedges as they hurried onward.

None of the other couples were in sight, and it wasn't long before the lake appeared through a bank of trees before them. A few swans and ducks disturbed the glassy surface, and Lenore's eyes widened at how large it was.

"The boat house is over there, behind those rhododendrons," Rhys pointed.

The land sloped steeply down toward the lakeshore, and together they skidded down the embankment, taking care not to fall. Lenore was glad that beneath her impractical dress she'd had the foresight to wear a pair of far more sensible ankle boots. If she'd been wearing pretty, silk slippers they would have been ruined by now.

She thought she heard someone crashing through the undergrowth, off to their left, and increased her pace, but they reached the boathouse unchallenged.

The shed was built into the side of the hill, with the far end almost completely below ground, and the front giving onto a shingle 'beach' that acted as a launch for the boats.

Lenore peered cautiously inside, but the scrape of wood and a splash from the far side of building made Rhys hurry forward to investigate.

He let out a hiss of annoyance as Morgan and Harriet suddenly drifted into view, floating in a rowboat that must have been tied to the small wooden dock beyond the boat shed.

"Damn it!" Rhys muttered as Harriet sent them a cheerful wave while Morgan plied the oars to take them further out into the lake.

"See you on the island!" Morgan called cheerfully.

"Quick," Lenore hissed. "There are more boats in here. And we should look for the flag from the 'boat' clue, in case they haven't found it."

She stepped inside, quickly examining the three little rowboats that were illuminated by the light streaming in from the windows set in the roof. Two were upside down, stored on wooden stands, and she checked beneath them. There was no flag hidden there, nor behind the piles of oars, assorted garden tools, or under the stack of picnic blankets folded neatly on a chair in one corner.

Rhys had just grabbed the front of the boat closest to the door, ready to drag it out onto the shingle, when the wooden doors slammed shut with a bang, and a guffaw of masculine laughter sounded from outside.

"What the—?" Rhys exclaimed.

Another loud bang, this one clearly the scrape of something heavy being placed against the outside of the door.

"Morgan!" Rhys bellowed. "I'll strangle you!"

"Not if you're stuck in there, you won't," Morgan shouted back gleefully.

Lenore bit back a laugh as she realized how they'd been duped. Morgan had only pretended to start rowing out to the island and must have doubled back to land when he saw the chance to trap them in the shed.

"Harriet!" she called out, a pleading tone in her voice. "Cousin!"

"Oh, dear. Look at that. The wind must have blown the door closed."

Harriet's dry, amused voice floated through the gaps in the planks. She didn't sound the least bit contrite. In fact, she was clearly struggling not to laugh. "And a big branch seems to have fallen right across the doors. How unfortunate. Sorry, Lenore, my love. But all's fair in love and treasure-hunting. We'll come and let you out if you're still there when we get back from the island."

"Don't promise them that," Morgan scolded her, with mock-severity. "They can stay in there all night, for all I care."

Rhys slammed his palm against the inside of the door, rattling the hinges, then pushed against it with his shoulder, but whatever Morgan had placed to block the doors held fast.

"We'd love to stay and chat," Morgan taunted, "but you know how much we Navy boys like the water. It's our second home, and I have the most amazing urge to get back out there and feel the wind on my face."

"You'll feel my *fist* on your face if I ever get out of here," Rhys bellowed through the door. He took a step back and rammed the wood again with his shoulder, but while the two doors did buckle outwards a bit, it was not enough to break whatever had been braced against them.

"Stop!" Lenore urged him, half amused and half impressed at his display of brute strength. "You'll hurt your shoulder. There must be another way out."

"Fine," Rhys huffed, turning from the door with a final glare, as if his fury could singe his brother on the other side. "Sneaky bastard."

"You're just annoyed you didn't think of it yourself," she said, and was rewarded with a curl at the corner of his lips.

"True enough," he conceded. "I would have done exactly the same to him, if our positions were reversed."

In truth, Lenore wasn't all that dismayed at being locked in another gloomy space with Rhys, but any hope that they could resume kissing was dispelled by the way he started to prowl around the space, looking for an alternative exit.

Her spirits deflated a little.

Was he tired of kissing her already? Had once been enough to satisfy his natural male curiosity? Had he not enjoyed it as much as she had?

He stomped to the back of the shed and stood, hands on hips, looking up at the small, semicircular window set high up on the back wall.

The slope of the hill meant that although the window was about six feet up the back wall of the shed, it was only a couple of feet above the grassy hillside outside. The bobbing heads of foxgloves and cornflowers could be seen tapping against the glass.

"You're going to have to climb through that," Rhys said decisively. "My shoulders are too big."

Lenore smiled, delighted by the way he didn't question either her ability or her willingness to do such a thing. The fact that he regarded her as a capable member of his team, as opposed to a fragile female who would be scandalized at the thought of climbing out of a window, made her inordinately happy.

She dragged the chair from the side of the room, and stood on it, but while she could reach up and undo the window latch and push open the large pane, she wasn't high enough to climb out.

She glanced at Rhys over her shoulder and found him studying her backside, and bit back a grin. Hopefully he was enjoying the view.

"You're going to have to give me a boost."

He nodded, and she sucked in a breath as his strong hands slid around her waist. "No," he muttered pensively, "that's not going to work. You won't get high enough. I'm going to have to lift you from lower down.

"Go on, then."

He bent and wrapped his right arm around the front of her knees, pressing her legs together. The position put his cheek flush against the outside of her thigh, her bottom resting on his shoulder.

"This should do it. Up you go!" He straightened, and Lenore grabbed the window frame with both hands. She pushed her shoulders through the open casement, then her upper body, as Rhys pushed her lower half, his hands gripping her legs.

It was definitely not the most elegant position, and she struggled not to laugh as he abandoned all attempt at propriety and gave her bottom a firm push. His hands lingered much longer than necessary, too, and her stomach flipped at the feel of his broad palms cupping her hips, then sliding over the rounded curves of her arse. He gave them a gentle squeeze.

"Sorry!" He muttered from behind her. "Can't be helped."

Lenore kicked her heels to try to wriggle through the gap, and her left foot connected with something hard.

"Ow!" Rhys yelped. "Bloody Hell, woman, that was my nose!"

"Sorry!"

With one final push to her ankles, she managed to pull herself fully out of the window and collapsed, panting, on the grassy bank. She turned and peered back in at Rhys. He was holding his nose, and her eyes widened at the trickle of blood that seeped from beneath his cupped hand.

"Oh no! I'm so sorry!" she gasped again, filled with genuine remorse. "I couldn't see what I was kicking. Is it broken?"

He felt along the ridge with his fingers, then wiped away the smear of blood with his thumb. "It wouldn't be the first time," he said, "But no. Not from a little tap like that."

She studied his nose intently, trying to see if there was a telltale kink in it, but he seemed to be telling the truth. His nose was as straight and as perfect as ever. Although he'd probably look just as handsome with a crooked nose, curse him. Like a rugged pirate.

Their positions, with him below, and her above, made her think of the famous balcony scene from Shakespeare's Romeo and Juliet, but Rhys was hardly the sort of man to linger outside a maiden's bedroom window mooning over her beauty. He'd be more likely to scale the walls and claim a kiss, and more.

He waved his hands in an impatient gesture. "Don't just stand there looking at my nose. It's fine. Go around the front and see what Morgan's barred the door with."

Lenore scrambled to her feet, embarrassed at having been caught gazing at him like a lovesick puppy.

The doors had been blocked with a stout log, angled to prevent their opening from within, and with a grunt she managed to roll it aside. Rhys emerged and she let out a shocked shriek as he caught her by the waist and spun her round in a celebratory little dance.

"Excellent work," he said, his eyes crinkling at the corners. "My hero!"

He released her abruptly, as if suddenly realizing the informality of what he'd done and sent a dismayed glance at the front of her dress. Lenore looked down to see what he was looking at, and found the pale fabric covered in streaks of black dirt, dust, cobwebs and green grass stains.

She brushed at it, but it was a futile effort.

"I'll buy you a new one," Rhys promised. "Since the window was my idea. That one's ruined."

Lenore rolled her eyes. "You'll do no such thing. What would people think, if word got out that you'd bought me a dress?"

"Nobody would have to know."

"Men only buy dresses for women they're intimately acquainted with."

"I just had my hands on your arse, Montgomery," Rhys said

with a wicked grin. "I'd call that intimate acquaintance, wouldn't you?"

Lenore turned away to hide her blush. "I can buy my own dresses, thank you very much. I don't need your Davies charity." She pointed across the lake. "Look! Morgan and Harriet are already halfway to the island already."

"Then let's get after them. I have a bone to pick with that brother of mine."

CHAPTER 13

Despite their slow start, and Morgan's undoubted familiarity with a pair of oars, Lenore and Rhys made excellent progress across the lake and managed to close the distance between the two boats quite considerably.

Since Rhys was facing backward to row, Lenore kept him updated on their progress as the muscles in his forearms rippled in time with his powerful strokes.

He'd removed his jacket and thrown it on the wooden plank that served as a seat, and she couldn't help but be impressed by the smooth motion of his body as he reached forward and pulled back. The oars cut into the water, and they sped across the lake, pushing through the lily pads that clustered in the shallows.

"We're gaining on them!"

"Not quickly enough," Rhys panted.

"What's on the island, anyway? Is it just trees?"

"No. There's a little stone temple thing in the middle. You can see the columns through the leaves if you look closely. I bet the flag is hidden up there."

A flash of color at the opposite end of the lake caught

Lenore's eye, and she gave a disbelieving gasp as she identified who it was.

"Gryff and Maddie are over there, on the far side."

"No boats over there," Rhys gloated.

"I don't think that's going to be a problem. Your brother's stripping off his clothes. I think he means to swim!"

Rhys turned around his seat to look, then let out a growl of disbelief as he, too, saw Gryff tug off his boots, then discard his jacket, cravat, and shirt. Maddie, his willing co-conspirator, grinned as he handed her the clothes.

Lenore raised her brows. "I say, your brother keeps himself very fit, doesn't he?" She glanced at Rhys and was delighted to see an aggrieved frown flash across his handsome face.

"You shouldn't be looking at his physique," he scolded. "Avert your eyes!"

Lenore snorted. "I've seen hundreds of shirtless men, Rhys Davies. Sailors, porters, fellow shipwreck survivors. I don't think I'm in any danger of swooning just because your brother happens to show some chest."

Rhys gave the oars a particularly hard pull.

There was an audible splash as Gryff dove into the water, and a shout from the boat up ahead as Harriet and Morgan obviously realized they had competition.

The island they were all heading for was large and tree-covered and situated far closer to Gryff's end of the lake than the boat shed. There was a definite possibility that he would reach it first.

"Row faster!" Lenore ordered Rhys with a laugh.

There was an audible crunch as Harriet and Morgan's boat reached the shore on the island. Morgan leaped out.

Gryff had disappeared from view around the back of the island.

"Go!" Harriet shouted to Morgan, gesturing frantically into the trees toward the center if the island. "Don't wait for me."

Morgan started off through the undergrowth, and Harriet sent Lenore a laughing glance as their boat slid onto the same stretch of beach. "Afternoon!"

Rhys didn't even wait for the boat to come to a complete stop. He threw down the oars and jumped out after Morgan in hot pursuit, careless of his expensive boots splashing in the water.

Harriet obviously planned to stay with their boat, but Lenore decided that two sets of eyes were better than one. She hitched up her skirts, tucked the excess fabric into her waistband, climbed out of the boat, and dragged it higher up the beach so it wouldn't float away.

Then she set off after Rhys and Morgan.

The trees and grasses were incredibly overgrown, but she pushed ahead, uphill, batting branches out of the way and stepping over fallen logs. The sound of snapping twigs indicated that someone was up ahead, and then the peace was shattered by a cacophony of male shouting.

"Got you!"

She rounded a large pine just in time to see Rhys running towards Morgan's retreating back. He launched himself at his brother and tackled him with arms around his chest, and the two of them tumbled to the ground in a blur of limbs.

"Oi! Get off, you bugger!" Morgan rolled and tried to push him off, but Rhys clung to him like a barnacle, and the two of them rolled over and over through the mud and leaves, scrambling in the most undignified manner.

Morgan managed to get one arm free and grabbed Rhys's hair, which he gave a brutal tug.

"Owww!" Rhys howled. "Not the hair!"

He retaliated by elbowing Morgan in the stomach.

Morgan grabbed the waistband of Rhys's breeches and gave a sharp tug, and Lenore winced as he heard the rip of fabric.

Since both men were of a similar size and weight, they were evenly matched, and they'd clearly been scrapping like this since they were boys. They obviously hadn't lost the relish for it now that they were in their twenties. Lenore almost rolled her eyes.

Rhys had just pulled his right arm back to punch Morgan in the face when Harriet's scolding tones carried clearly through the trees.

"No punching, Davies boys!"

Both Rhys and Morgan stilled, and Lenore turned in surprise to see Harriet pushing through the greenery to her left.

Harriet sent the two men a look of withering disappointment that made Lenore suppress a chuckle. She'd clearly witnessed such chaotic scenes from the Davies siblings before.

"Rhys Davies, don't you dare give my husband a black eye. We have to go to Lady Pilton's garden party next week and I won't have him looking like a pirate."

She turned to her husband. "And you. Have you forgotten he was boxing champion at Cambridge for three years in a row? Why on earth would you get into a scrap with him?"

"Just helping him stay on top form," Morgan grinned.

Rhys sent Morgan a gloating look for Harriet's apparent admiration of his boxing acumen, but it faded with her next comment.

"He's probably received so many blows to the head that his brain's stopped working properly."

"Hey!" Rhys objected. "My brain works perfectly well, I'll have you know."

Morgan sent his wife a laughing glance. "And if I remember correctly, there have been times when you've quite *liked* me looking like a pirate." He waggled his brows and sent her a comically suggestive leer.

Harriet's cheeks turned pink, and she sent him an embarrassed glare. "Oh, hush, you!"

Lenore caught Rhys's eye and gave her head an almost imperceptible tilt toward the center of the island to indicate that she was going to make a run for the temple while he detained Morgan. He understood her intent immediately.

"Go!" he shouted, just as he grabbed Morgan's shirt collar and gave it a brutal yank backwards.

Morgan let out a howl as there was more ripping of fabric. "I paid ten shillings for this jacket, you arse!"

Lenore didn't wait to hear Rhys's reply. She lifted her skirts and leapt over their tangled legs and raced onward.

The pale stone pillars of the temple came into view between the trees and she quickened her pace, fearful that Harriet would be right behind her.

She'd just reached the lowest of the curved steps that ringed the base of the circular temple when a dripping and shirtless Gryff Davies emerged from behind a pillar with a whoop of triumph.

"No!" she gasped, her chest heaving with exertion.

Gryff waved the little blue flag down at her. "Give Rhys my thanks for taking care of Morgan."

With a grin, he trotted down the steps and plunged back into the trees.

Rhys arrived just then, panting as he reached her side. His cheeks were flushed, and his hair was a tangled mess, but her heart gave a traitorous little flutter all the same. She liked him all mussed and disreputable.

"What's the matter?" he demanded. "Why have you stopped?"

"Gryff got here first." She pointed to the incriminating wet puddle in the middle of the temple.

Rhys bent over and braced his hands on his knees, trying to catch his breath.

"Bugger and arse. That was well played of him."

The words were more stoic than angry, and when he straightened back up his eyes were glinting with good humor. He clearly didn't bear either Morgan or Gryff a grudge.

"Gryff beat both of us to it!" he called back to Morgan, who offered a muffled curse of his own through the trees.

Lenore heard a murmur of commiseration from Harriet, and then the rustle of undergrowth as the other couple started back to their boat.

Rhys, however, seemed in no particular hurry to leave. He leaned against the nearest column, and Lenore's tummy fluttered at the sight he made.

She ascended a step to they were almost eye to eye and reached out towards him. He stilled, his eyes darkening in surprise, but she merely pulled a stray leaf from his hair.

"You had a leaf," she muttered.

She'd stepped close to him, close enough to see the flecks in his dark eyes and the way his pupils expanded at her nearness. His gaze flashed down to her lips as if he was remembering them against his own, and she leaned forward even more, hoping he'd take the hint and close the distance between them, but he cleared his throat and pushed off the pillar, breaking the spell.

Her spirits plummeted. He didn't want to kiss her again.

What had she done wrong?

"I think that was the last flag." He glanced up at the sky, where the sun's low position indicated the lateness of the afternoon. "And it's getting late. We should probably head back to Newstead Park and find out who's won."

Lenore hid her disappointment with a wide smile. "Yes. Of course."

They walked side by side back downhill, with Lenore's thoughts a jumbled whirl, but Rhys's outraged gasp snapped her from her introspection.

"They've stolen our oars!"

They both squinted out across the water, to where Morgan and Harriet were making a rapid escape. Harriet lifted one of the purloined oars above her head and sent them a cheeky salute.

"All's fair in love and war!"

Rhys's growl of irritation did funny things to Lenore's insides. "Bloody brilliant. We're stranded."

CHAPTER 14

"I wish I could say this is a new experience," Lenore said lightly, determined not to appear downcast at being stuck with a man who'd obviously changed his mind about her. "But I've been stuck on an island before. That one was quite a bit bigger than this one, of course. More tropical, too."

A shout from the lakeshore off to their right interrupted whatever Rhys had been about to say, and they both turned to see Carys and Tristan waving at them. There was no sign of Gryff and Maddie.

"Lost your oars?" Carys called out, her laughing, throaty tones carrying across the water like a peal of bells. "Oh, bad luck!"

"Any chance you want to row out here and bring us some?" Rhys shouted.

Gryff and Maddie emerged from the trees to Carys's left. Gryff had put his shirt back on, but he cupped one hand behind his ear.

"What's that, Rhys? Can't hear you, old chap. Must have water in my ears."

His amused laugh echoed across the lake.

"Carys!" Rhys cajoled, ignoring him. "Favorite sister!"

Carys grinned at his pleading tone. "I'm your *only* sister, you dolt. Of course I'm your favorite. Which means that I'm also, by default, your least favorite, too."

"Where's your loyalty?" Rhys bellowed, clearly abandoning his attempt to charm her. "I've always been nicer to you than Gryff."

Carys shrugged. "My loyalty's to winning. You're on your own."

She turned and ushered Tristan back into the woods.

"And I'm afraid I can't help you either," Maddie called out. "Gryff needs to get home and dry his hair. I'd hate for him to catch a cold."

"Such a thoughtful wife." Gryff grinned, bending to press a kiss to her lips before he turned back toward Rhys and Lenore. "Have fun!" With a final wave he took Maddie's hand and tugged her back into the trees.

Rhys let out a long, frustrated sigh and Lenore watched with flagging spirits as Morgan and Harriet reached the boat dock and made a big show of putting both sets of oars safely back into the shed. With a wave, they too, disappeared from view.

She took a deep breath. "So. What's the plan? Find a couple of branches and use them to row back to shore? Swim?"

Rhys sat down on the strip of thick grass that bordered the shingle beach and stared out across the water. "Are you any good at swimming? Most ladies don't know how."

Lenore sank down next to him. "Of course. Father made sure we knew how before we set sail on our very first expedition. We had lessons in the river, right here at Newstead."

She sent him a sideways glance, unable to resist teasing him. "Of course, if we're going to swim, we'll need to take off most of our clothes."

She heard him suck in a breath, and continued breezily, "These skirts and petticoats would just hamper my legs and drag me down when they get wet. And my stays would have to go, too. Very restricting, trying to swim in stays."

A muscle ticked in his jaw, and she stifled a laugh, certain she was getting to him with her mental undressing.

"In fact, I'd probably have to strip right down to my shift and my stockings." She paused for dramatic effect. "It would be quite scandalous, actually. I bet my shift would turn completely transparent."

Rhys stood abruptly and turned away. "You're not swimming anywhere."

"You mean you're going to strip off and go?"

Oh, she was wicked. Half of her wanted him to do just that, purely so she could see him as gloriously undressed as Gryff had been, but if he did choose to swim, she'd be left here alone, and their adventure would be over. She didn't want that. She wanted to steal as much time with him as she could,

"I don't think you should go," she said decisively. "The water must be very cold."

"Gryff managed it," Rhys growled, still with his back to her.

One of the inside seams of his breeches had split during his brawl with Morgan; she could see the most tantalizing sliver of bare, tanned skin on the inside of his left thigh, just above his knee. Her fingers itched to touch it.

"Why don't we just wait a while and see if someone else comes along?" she suggested.

He didn't reply, which Lenore took to be reluctant assent, so she bent and picked a daisy and started to pull off the petals one by one.

He loves me. He loves me not.

Which would it be?

"You should see the color of the sea on the islands near Madagascar," she said, determined to avoid an awkward silence. She always chattered when she was nervous. It was one of her worst traits. Women were always thought more alluring if they stayed silent and mysterious. But she was past using such wiles with

Rhys. If he'd changed his mind about wanting her, then she might as well talk as much as she liked.

"It's an incredible turquoise color, and the sand is almost white. The water's so clear you can see the bottom even when it's very deep, and the fish come in every color of the rainbow. Spotted and striped, all shapes and sizes. They make our British fish look very dull in comparison."

Rhys rolled his shoulders. "The coast of Portugal was like that. Not that I saw it for more than five minutes before we all marched inland."

She cast around for something positive to say about their predicament. "At least there are no snakes here. Or insects that might kill you. The jungle's full of snakes and spiders that are deadly. The *fer de lance*, for example, can kill a person with just one bite."

Rhys seemed to have recovered his previous good humor. He turned around and sat back down next to her. "That's true. We only have a few adders over here in Wales. I've never seen one."

"And no water snakes either. I wrestled one once, you know. In Brazil."

"Why am I not surprised?" His tone was dry and slightly mocking, but she took it as a compliment, not an insult.

"I didn't *mean* to," she protested. "But it seized one of the village dogs and I couldn't just let it just squeeze the poor thing to death right in front of me, could I?"

"Course not," Rhys said. "Totally reasonable reaction. Anyone else would have run screaming into the jungle, but not you. Not a Mad Montgomery. You decide to wrestle the thing. With your bare hands, no doubt. Or did you employ the same method you used with the panther, and use your shoe?"

Lenore looked out over the lake, not quite sure if he was mocking her or not. He sounded more amused than censorious.

"Well, first I hit it with a stick, and when that didn't work, I put a rope around its throat and tugged until it let go of the dog and slithered off into the jungle." She shrugged. "It was quite a small anaconda. A male, probably. The females can get to be enormous."

Rhys gave a theatrical shiver. "I have never been more glad to be back on Britain's boring, rainy shores."

Lenore chuckled. "The only snakes you find here are the ones slithering around the ballrooms of Mayfair, trying to snare a rich wife."

She sighed and picked another daisy. The last one had finished on *he loves me not*, which was . . . unacceptable.

She'd try best of three.

"I'm sure we won't be here for long," she said bracingly. "Someone will come and rescue us. It's not as if they're going to make us stay here all night."

"You're probably right."

"I had to wait weeks to be rescued near Madagascar, but it wasn't that bad. There were plenty of people to talk to, and enough food. Only Caro had the misfortune to be separated from the rest of us. She and Max were swept onto a different island, just the two of them."

"And now he's her husband," Rhys growled.

Lenore shrugged. "Being stranded is obviously a good way for people to bond."

"Or to convince them that murder isn't such a terrible idea after all," he said dryly.

"Oh, hush. This isn't so bad. It's a pleasant way to pass the evening."

To prove her point she leaned back on the springy grass and put her hands behind her head. The late afternoon sunlight dappled her face through the fluttering leaves and sparkled off the rippled surface of the water.

Rhys gave a deep sigh of resignation. "You're right. It could be a lot worse."

Lenore wasn't sure how to take that comment.

CHAPTER 15

*L*enore watched as Rhys tugged off his wet boots and set them in a patch of sunlight to start drying, then peeled off his stockings.

She turned her head and sneaked a glance at his long, tanned feet as he wriggled his toes in the grass, then went to cool them off in the water. Not to be outdone, she sat up and unlaced her ankle boots and removed her own stockings, relishing the naughty thrill of undressing, even partly, next to him.

But he only glanced her way once as she hitched up her skirts and waded into the shallows, then bent to inspect a patch of little yellow lily flowers floating nearby.

"In Brazil they have lily pads that are big enough for a person to sit on," she said, desperate to keep his interest. "Like little boats. And quite a few of the tribes have legends about them."

"What kind of legends?"

"Of how the lily flowers are the spirits of beautiful maidens who've drowned in the water."

"That's cheerful," he said dryly.

"My favorite was the story about a mermaid, called the Iara.

She lures men to their doom with her singing and false promises of great riches at the bottom of the river."

"I think most cultures have legends about beautiful women luring foolish men to their doom. The ancient Greeks had their sirens and their naiads. We Welsh have Gwenhidw, a magical mermaid queen. Some say she's the inspiration for King Arthur's Guinevere. Men have made fools of themselves over pretty faces for thousands of years."

He sent her a wry, sideways glance that made her pulse pound.

If only he'd make a fool of himself over her.

"It's not always women." She sent him an answering smile. "There's also a male river spirit, an unnaturally handsome warrior who comes out of the water at the full moon and seduces all the prettiest girls in the village. He makes love to them at night, but in the morning, he's gone, turned back into his true form, a pink river dolphin."

Rhys's expression was one of laughing disbelief. "A pink dolphin?"

"They exist. I've seen one, in the Amazon River."

"And were you captivated by this scarlet seducer?" he teased.

"I was not."

His mouth opened as if he was about to ask another question, but then he seemed to change his mind and glanced away, and Lenore bit back a wave of disappointment.

She gazed out across the lake. The sun was dropping toward the horizon, slanting its peachy rays across the land and turning the sky purple and gold. A few ducks paddled about, upending themselves in that comical way they had to search for pond weed. The water reflected the darkening sky and the fluffy white clouds above. It was an idyllic spot.

"You must have had some exciting adventures yourself, though," she prodded softly. "You went to Portugal, Spain, and France."

Rhys splashed back to the shore and sank down on the grass again. "I did. But I had quite a few close brushes with death, too. I was in the same regiment as Gryff, the Royal Welsh Fusiliers. We saw action at Salamanca, Nivelle, and Toulouse. Gryff left just before Waterloo because our father had died and he needed to come back and take over as earl, but I stayed to get the job done. Or until I met my maker, whichever came first."

Lenore lowered herself down next to him. "Brave men like you are the reason we're not all speaking French right now."

He gave a self-deprecating shrug, uncomfortable with her praise, but she'd wanted to tell him this ever since she'd met him.

"Waterloo was such a close-run thing," he said quietly. "It could have gone against us so easily." He selected a flat stone and sent it skimming over the surface of the water with a practiced flick of his arm. "I feel incredibly lucky to have survived, when so many of my friends didn't get to come home."

Sadness flashed across his features, and she reined in the impulse to put her arms around him and give him a hug. She pressed her shoulder against his instead, in a wordless show of sympathy, and he sent her a smile to show he appreciated the gesture.

His humility was humbling. He was so much more than just his good looks. He had depths to his personality, a hundred different facets, and she wanted to discover them all. She wanted to know his likes and dislikes, what made him laugh, what made him cry.

She already knew he liked physical activity, like boxing. But did he also like to read? To ride? Was he musical? Could he play an instrument? What was his favorite book?

She couldn't pepper him with a thousand questions now, though, however much she wanted to.

She picked up her own stone and managed a very creditable four skips before it sank into the lake. He shot her an impressed look, eyebrows raised.

"I think travel has changed me," she said pensively. "Well, maybe not changed me, exactly, but certainly *shaped* me. It brought out aspects of my character that probably already existed but made them stronger. My resourcefulness, for instance." Her lips quirked. "And my stubbornness. And despite all the misfortunes—some frightening, some even life-threatening—I can be proud of the fact that I survived. I am stronger than I thought I could be. I can endure more than I ever imagined."

"War changed me," Rhys admitted. "It made me realize that people can do the most incredible things, both good and bad."

"Do you believe in fate?" Lenore asked, curious.

He shook his head. "Not really. I mean, I don't think I was destined to live while other men around me died. I think there were a hundred times when my life hung in the balance, and I couldn't say whether I survived because of some action I took, or because of sheer luck."

"Well, whatever it was, I'm glad," she said with a smile. "Just think of the millions of tiny incidents that have led to the two of us being here, at exactly this point in time. It's enough to make your head spin, really."

"Best not to think about it too hard," Rhys grinned. "I've heard too much thinking can addle the brain."

She gave him a playful punch on the arm. "I'm not the one whose grey matter is scrambled from all those punches to the head."

He chuckled. "I'm beginning to think there's more to us being stuck here than just our siblings' desire to win this treasure hunt. I think the lot of them are throwing us together for their own amusement. Because we're the only two unmarried ones left."

Lenore felt her cheeks heat with a guilty flush, as if that wasn't precisely what she'd asked her aunts to do. "Interesting theory."

"They all seem convinced the Davies-Montgomery enmity is

a thing of the past. That we've been enemies for so long that the universe is righting itself now by having us all fall in love."

Lenore managed a snort. "That's ridiculous."

He raised his brows. "Is it? All three of my siblings have fallen for Montgomerys. Gryff with Maddie, Carys with Tristan, and Morgan with Harriet."

"You make it sound as though we're doomed."

He shrugged, and her heart gave a funny lurch at the fact that he wasn't outright denying the possibility that he could fall in love with her. Perhaps there was hope after all?

She skimmed another stone and kept her tone carefully neutral, praying that she wasn't about to make a complete fool of herself.

"Andover keeps asking me to marry him. He won't take no for an answer."

Rhys's shoulder lifted in a casual shrug, but there was a thread of steely tension in his voice when he spoke.

"Why don't you marry him, then? Put the poor sod out of his misery. And the rest of the country's unmarried men, too, for that matter. Once you accept Andover, the rest will stop thinking they have a chance of capturing your heart."

"That's just the problem," Lenore said, her pulse pounding in her throat. "Andover doesn't have my heart."

Rhys didn't even bother to skim his stone. He just threw it as far into the lake as he could. He almost hit a duck.

"Why not? He's got a ducal title, a huge estate in Wiltshire, and a healthy bank balance."

"Is that what you think I'm looking for in a husband?"

"Isn't that what *every* woman's looking for in a husband?" he countered cynically.

"Not me. I mean, it would be *nice* if the man I eventually marry isn't a pauper, but I really don't care much about material things. I've spent a large part of my life without what most people would call creature comforts, even necessities. There are no lovely hot baths in the middle of the rainforest, no chefs to cook up whatever delicious puddings your brain can conceive. In Brazil, I only had three dresses to last me an entire year."

She twitched the skirts of her dress, which was now ruined beyond any hope of salvation. "And while I certainly appreciate pretty things, they're not the most important thing in life."

"What is?"

She tilted her head and waited for him to look directly at her. "Why, love of course."

He rolled his eyes in typical male exasperation.

"You mock," she said severely, "but that's precisely what kept my parents together all these years, through thick and thin. It's what kept us all from going mad and giving up hope for those weeks we were shipwrecked. I had a loving family to support me and comfort me. I'd trade a boatload of jewels for someone who loved me and cared for me."

Rhys turned to look at her again. "And Andover doesn't love you?"

She shook her head. "He does not."

"And you don't love him?"

"No."

"What will you do if you don't find someone who loves you?" he asked curiously.

"I suppose I'll just stay a spinster, like Aunts Prudence and Constance."

"A lot of women in your position would marry him just for financial security. Or to call themselves duchess."

"Not me. He doesn't make my heart flutter."

Rhys's dark eyes were steady on hers. "Have you ever met a man who does?"

Lenore couldn't look away. "I have."

"Do I know him?"

Lenore threw caution to the wind. "Intimately."

She held her breath, bracing for rejection as she waited for him to realize the import of what she'd just said. His eyes widened, then he frowned, as if questioning his own judgment.

"You might have been right about my brain and all those hits to the head," he said. "Are you saying the person who makes your heart flutter is *me*?"

CHAPTER 16

*L*enore nodded, not trusting her voice, but Rhys's lips curved into the most relieved, wicked smile she'd ever seen.

"Was that when I kissed you, in the wine cellar?"

"Yes," she admitted. "And every time before that, too. Ever since that very first time we met, in Lady Chessington's garden."

His jaw dropped open and she relished his look of shock as he finally understood what she was admitting.

"You love me? Right now? And you've *been* in love with me for almost an entire year?" His tone was an amusing mixture of triumph and irritation. "Bloody hell, woman! Why didn't you say something?"

She sent him a laughing, scolding glance. "When did I have the chance? You avoided me at almost every single event. You barely even deigned to talk to me."

"Because I was in love with *you*," he said, his voice rough with frustration. "And I didn't want to admit it, even to myself. It was self-preservation. I told myself it was ridiculous to fall in love with someone I'd only just met. I was convinced a woman as beautiful and as clever as you would have nothing to do with me.

That if I left you alone, you'd eventually marry some stuffy old duke and I'd just go and drink myself into an alcoholic stupor and die of a broken heart like all the best tragic heroes."

Lenore let out a peal of laughter. Her own heart was racing so fast she could hardly breathe.

Rhys reached out and caught her face between his palms, his eyes wide.

"You really love me?"

"I'm afraid so. The Davies-Montgomery curse has struck again."

"Lenore Montgomery, will you *marry* me?"

Lenore returned his incredulous smile with one of her own. "Rhys Davies, I'd be *honored*. And I really don't care if you don't have a title, or any money. We'll manage."

Rhys actually looked a little guilty. "Ah. About that."

Her heart dropped. Was he about to admit to a mountain of debt? A slew of illegitimate children? A terrible addiction to gambling or laudanum?

Whatever it was, they would deal with it. Together.

"I'm not entirely penniless," he said. "I'm actually quite rich. You remember all that wine in the cellar? That belongs to me, not Gryff."

Lenore gaped at him. "But—How—?"

His grin somehow managed to be both shy and cocky at the same time. "Turns out this poor scrambled brain of mine is quite good at investing. I've made some decent returns on the stock exchange over the years, and that wine is one of my longer-term projects. Most of those bottles will increase steadily over the next five to ten years. Far less volatile than stocks and shares."

Lenore stared at him. "I don't know what to say. I always assumed you were a penniless second son."

Rhys's eyes bored into hers. "Say you'll still marry me, even if I have a fortune. Prove you weren't lying when you said you didn't care about a man's financial position as long as he loved you and you loved him."

Lenore let out an exasperated laugh. "Oh, you are impossible! Yes, I'll marry you, you rogue." She leaned forward and pressed a kiss to his lips.

He stilled, just for a moment, as if still afraid to trust his good fortune, then he returned the pressure with thrilling enthusiasm.

Lenore groaned as his tongue darted into her mouth, tasting her with an urgency that made her blood sing in her veins. She wound her arms around his neck and tugged him back with her onto the grass, loving the urgent sound he made deep in his chest.

"You're not just offering to marry me because I've been compromised, are you?" she murmured with a laugh, pressing feverish kisses along his jaw, his neck.

"Nobody except our families knows we're here," he panted between kisses. "So obviously not."

"Pity," Lenore sighed. "Because I'm not at all averse to being compromised, you know. In fact, I think I'd quite like it."

He stopped kissing her and rose up on his forearms to study her. His eyes were almost black with desire. "Are you sure?"

Lenore nodded. She'd never been more certain of anything in her life. She wanted him with a desperation that was a fire in her veins. And she trusted him not to love her and leave her.

"I've been dreaming of you kissing me, touching me, for months," she breathed. "Every time you looked at me from across a crowded room, I wanted to know what it would be like to have you make love with me."

"Wicked girl," he said softly. "But you deserve silk sheets and a feather mattress, not grass and—"

She arched her neck and kissed him again. "I deserve *you*," she murmured. "All of you. Right now. I don't want to wait."

He shook his head, but his lips quirked in that teasing way she adored. "Oh, love. Your wish is my command."

He lifted his body off hers and she frowned in confusion, only to smile as he caught her hand and pulled her away from the shore and into the privacy of the trees.

"Just in case they decide to come and rescue us, after all."

As soon as they were safely hidden, he pulled her against his body for a kiss that set her heart racing all over again. The mossy grass was soft beneath her as he lowered her to the ground, his hands roving over her as if he was searching for a flag hidden on her person.

Lenore gasped as his lips slid down her throat and over her collarbone, then lower, over the curves of her breasts. The slight stubble of his jaw raised goosebumps on her sensitive skin and her belly clenched in excitement.

He pushed down the front of her dress and his tongue swirled over her nipple a moment before he took it in his mouth, and she grasped his hair as his wicked tongue laved and circled, teasing it into a tight little bud.

"Rhys!"

"God, you're so beautiful," he murmured against her skin, his hand cupping her other breast, so she arched up into his touch like a cat. "I've wanted you from the very first moment I saw you, and I haven't stopped for a single day since."

His mouth nipped and teased.

She'd suspected making love would be nice, but she'd never dreamed it would feel like *this*. Hot and cold, like a fever, a clawing hunger in her belly and a pulsing throb between her legs.

"Please," she panted, not entirely sure what she was asking for, but desperate for more, all the same.

His low chuckle made her shiver. "Patience, my sweet. I don't want to hurt you. We're not going to rush."

He sat up and tugged off his jacket, then his cravat, and tossed them aside, and she ran her hands greedily over his shoulders, then stroked his chest through his shirt, loving the twitch of his muscles beneath her palms.

"Shirt off," she demanded, and he laughingly obliged.

His chest was even more impressive than his brother's, all muscled curves and intriguing ridges thanks to his boxing regimen, and Lenore couldn't resist pressing her lips to the flat plane of his pectoral. She flicked her own tongue playfully across his tawny male nipple, reasoning that whatever he'd done to her would feel equally nice to him, and was rewarded with a deep groan and another ravenous kiss.

He untied the lacing at the back of her dress with deft fingers, then undid her stays, and his reverent gaze roved over her body as she wriggled out of the fabric.

Lenore's cheeks heated in embarrassment to be left in just her sheer shift, but the hot look in his eyes as he looked down at her made her feel like the most beautiful woman in the world.

"One day I'm going to take you swimming in this, just so I can see you looking like a mermaid," he breathed, his hands skimming over her ribs and down the outside of her thighs.

She arched restlessly. "And I'm going to make you work for me in the butterfly house without your shirt, just so I can ogle you in the most shameless manner."

His brows quirked. "How scandalous."

He moved down her body, his palms skimming her breasts, then shaping the curve of her waist. Lenore opened her legs, desperate for him to touch her there, and his deft fingers slid up under the hem of her shift against the smooth skin of her thighs.

His eyes were almost black as he looked at her in wonder. "When you were up on my shoulders, all I could think about was pressing my mouth right here."

He bent his head and kissed her on the inside of her leg, just above her knee, then higher.

Lenore grabbed his hair to try to drag him even closer, and felt the warm puff of his laughing exhale against her thigh.

"I wanted to taste you so badly," he groaned, his breath fanning her most intimate place.

He kissed her again, even higher, and she squirmed at the delicious sensation. She'd seen such scandalous acts depicted in erotic engravings, but the reality was even better than the theory. Her eyes rolled back in her head as his fingers slid against her folds, teasing and circling, and when he leaned forward and added his tongue, she arched into his touch, trying to find some relief from the coiling tension inside her.

He made a hum of pleasure against her and the vibration made her shudder, and then his finger slid *inside* her, and she gasped at the strange sensation.

"All right?" he breathed.

She nodded. "Yes. It's just . . . different, that's all."

And then his hand began to move, slowly, sliding in and out of her, and the heat and the tension increased even more.

"Oh! That's very nice."

He rose up and took her lips again, and his tongue delved into her mouth in the same wicked, insistent rhythm as his finger. Every inch of her body felt hot and restless, and she held her breath, tensing, moving against him, reaching for something just out of reach.

"Let go, Lenore. That's it. Come for me," Rhys growled against her neck, and the pleasure burst over her like a great wave. She tilted back her head and groaned in astonishment as pulses of blissful relief suffused her whole body, happiness exploding like fireworks behind her closed eyelids.

"Rhys!"

He chuckled against her temple at her astonishment, and she relaxed against the grass, entirely spent. She'd never been so relaxed, so boneless in her life.

So that was the mysterious 'crisis' she'd read about in books. How glorious.

A satisfied smile spread across her face, and she opened her eyes to find Rhys gazing down at her, a pleased, tender expression on his face.

"I had no idea," she breathed. "It was like running and jumping off a waterfall, and then landing in the most glorious pool of happiness." She narrowed her eyes at him. "Are you sure you're not secretly a pink river dolphin in disguise?"

"Just a man." Rhys pressed a kiss to her flushed cheek, then another to her lips. "Who happens to love doing that to you. Do you think you can bear any more?"

Lenore widened her eyes. She knew he hadn't found his own pleasure yet, and to her surprise her body tingled with renewed excitement at the thought of him joining his body with hers.

"I want you, Rhys Davies. Body and soul. Make me yours."

Her words seemed to release some pent-up spring inside him, because he groaned and pressed a passionate kiss to her lips. "God, I really want to be gentle, to make this good for you, but I've wanted you for so long. I don't think I can wait."

She stroked her fingers through his hair. "Then don't. Show me what to do."

"Let me see you. All of you. Please." His voice was hoarse, and wonderfully desperate, and her heart sang at his indisputable desire.

With fumbling hands she helped him pull her shift up and over her head and she lay back, unashamed to lie before him naked. The cool breeze peaked her already-sensitive nipples and the dappled sunlight made shifting patterns across her stomach and chest.

He swallowed, then rolled to his back and discarded his breeches, and she sucked in a breath as she finally saw him naked.

He was beautiful, an animal in its prime, as sleek and as lean as a panther. His skin was tawny, and his limbs all flowed in muscled lines. His cock stood to attention against his flat belly, and when he wrapped his hand around it and gave it a squeeze, she reached out, desperate to touch him herself.

She'd never seen an aroused man before, and she was

intrigued by the difference between his body and her own. Men were such strange creatures.

He let her fingers close around him, and the contrast between velvet-soft skin and iron-hard muscle was fascinating.

"That's enough of that," he half groaned, half laughed, when she gave him a little stroke. "Or this will be over far too soon."

He settled himself over her, taking most of his weight on his elbows on either side of her head, and the sensation of his big body against hers, his ridged belly and strong thighs pressing her down into the earth, made her breathless with excitement.

She widened her legs to let him in, but when his cock nudged against her entrance he paused. "Still sure? We can wait until we're married, if you like."

Lenore laughed. It was clear he was desperate to continue, and the fact that he'd deny himself, even to the point of pain, just to reassure her of his honorable intentions, was all the evidence she needed that he was a good man.

Luckily for him, she was a very *bad* woman, and now she had him here, there was no chance she'd let him go without finishing what he'd started.

"You can't stop now," she said, wriggling her hips so they both groaned at the delicious friction. "That's like setting off on an expedition and giving up a few miles from the end. I want the whole adventure."

He let out a breathless laugh. "Whatever the lady wants."

He rocked forward, entering her slowly, then pulled back, watching her face for any sign of discomfort. She tilted her hips, instinctively seeking a better angle, and the next time he slid in a little further.

There was no pain, just a slight stretch, and soon he was seated to the hilt inside her.

"So good," he groaned, sounding as if he was barely holding on to his control. "Hold on."

Lenore wrapped her arms around his neck and kissed him as

he started to move, slowly at first, then with ever-increasing speed. Her body clenched around him, and the friction of him inside her was even better than that of his fingers.

She stroked her hands along his sides, over the ridges of his ribs, then down to the smooth mounds of his backside, and he groaned against her shoulder when she gave his arse a cheeky squeeze, just as he'd done to her at the boat shed.

He quickened his pace, hitting a spot inside her that made her teeter on the edge of that wonderful drop again, and then she fell, arching her back and crying out as another surge of pleasure racked her body.

Her convulsions must have finished him off, because with a deep groan he tensed within her, and his whole body pulsed with his release. He groaned her name as he came, loud enough to be heard right across the island, and she smiled up at the canopy of trees above her head, entirely satisfied.

He collapsed on top of her, squashing her for a brief moment, then seemed to come to his senses and rolled to her side, withdrawing from her body.

Lenore felt wonderful, sated and tingling and utterly replete. She'd always suspected being ravished by Rhys would be delightful, but this had exceeded her expectations.

"Well, I'm definitely compromised now," she wheezed.

Rhys let out a weary chuckle and rolled onto his back to stare at the sky. "Bloody Hell, woman. Do you know how long I've wanted to do that?"

"Since the first moment you saw me," Lenore chuckled. "You said."

"It bears repeating. I didn't even think you were real, at first. I thought maybe I'd dreamed you up. My perfect woman. But then you spoke, and told me your name, and I started being an idiot."

"It's only taken you a year to realize it," she smiled. "And I did everything I could to show you I was interested. I wore the most beautiful dresses, encouraged a score of men fall in love with me, just to spur you into competing."

Rhys let out a heartfelt groan. "I told you. Scrambled brain. You're going to have to do most of the thinking."

He turned his head to look at her. "Where do you want to get married? Here? Or back in London? I don't care which."

"Here. I always thought the little church in the village was pretty, and I've never wanted a big public society wedding."

"Done," he said. "I wish we didn't have to wait the three weeks required to have the banns read, but it can't be helped. I think we Davies have used up our share of special licenses for a decade. The Archbishop of Canterbury must be sick of us."

"Will we live at Trellech?" Lenore asked.

His brows rose. "Would you like that? I thought you'd want to keep traveling the world."

"I'd like to travel a bit, but only with you. And I'd love to live at Trellech. Then, I could easily work in the butterfly house at Newstead."

"In that case, yes. Although I do have quite a nice town house in London, just off Grosvenor Square."

Lenore sighed in happiness. "I have a confession to make."

His lips quirked in amusement. "Oh really? Do tell."

"I asked the Aunts to contrive ways for us to be alone together. This entire treasure hunt was a way for me to spend time with you to see if I could convince you to love me."

Rhys blew a lock of his hair off his forehead and laughed. "I needed no convincing. And, well, I have a confession to make too. I asked my siblings to take every opportunity to push us together. Morgan was kind enough to lock us in the boat shed, and even kinder to leave us here without any oars. I think I owe him a drink."

Lenore gasped. "We're as bad as each other," she giggled. "I knew you were dastardly, Davies."

Rhys rolled onto his side and pressed a tender kiss to her lips.

"We're perfect for one another," he grinned. "Now, get dressed, in case someone decides we've been here long enough and decides to come and get us."

"Please say we can do this again before the wedding."

"Oh, we will definitely do this again before the wedding. We Davies are excellent at sneaking around. I'll show you all the ways to get into Trellech without being seen. As nice as this was, I can't wait to make love to you in my bed. I want you naked on my sheets, exactly as I've imagined."

His eyes sparkled. *"Now* can I buy you dresses?"

Lenore bit her lip and pretended to consider. "Well, I suppose this does count as intimate acquaintance. I just had my hands on your arse, Davies."

He shook his head at her cheek. "You have a wicked tongue, Lenore Montgomery. And the next time we're together, I'm going to put it to good use."

"I can't wait."

EPILOGUE

The treasure hunt was a four-way draw.

Four of the couples managed to find two flags each. Carys and Tristan found the ones at the folly and on Geoffrey the peacock. Maddie and Gryff claimed the ones at the wishing well and on the island. Morgan and Harriet found the bridge flag and the one hidden in the library at Trellech, and Rhys and Lenore found the ones at the butterfly house and in the clock tower.

Caro and Max found the one in the cellar at Newstead, and Will and Lucy discovered the boat house flag before anyone else.

Lenore still considered herself victorious, however, as did Rhys, especially when they said their vows in the tiny, ancient church a few miles from Trellech in front of a select handful of friends and relations.

Aunts Prudence and Constance sat in the front pew in pride of place, mopping the happy tears from their eyes and telling everyone who would listen that they always knew Lenore and Rhys were destined to be together.

Since Rhys and Lenore both secretly thought the same thing, they simply smiled, and spent the weeks after their wedding making love in every one of the places they'd visited in the treasure hunt.

This required Davies and Montgomery levels of sneaking about, since many of the other couples had come up with the same idea, and they all frequently encountered one another in various amusing stages of undress.

Rhys enacted a little sweet revenge on Gryff by stealing his clothes while he and Maddie were swimming naked in the river, and locked Morgan in one of the large enclosures with Geoffrey, just for the entertainment of seeing him try to scale the metal gates.

Geoffrey was not amused.

A few months after their wedding, Rhys and Lenore set sail on their next adventure, a caterpillar-gathering expedition to Martinique, on a ship captained by Morgan, and accompanied by Harriet.

Lenore discovered eight new species of butterfly, one of which, the Madagascan blue-winged Charaxes, she gave the latin name *Charaxes Daviesi*, in honor of her husband.

Rhys bought her a ridiculous number of beautiful dresses, an inordinate amount of jewelry, and named a ship after her, the *Siren Lenore*, a sister-ship to its twin, the *Destiny*.

* * *

Thank you for reading *A Scandal In July*. I hope you enjoyed Rhys and Lenore's adventures as much as I enjoyed writing them. Please consider leaving a review on any (or all!) of the online retail sites: every review is greatly appreciated.

To find out more about the Rake Review series, visit here: https://therakereview.wordpress.com

Find more of Kate's books here: and on all the major retail sites.

FOLLOW

Follow Kate online for the latest new releases, giveaways, exclusive sneak peeks, and more!

Follow Kate Online at your favorite retailer

Sign up for Kate's monthly-ish newsletter via her website for news, exclusive excerpts and giveaways. At www.kcbateman.com

Join Kate's Facebook reader group: Badasses in Bodices

Follow Kate Bateman on Bookbub for new releases and sales.

Add Kate's books to your Goodreads lists, or leave a review!

ALSO BY KATE BATEMAN

Her Majesty's Rebels Series:
Road Trip With A Rogue
Second Duke's The Charm
How To Fall For A Scoundrel

Ruthless Rivals Series:
A Reckless Match
A Daring Pursuit
A Wicked Game
Desert Island Duke (novella)
The Phantom of Drury Lane (novella)
A Scandal In July (novella)

Bow Street Bachelors Series:
This Earl Of Mine
To Catch An Earl
The Princess & The Rogue

Secrets & Spies Series:
To Steal a Heart
A Raven's Heart
A Counterfeit Heart
Orchids & Mistletoe (novella)

Italian Renaissance:
The Devil To Pay

Novellas:
The Promise of A Kiss
A Midnight Clear

ABOUT THE AUTHOR

Kate Bateman is a bestselling author of Regency and Renaissance historical romances, including the Her Majesty's Rebels series, Ruthless Rivals series, Bow Street Bachelors series, and Secrets & Spies series. Her books have received multiple Starred Reviews from Publishers Weekly and Library Journal, and her Renaissance romp The Devil To Pay was a 2019 RITA award nominee.

Her books have been translated into multiple languages, including French, Italian, Brazilian, Japanese, German, Romanian, Czech, and Croatian.

When not writing, Kate leads a double life as a fine art appraiser and on-screen antiques expert for several TV shows in the UK. She lives in England with a number-loving husband, three inexhaustible children, and a naughty toy poodle named Monty.

Kate loves to hear from readers. Contact her via her website: www.kcbateman.com and sign up for her newsletter to receive free books, regular updates on new releases, giveaways, and exclusive excerpts.

www.ingramcontent.com/pod-product-compliance
Lightning Source LLC
LaVergne TN
LVHW091713070526
838199LV00050B/2375